Love¹⁰

Based on a true story

Theresa Konwinski

ISBN: 1-7335076-2-0
ISBN 13: 978-1-7335076-2-2
Library of Congress: 2020907567

DEDICATION

This book is lovingly dedicated to my grandparents, Robert and Edith Riedel, as well as to all of their children—my dad and my aunts and uncles. I don't remember ever seeing my grandma without a smile on her face, and my grandpa was funny and loving. Our family get-togethers are a source of joyful memories for me.

Though Grandma, Grandpa, my dad and my Aunt Clara have passed on, I hope that somehow they're aware that this story is finally on paper, and I hope they are proud of the manner in which it is told.
This book is meant to honor them all.

ACKNOWLEDGMENTS

I want to express my deepest gratitude to all of my aunts and uncles who took the time to provide me with information about my grandparents' lives, both in written and verbal form.

I especially want to thank my Aunts Mary, Phyllis, and Kathy for inspiring me to write this story and for giving me moral support to carry on.

Based on the story of my grandparents' lives, this book represents a fictionalized telling of a mostly-true tale where conversations and exact details of many proceedings cannot be accurately recounted. That said, the reader may rest assured that about 90% of these events really happened.

1
AUGUST 1928

At the Sycamore United Brethren church, William Franklin Wagner entered a small Sunday school classroom where new brides waited to walk down the aisle. He saw his daughter Edith, seated near a window, beaming, her beautiful hair backlit by the rays of the setting sun shining through stained glass.

Just sixteen, she had already carried the burdens of motherhood. Her mother—his wife, Alverta—died when Edith was only seven. Even as a young child, Edith understood what was needed to run a family and accepted responsibility far beyond what a seven-year-old should have to shoulder, helping care for the other children in the family. *She became the sunshine that went out of our home when Alverta died,* he reminisced. *I hate for Edith to leave us, but she deserves to be happy.* He shook off his melancholy and forced a smile.

"Girls, it's time to go out," he said, offering his arm to his daughter.

Edith smoothed the skirt of her soft, pale green georgette dress and stood up. She looked at her best friend, Juanita, whose maid-of-honor dress was plum. *Complementing colors,* Edith thought. *I hope Robert likes them when he sees us coming down the aisle. Such pretty shades.* She stopped herself. *Why am I thinking about this now? Why am I so nervous? I wish Mama could be here today.* She gripped her father's arm.

Juanita gave Edith a quick peck on the cheek. "Here we go," she said, smiling, handing Edith a small nosegay of mixed, late summer flowers tied with a green ribbon. She walked through the doorway. "Come on, now—you don't want to keep him waiting!" She winked and turned into the hallway that led towards the sanctuary.

William put his hand over Edith's smaller hand. Her grip was tight, and he knew she was anxious. "This will be one of the happiest days of your life," he said. "Try not to be nervous and enjoy it all."

"I love you, Daddy." Edith's voice was an unsteady, near-whisper as her father started into the hallway.

The traditional bridal march was already playing, and Juanita was a few steps down the aisle. Robert was facing the front of the church, his spine straight, as he always held himself. She could see him shifting his weight from foot to foot as she and her father entered the sanctuary. *He's probably as scared as I am*, Edith thought. *But we'll be all right.*

***

A small group of guests were seated in the pews. One of them caught a glimpse of the bride with her father and stood up. The rustling caused other guests to look back and stand up, too. The noise alerted Robert, who turned around to face his bride. As he turned, he caught a glimpse of his Uncle Wesley, the man who had loaned him the money for Edith's ring. Uncle Wesley grinned at him. Robert winked in reply.

Edith was glowing. *She's beautiful. How did I get so lucky?* he thought. He smiled, keeping his full attention on the wonderful girl he was about to make his wife, but his thoughts went back to how they had met and how impressed he was with Edith right from the beginning. First attracted by her beauty, he bothered Evelyn Geary till she finally introduced them. He soon found that Edith wasn't just beautiful outside. She was beautiful *inside*. Despite her hard life, she had a quick laugh, and she could tell a joke or story with the best of them. She was a Christian girl, smart, a hard worker, taking care of her whole family. Robert was smitten. He invited her out as often as her father would allow her to go with him. After six months, he got down on one knee and asked her to marry him. She consented. *Now the day is finally here*, he thought, and as he watched her come down the aisle, he silently thanked God for his good fortune.

***

The two young people who came from similar backgrounds stood together at the front of the church. Candles lit on either side of the altar cast a warm glow all around them. Before God and their families, they uttered their vows, making promises to each other that would never be broken. Vows to love, honor, and cherish. Vows to stay together and work as partners for better or worse, richer or poorer. Vows that in sickness and in health, they would stick by each other.

In that solemn and joyous moment, they had no idea how

those vows or their individual strengths would be tested—no concept of the challenges they would face together or how their upbringing would give them strength and resilience to weather every storm.

2
PAST IS PROLOGUE
1916 – THE RIEDELS

"Cora! Robert! Virgil! C'mon…let's get out in the field! It's past time to get busy."

Wooster Riedel had no time to dally. Farming his eighty acres, plus the 160 he rented, meant every able-bodied son and daughter had to help. He was fortunate that Cora, the oldest of his children, enjoyed outdoor chores—she usually begged to be out in the field. Otherwise, it would have been just him and the boys. Robert was only ten years old; Virgil, seven. The youngest of the boys was Ross, but at age five, he was no help at all, remaining Verna's concern all day long. Wooster chuckled at the thought of Verna trying to keep up with Ross, who could be a handful.

Married for twelve years, Wooster and Verna were making a good life together. They both made sure the children knew what it meant to work. Cora started helping drive horses in front of the plow by the time she was ten, and Robert was now learning the skill too, though Cora objected.

"He's a year younger than me! I should get first pick of the chores!" she argued.

Robert really didn't mind Cora's claim. He liked helping his mother inside the house. Early on, he learned how to dust, iron, wash the dishes, and carry water from the cistern for doing the family's laundry. He took pride in filling the reservoir on the end of the cookstove with water every single day, making sure there was always plenty to aid in his mother's meal preparation. The only thing he didn't enjoy was splitting wood for the parlor stove. *That* felt like a chore, one that quickly wore him out.

With the acreage the family worked, most every spring Wooster hired farmhands. This year would be no different.

"You know, Verna, our Cora works hard, and the boys are learning, but I need some older boys or men to help with this much land and all these animals," Wooster told his wife.

"Better go ahead, then. Find some good ones before they're all hired out," Verna said. With farming the main occupation of the region, able-bodied men went fast.

However, Wooster never had trouble finding hired hands. He was a good employer—fair and honest. Young men learned a lot about farming by working for Wooster Riedel.

Each evening, the workers came in from the fields tired. Supper consisted of whatever vegetables were in season and whatever meat had been killed in that week's hunt or had been smoked during butchering days the previous fall.

Working outside with Wooster meant the children had to take a bath more than once a week because of the dust kicked up by the plow and the horses. Typically, the children bathed only on Saturday nights so they could be presentable for church the next day, but when they were working the fields, it was a different story.

"I get to take a bath first!" Cora would argue. Often, Robert was forced to use the same water his sister had used, especially if there wasn't enough hot water available for all the baths that needed to be done.

"Why do I have to use *her* water?" Robert complained. "It's not hot by the time she gets done with it!"

"You children will drive me to distraction!" Verna said, weary of this frequent argument. "C'mon son. We'll put the tub in front of the stove door. That will keep you warm."

"Mom, that never works!" Robert said. And it didn't. On top of that, the kids had to dry off with linen towels, which didn't absorb water like terrycloth.

Verna was undeterred. "Robert, get in that bathtub and quit complaining or I'll skin you!"

Robert did as he was told. He knew better than to smart-talk his mother. Either she or his father or *both* would make him pay for it.

Not that Wooster or Verna were mean. They were *focused*. Keeping body and soul together meant hard work from sun-up till sundown. Nothing could be wasted. That included bath water.

After baths and before bed, it was time for Bible reading. The older kids took turns reading out loud, and Verna said prayers. No one stayed up too late. Tomorrow would bring more of the same exhausting routine.

Sun-up. One girl and three boys got out of bed in the morning, rubbing their eyes and stretching. Cora had her own bedroom while the three boys shared a room. They met in the hallway and made a beeline for the dry sink where faces were washed, and teeth were brushed. Then pajamas were exchanged for dungarees, and breakfast was quickly consumed. The fields called for attention.

All summer long, life consisted of a similar routine every day unless it rained. Then there were inside chores to contend with, and once they were done, there might be time for games.

As summer drew to an end and they began to talk about school starting up, Verna realized how much the children had grown.

"Wooster, these children need some new clothes. Robert's pants are so short they're clear above his ankles now, and his shoes are getting tight. The same is true for Virgil. And Cora! I've got to get a dress or two made for her."

"I'll go pick up Mrs. Feltus," Wooster said. "Maybe she can stay for a few days and get the sewing caught up."

Mrs. Feltus was a good local seamstress who kept busy year-round. Sewing was not Verna's best skill, and Mrs. Feltus was not only good at it, she was *fast*.

Wooster went upstairs to his childrens' rooms. "Does anyone want to go for a ride to the Feltus place? Your mother says it's time for some new clothes."

"I'll go, Pop," Robert said.

"I will, too," said Cora.

"All right. Virgil, you stay with Mother and help take care of Ross, all right?"

"Yes, Papa. Am I going to get some new clothes, too?"

"You might. Then again, you might get Robert's old ones."

"Aw, geeminy. Why can't I ever get anything new?" Virgil asked.

Wooster squatted down and looked his son in the eye. "Virgil, we all have to make do with what we have for as long as we have it. We can't be wasteful. I'm sorry son. It's not always fun to be the younger brother. Maybe Mrs. Feltus will be able to make you your very own new jacket, but truth be told, you'll probably have to just use Robert's old dungarees. Think that'll be all right for now?"

Virgil didn't want to complain. "Sure, Papa."

Wooster patted him on the head. "You're a good boy. You know, you might have to get a new pair of boots all your own. Yours look like they're getting tight and your feet are too little to fit into Robert's boots yet. We'll see what we can do, okay?"

Virgil's face brightened. "Thanks, Papa!"

The day was saved. Wooster smiled to himself.

As he drove their hay wagon to Mrs. Feltus' house, Wooster thought about how well his family managed. They weren't rich by any means, but neither were they struggling. They just knew how to be thrifty and make things last. Extravagances were saved for Christmas or maybe a birthday.

They arrived at a white clapboard house. The residence showed the care and nurture of Mrs. Feltus. Flowers of every variety and color grew along the front of their home. Cora ran for the house.

"Mrs. Feltus," she called, knocking frantically on the screen door. "Mrs. Feltus, are you home?"

Making her way to the door, Mrs. Feltus said, laughing, "Lands, child. Is there a fire somewhere?"

"No, but we need some clothes, *bad*," the young girl told her.

"Well, most women feel that way sometime or other, I suppose," she chuckled as Wooster walked up the steps to the porch with Robert in tow.

"Good day to you, Mrs. Feltus. Verna asked me to stop over and fetch you if you can come for a few days to do some sewin' for us. These youngsters are outgrowin' everything they own."

"You've come at a good time. I'm not up to my eyeballs in housework or gardening right at the moment. In fact, everything's pretty smooth around here. Why don't you all just sit down on the porch, and I'll go let the mister know that I'm going over to your place for a few days. Do you know if Verna already has material and threads?"

"I believe she has everything you'll need. You know, sewin' just isn't in her bag of tricks. She can cook better'n anybody I know, and she works like a dog keepin' up the house and workin' in the garden, but she can't sew worth a hoot."

"Well, you've come to the right place. I'll be back in a minute." Mrs. Feltus smiled and went to find her husband and pack up a few things for her trip to the Riedel farm.

7

"Will Mrs. Feltus sleep in my room?" Cora asked Wooster as they moved the porch glider back and forth with their feet.

"No, Cora. She'll sleep where the hired hands usually sleep—out in the workhouse."

"If she sleeps in my room, maybe she could teach me some sewing."

Wooster considered this. It wouldn't hurt for Cora to know how to sew. "That's not a bad idea. I'll talk to her about it on the way back home."

Before long, Mrs. Feltus appeared at the door with a carpetbag filled with her belongings and a wicker box with an oak handle.

"Robert, take Mrs. Feltus' bag to the wagon. Cora, you take the sewing box." Wooster turned to the seamstress and offered his arm to assist her over the rocky ground to a horse-drawn wagon that was their transportation back to the Riedel farm.

As they rode back home, Wooster asked Mrs. Feltus, "I was wondering…would you consider teaching Cora a bit about sewing? She's anxious to learn." The horses clip-clopped along, the rhythm of their canter relaxing the riders. The kids were stretched out in the wagon and beginning to nap. "You know," he continued, "I never dreamed I'd have a daughter like Cora. She wants to be out in the fields working most of the time, and she doesn't usually like learning how to do things inside the house like most other girls want to do. When she asked me about you teaching her to sew, I was surprised. Since she took an interest, I thought I'd ask you."

"Heavens, yes! I'd love to teach her some sewing." Mrs. Feltus thought *all* girls should know how to sew. And cook. *And* clean. "Why does she like being outside so much?"

"I don't know, but she's a worker. You should see her. Well, you *will* see her over the next few days. She often drives the plow horses for me."

"Since Verna doesn't sew, Cora's learning could be very helpful, I'd say. And if Cora decides she likes the work, this could turn into an occupation for her someday," Mrs. Feltus said.

"My thoughts exactly," Wooster said. "It's good for people to be self-sufficient."

"Exactly right," Mrs. Feltus replied, and they fell silent for the rest of the ride home.

***

In the fall, all four children had at least one new item of clothing all their own. Cora had a new dress for school, as well as one for church. Robert and Virgil each had a new shirt, and Robert had new dungarees. As predicted, Virgil owned a patched-up pair of Robert's old pants, but he got his jacket, too. And little Ross made out like a bandit. Not only did he have a new shirt and pants, but he got a teddy bear made from one of Wooster's old flannel shirts. Best of all, Cora had learned a new skill.

"Look, Mom. I made you an apron!" Cora was proud that she could do something her own mother didn't care to do.

"It's lovely, Cora!" Verna exclaimed. "Just in time for the apple butter stir!" She was as proud of Cora as Cora was of herself.

Making apple butter was a family affair, beginning with picking red and yellow delicious apples from the large orchard they owned. Grandma and Grandpa Riedel showed up, and so did Uncle Chet and Aunt Alicia. Everyone was busy choosing the best apples for the apple butter. The smaller, knotty apples would be saved for feeding livestock.

"Boys go get the fire going, and be careful," Wooster told Robert and Virgil. "Keep Ross away from it!"

Robert and Virgil got to work building a fire, just as they had seen their father do over many apple butter-making events before. When the fire was good and hot, Wooster and Chet hung a copper kettle over the blaze on a metal bar held between two poles. The women peeled apples while the men and the children picked, and it was often a race to see who could out-work their competitors.

"You children are behind! You've got to move faster than that!" Verna kidded.

"And you men aren't doing much better!" called Alicia. The women were whizzes with a paring knife.

All afternoon, the smell of apples filled the air at the farm. Bees buzzed around the apple scraps—peelings and cores—and were undeterred by the smoke from the fire. A hot, tiring job, canning was completed in the evening, and everyone split the apple butter evenly.

"Wooster, you and Verna keep some more of this, this year," Grandpa Riedel said. "We've got just the two of us to feed now. You've got five mouths to fill."

"Well, Dad, if you insist. We appreciate all the help you provided, though, and I don't want you to feel like you didn't get your fair share."

"No, no, son. We've got plenty," Grandma said. "We had fun today. Apple butter-making time has always been my favorite time of the year, really."

"Better than butchering day?" Wooster asked.

"Better than butchering day," Grandma answered.

And no wonder. Butchering day was really for the men. The heavy lifting of hogs onto hooks to hang upside down, the gutting and scalding and scraping of the hides—that was men's work. Even the hired hands helped with that job. Young Robert and Virgil learned how to scrape the hides while the women stuffed the sausage and preserved the meat by rubbing it with a mixture of salt, brown sugar, and pepper. It was far less pleasant than making apple butter. But then, there were no complaints in the winter when Mother cooked up sausage and eggs for breakfast before they trudged off to school, almost two miles away. A good breakfast before going out in the snow made up for all that hard work.

The children went to Buffalo School Number 1. Eight grades in the same room made it challenging for the teacher, but the Riedel children were well-behaved.

"If you get a spanking at school, you'll get one when you come home, too," Verna warned. "I'll have no tomfoolery when you're supposed to be learning," and she meant it. "And no tomfoolery at church, either!"

On Sundays, the family walked to the United Brethren Church in Sycamore except in the winter, when they took a horse-drawn sleigh. Going to church was an expectation, and the kids didn't argue, but they groused among themselves.

"It's too darn cold to ride to church. Why can't we just skip once in a while?" Virgil said.

"Yeah, like maybe when it's really, really cold," Robert said.

"You boys know better than that. The only way you'll skip church is if you're sick."

It was hard to keep warm in that sleigh until one Sunday in the winter of 1916, when Wooster came up with the idea of using a drum heater.

"You children can keep this by your feet, and it will help you stay warm. Put some horse blankets or cow hides over you."

The whole family piled into the sleigh. Since it had snowed the night before and was now bitterly cold, they were delighted to find that

Wooster's idea worked. Blowing snow still stung their faces until they pulled the horse blankets up so that only their eyes showed. They could hardly wait to get to their destination and were not far away from the old brick church when one of the sleigh runners hit a drift. The horses kept pulling forward, but the runner was stuck, and before Wooster could rein the horses back, the sleigh tipped over, dumping every last person on the ground.

The boys laughed and started making snow angels. Wooster jumped up and tried to set the sleigh to right, hollering at the boys, "You kids get over here and help me with this."

Cora was mortified, pulling at her coat and her dress, trying to straighten up her clothing while Ross cried a full-throated wail.

"Mama, I'm cold. My teddy bear is cold, too," the little fellow bleated.

"Wooster Riedel, if you didn't try to go so fast!" Verna said. Then the silliness of it all got the best of her—the boys on the ground, waving their arms and legs like wild things, Cora harrumphing around in the snow, Ross crying his eyes out—and she began to laugh. Surprised, Wooster stopped what he was doing and looked at her.

"Are you all right, woman?" he said. "Did you bang your head on something?"

"No, husband, no. Here, let me help you," she said, continuing to laugh.

After a short struggle, the two of them set the sleigh upright.

"You boys get in here!" Cora was first to return to the sleigh.

They continued to church without further incident, but Wooster noted that Verna continued to giggle at odd times throughout the sermon.

***

Christmas time…there weren't a lot of presents, but there were plenty of treats. Grandma Riedel's house perpetually smelled of sugar cookies or molasses cookies or taffy. Robert and Virgil knew exactly where they were kept, and Grandma Riedel let them have all they wanted. They didn't even have to ask permission.

"It's only once a year, Verna," she reassured the boys' mother. "It won't hurt them once a year as long as they brush their teeth."

Verna wasn't so sure, but she had to admit she loved watching the boys savor every crumb of every cookie. The taffy was a little different story….

"Mother, Virgil got taffy in my hair," Cora griped one afternoon.

"I didn't do it on purpose," Virgil spoke up, following his older sister into the kitchen. "I coughed, and it flew out of my mouth."

"Why did you start coughing?"

He looked down at his feet. "Because I put too many pieces in my mouth at once. I was afraid Robert would take it if he saw it."

"Good grief. Where did you get taffy today anyway?" Verna asked her son.

"I kept it on the windowsill when we got home from Grandma's the other day."

"Oh, for pity's sake. You boys! Do you *want* to attract mice?"

"No, mom. I just wanted to keep some of my taffy for later."

"What about my *hair*?" Cora whined.

"Let me see if I can get it out," Verna sighed. She got her narrow-tooth comb and began working on the sticky mess. Thank heaven it was only stuck at the ends of Cora's hair.

"Cora Alice, I don't know if I can get this out of here without cutting it."

"But my currrls…" Cora continued to whine.

"Virgil, go get my scissors," Verna said. "Cora, settle down. We're not going to have to cut too much."

Virgil brought the scissors, and Verna set to work clipping as little of Cora's hair as possible, but it was hopeless, requiring more trimming than she had anticipated. Cora winced and moaned with each snip of the scissors.

"There. No one will be able to tell the difference."

Cora took off for the bathroom to find the looking glass. They soon heard a screech.

Verna looked at Virgil. "If you ever decide to save taffy again, don't put so much in your mouth, all right? I'd truly love to avoid this pitiful scene in the future."

"Yes, Mother."

1916 was about to end. Cora managed to put her trauma behind her before the new year. Robert and Virgil went hunting with Wooster and learned how to shoot straight and true, providing many good meals for the family. Ross, along with his older brothers and sisters, heard Bible stories every night from his mother, who, unlike her daughter, never did learn how to sew worth a hoot.

3

1920 – THE WAGNERS

On a small farm four miles west and one mile south of Sycamore, the Wagner family was in mourning. Muffled sobs could be heard throughout the white-washed, five-room house. William Wagner sat in the bedroom that had once been the home's parlor and stared straight ahead, listening to the sounds of grief. Though some of them were grown and married with children of their own, twelve children suddenly had no mother. No one had expected it.

Upstairs, Edith Wagner, numb with sorrow, couldn't cry any more. Her beloved mother was gone. *Forever.* How could it be? She got up and paced around the bedroom she shared with her sisters Jeannette and Doris. They were older, but it was Edith—just seven years old—who was thinking about the future. How would they survive without Mama?

Mama taught them everything. How to churn butter and clean the cream separator. *Oh, that chore is going to Claude now! I've had my share of that job!* Mama had showed the girls the most effective way to wash clothes on their old washboard, using rain they caught in a barrel. It was an all-day job at minimum. Mama—she was the one who encouraged all the children to learn to read by reading the Bible aloud after supper. Mama, with long, brown hair that Edith helped to brush after those evening readings were done. Their mother was beautiful, always humming or singing as she worked, and laughing—always laughing. Her death crushed them all. As Edith paced, the word echoed in her mind—Mama. *Mama.*

She stopped pacing and straightened her shoulders. *Mama taught us the things we need to know. I can't let her down. I'll take over. I can help*

Dad. I know how to cook and clean and do everything a grown woman can do. I can take care of the children. I'll read the Bible every night. She started her plan, then remembered what Mama would have told her to do—pray.

She got down on her knees by her bedside, folded her hands, bowed her head, and prayed in earnest. "Dear Heavenly Father, I don't know why you had to take Mama. It was so hard putting her in the ground today! You must know how much we all loved her. But I'm not going to ask you about it anymore. Thy will be done, on earth as it is in Heaven. That's what Mama taught us, and she would not want us to be mad at you. She would want us to pick up and carry on. She wouldn't want us to complain. And I won't, Lord, only I *am* going to ask you to help me. With Sally and Viola and the older boys gone, it's just me and Jeannette and Doris to do the women's work. Ralph, Claude, Del, Ricky—they're going to have to help out, too, but it's hard because they're still so little. Well, except for Ralph...he can help Dad, but he can't do it all. Lord, you're just going to have to help us! I'm worried about my father. He's so sad. Please help me, Lord. I promise to be good, and I promise to remember everything Mama taught me, but I'm gonna need your help, and that's all there is to it. I know you love us, so I'm counting on you. Amen."

She hadn't heard Jeannette enter the room. Edith looked up in time to see her changing out of her Sunday dress. She had a hard, grim look about her face.

"Jeannette, I'm going downstairs and see what there is to cook for dinner."

"Edith, no one's going to even *want* dinner. What in the world are you thinking?"

"Dad is going to need something to eat. He has hardly eaten anything for three days. He'll be too weak to run the plow or do much of anything else. You know that."

"I can guarantee he won't eat anything, Edith. You may as well not waste your time."

"What about the boys? *They'll* need something to eat!"

Jeannette turned to face her. "Listen, I know what you're doing. You can't replace Mama, no matter how hard you try, so just stop it. Today's not the day for you to get all bossy."

Edith dropped down to sit on the bed. A chill passed over her, and she shivered. She rubbed her arms and thought about what Jeannette had said.

"Jeannette, I'm not trying to be the boss. You're the one whose fourteen. You can be the boss, I don't care. Or if you don't want to, Doris can be the boss. She's ten. I might be the youngest, but I know what Mama expected from us, and I'm not going to let her down."

Jeannette carried her everyday dress in her hand as she walked over and sat down beside her little sister. "I'm sorry. I really am. I know you're trying to be brave and strong, but I'm *scared*. Aren't you? Just a little? Edith, Dad isn't acting like himself at all. Our older sisters and brothers have their own families to worry about now. It's just us by ourselves."

"That's exactly what I mean…it's up to us, now. You, me, Ralph, Doris…we've gotta take care of Dad and the boys. We can do it! You know we can! Mama made sure we know how to do everything that a family needs, and we can teach the little ones," Edith insisted. "It's hard, but if we don't buck up right now, this family will…."

"Fall apart," Jeannette finished her sentence. "You're right. You funny little thing! You act more grown up than any of us."

"We'll get through it, Jeannette. God will help us. I know that because I prayed for it." She headed for the stairs. "When you get finished changing, come down and help me get supper on the table. We've just got to get Dad to eat something today. Okay? Maybe then he'll feel better."

Childhood may be over for me, but I can't let it be over for her, Jeannette thought as she pulled her dress over her head. *She sure is determined.* She could hear the sound of pots and pans being pulled out of cupboards downstairs. *I hope God was listening to that one because she definitely knows what she wants!*

***

Months passed, and Edith learned even more about running a household than her mother had taught her. She helped get the children ready for school. She made sure the boys washed behind their ears. And she made sure that Bible reading continued every single night. She was mastering even the most difficult words of the King James version.

Jeannette and Doris learned a lot, too. They both became very good cooks. All three girls knew their way around a kitchen and made sure that the vegetables and fruits they grew were well-preserved for winter meals. The boys helped with chores like bringing in water as well as digging deep holes in the ground for storing the winter supply of potatoes, carrots, and apples.

The older kids came home to help whenever they could, but with families of their own, visits took place mainly on Sundays and holidays. There were exceptions like butchering day, a day that everyone in the family looked forward to. Neighbors and friends always showed up for butchering day. Edith was awake early in anticipation of this special event.

Before daylight, Emma and David Mueller knocked on the door. William answered it, not surprised to see them standing on the steps. He had helpful neighbors.

"We're here to help with the butchering! What do you want us to do?"

William hadn't smiled much since Alverta died, and he didn't smile now. "We're ready to go. The boys are out back getting the bonfire started. David, you can help me put up the iron kettle if you will. Emma, the girls are finishing the breakfast dishes, but maybe you could sharpen the knives?"

"I'll gladly do that," Emma said. "I can help get water out of the well for the kettle, too."

"We'll put Claude to that task," William said, "but he might need some help."

"How are you storing the meat, William?" David asked.

"I'm renting a freezer box. We'll smoke some of the meat—cure it and wrap it, but I'm going to rent a freezer box this year, too."

After the rest of the family and neighbors had gathered, the hogs were killed, then dipped in boiling water to loosen the coarse hair on their hides. The younger boys were assigned the job of scraping the hides to remove it all. Despite boiling first, that job was hard work.

"This job is disgusting," Ralph complained, "and it stinks."

"Trust me—it won't stink when the Christmas ham is in the oven." William had little sympathy for those who complained about work.

The men hung the hogs on large meat hooks and cut them into pieces. Some meat was set aside for smoking and curing—some would be ground for sausage.

Butchering day was long and tiring, but it was exciting and was always a feast day. Emma, Edith, and the other women and girls prepared a huge meal, which the men and boys ate outside at a table made of long planks of wood set up between two sawhorses. Tired as they might be, the men talked endlessly about fishing and hunting under the shade of the maple tree while the table was loaded with home cooking. When they were done devouring all they could consume, the women and girls ate a bite, and it was back to work. Once all the meat from the slaughter had been cooked and the sausages stuffed, other cuts of meat were salted and put into the smokehouse, where a fire of applewood smoked. Everyone worked together till the work was done—then everyone sat together for iced tea.

"I'd like to thank you all for helping today," William started. "This was always one of Alverta's favorite days...." He trailed off, looking down at his hands. There was an uncomfortable silence, neighbors looking at other members of the group for how to respond.

Edith jumped up. "C'mon Jeannette. Let's sing! How about if we do 'Yes, We Have No Bananas' for everyone."

Jeannette knew exactly what her little sister was attempting to do—distract everyone from William's sadness. She and Doris both stood up and joined her, singing loudly and a little off key. No one cared, and everyone clapped when they were finished.

"Girls, that's just about the best thank you we could have had," David Mueller said.

The girls giggled, and for the first time in a long time, William Wagner smiled.

***

Much the same crowd showed up for threshing day. William could not afford to hire any workers. He counted on the goodness of his neighbors and his children to help with the threshing.

Paul McMaster, a neighbor, owned a threshing rig. When the time for harvesting wheat was close, William went to see him and work out an arrangement.

"Paul, I've a favor to ask," William began. "Would you be willing to help us with the threshing this year? I can't pay you, but I can promise you a good meal."

"Well...when you thinkin'? I've got my own threshing to do, and I can surely help, but I need an idea of when your wheat is ready. Mine'll be ready this week. And frankly, I could use *your* help, too."

"Mine'll be ready next week. I appreciate it, and I'll be happy to return the favor. I'll bring the boys with me."

And so, the deal was struck. William and his children helped the McMaster family with their threshing—hard, hot, dusty work. The following week, a large crowd of neighbors assembled at the Wagner farm. The wheat had already been cut, bundled, and tied with string. William let it lay in long rows, drying in the sun until a day came when he and all the children set it up in bundles of eight. William and the older children completed the back-breaking work without help from anyone else, working long into the evening. Little Del and Ricky brought tin cups of water to the family as they worked in the fields, though the boys often spilled more than they carried. Everyone had to contribute, even the little ones. Now the wheat bundles were ready for the thresher.

On threshing day, the family woke up hot. The day was already sizzling. Edith, Jeannette, and Doris were hard at work in the kitchen, preparing a feast that could feed all the helpers who would be coming.

"Boy, I thought if we started early, we'd be done by the heat of the day. So much for that idea!" Edith said as she cleaned chicken for frying.

"Doris, do we have enough butter churned? Maybe you ought to start some more. I'm using quite a bit of what we have for the potatoes," Jeannette said, mopping her brow.

"We don't have time for that," Doris said. "We'll have to make do."

"I'm going to fry all this chicken," Edith said. "There's a whole army out there right now. They'll be famished in a few hours!"

The girls not only fried chicken and cooked potatoes for mashing, but they also cooked a big pot of green beans, with salted ham for seasoning. Jeannette made yellow squash, cabbage slaw, and sliced tomatoes. Doris finished frosting two cakes. The girls were ready for the noontime onslaught, and they took a short break before heading out for the fields.

"Jeannette, you're the oldest. Why don't you stay in here and keep an eye on the food? Doris and I will go out and help with the threshing," Edith suggested.

"Don't you think the food will be all right if we just cover it? We'll have to warm things up a bit when the men come in." Jeannette said. "They're going to need *all* of us out there."

"No, we still have gravy to make. You can work on that, and maybe if you have time, you can churn some more butter." Edith winked at Doris, who winked right back.

"All right you two! Are you telling me you'd rather work out in the field than churn butter? Fine and dandy. Have it your way. I'll pick churning butter any day over working out in the heat and dust!" Jeannette argued, but the other two knew she wasn't mad, and all three girls broke into peals of laughter.

"C'mon, Doris. We better get out there." Edith stood up.

"Here comes Mr. McMaster, anyway."

From the front steps, they could see Paul McMaster coming down the road. The thresher made a ferocious noise. Wheels on the machine went 'round. Belts and pistons moved. It looked like a beast to the girls, and before long, Del and Ricky had joined them on the steps to watch the mechanical monster make its way toward their farm.

It was still early morning, but McMaster knew what kind of work lay ahead of them. An early start was important. He saw the children, the boys jumping up and down. He waved. He was already perspiring profusely, the armpits and back of his shirt wet with sweat. He drove straight out to the field, where the men and women were waiting for him.

The work began without much delay, each person familiar with the task.

William paced back and forth, issuing orders like a general. "Claude… you fetch wood and keep it coming. Del, you bring the corn cobs—they're lighter, but that'll keep you right busy because they burn fast." William knew his boys could help but that they would be limited by their youth. "All right…Paul's runnin' the thresher, so Joe, you drive the water wagon and I'll drive the grain wagon. Stanley, can you keep the water tanks filled for the steam?"

"You bet," came the reply.

"Elijah and Daniel—you two be feeders for the hay wagon. Harold and Jim, you feed the thresher. If you need a break from it, let me know and we'll switch out." The repetitive motion of lifting bundles of wheat onto the belt of the thresher was exhausting and left even the strongest men with aching backs by the end of threshing day. "Who's driving the hay wagon?"

"Pop, let me, let me!" Edith said. "I'm old enough. I know how to handle the horses!"

"Indeed, you do. All right, you drive the hay wagon, but be careful. Doris, go back to the house and help your sister up there. We don't need you, young'un."

Doris glared at Edith. "Guess who's stuck churning the butter now?" she groused before heading for the house, disgusted. Edith laughed as Doris turned back to stick her tongue out.

"Samuel…Ralph…you two are young and strong and can unload the grain wagon, but I'll say the same thing to you as I did to Joe and Dan—if you need a break, let someone know. We can switch out. Till we get a full wagon, can you help the boys with the wood?" The young men nodded agreement to the plan.

"Daddy, can I help?" Ricky said. *Two years old and he's asking to help*, William thought.

"Son, maybe next year. This year, you ride on the wagon with me and help me drive the horses, all right?" He patted his son on the head. *The children have had to grow up fast with Alverta gone.* They might be growing up *too* fast.

With the thresher cranked up, they started down the rows. Elijah and Daniel worked as a pair, pitching the shocks of grain onto the hay wagon. Edith sat tall, like a grown woman, handling the horses well, taking the full wagons to the thresher. Harold and Jim kept a steady flow of hay onto a belt that fed the thresher's grinding teeth and winnowing grates. The machine blew straw and chaff out one long neck, while the grain poured out from the opposite side into the grain wagon, which sat alongside the thresher to receive its bounty. Ricky, riding along with his father, sat up tall, feeling like he was one of the men. He saw his big brothers hard at work, running wood and corncobs to keep the fire burning so that steam could be produced to keep the thresher working. Then he and his dad drove the wagon to the barn where his older brother, Ralph and his friend Sam unloaded the grain into the barn.

Threshing was hot, dirty work. By noon, the men were ready for a break.

"I'm 'bout to pass out, William. Let's go up for some water, at least," Elijah called across the field.

"Good idea," added another.

"I'm ready, too," William said. "Shut it down for a while." He knew Paul hadn't heard him over the noise of the thresher, so he walked over and hollered above the cacophonous machine. "Paul, time for lunch. Shut 'er down."

Edith had jumped off the hay wagon and was on a dead run for the house. Her job was hot, and she was sweaty and grimy, but she wasn't doing the heavy lifting the men had to do.

"Jeannette! Doris!" she yelled as loud as she could as she

neared the back door. "Here we come!" She burst into the house.

"Get out of this kitchen, you filthy thing! Go clean up and then get back out here and help us," Jeannette commanded.

Edith was happy to comply. She went to the dry sink, splashed water from her mother's favorite pitcher over her face and hands and ran back out to the kitchen. Her excitement about threshing day had not been diminished by the heat and dirt.

The girls carried dish after dish to the table while the men washed up. There was little chatter as the hungry workers mowed through extra helpings. Edith, Doris, and Jeannette continued to bring food to the table till every man was sated. Half of them stretched out in the soft grass under the maple tree to nap, while the other half sat in a small circle and talked about the day's work. The girls finally sat down and ate their own lunch. There was very little left by the time they were done.

"Doris said you're driving the hay wagon?" Jeannette asked. "Gosh. You doin' okay with that job?"

"Oh, sure. You know Dad taught me to drive a team of horses this year. I'm pretty good at it. It's fun being out in the field with the men. Everyone's working so hard!" She smiled, self-satisfied. "Mama would be proud of all of us right now. We didn't even have any other women to help with the lunch."

Jeannette reached over and squeezed her arm. "Edith, I can't get over a kid working like a dog the way you do. You're right—Mama would sure be proud. You're going to make a good mother, yourself, some day. And you'll know how to do so many different things!"

Edith smiled again. A long afternoon stood in front of them, but she didn't mind.

"You should see how beautiful the grain is! When it comes flying out of the thresher, it falls through the air like golden snow! And just think what we get to do tomorrow! Mattresses!"

Doris brightened up at the thought. "New mattresses! Remember how Mama would shake out the old straw and then we would stuff in the new?"

"Yeah, and the new straw always smells so good and clean," Jeannette said.

"I have a great idea. Let's make our mattress about a foot high this year!" Edith laughed.

"Then I won't be able to get up on it," Doris said, giving deep consideration to this possibility, a shadow passing over where a smile had once been.

Jeannette and Edith laughed. "Don't worry—we'll toss you up!"

William got up from his resting spot. "Lunch is over. Let's get this job done."

While Jeannette and Doris cleaned up the clutter that twelve men and boys had left behind, Edith and the men headed back out to the fields to glean the precious wheat that would be sold at market. With seven children still at home to feed, getting the best price possible would be more important than ever this year.

4
1923 – THE RIEDELS

"You girls are peeking! Mom! Pop! The girls are peeking at us!"

"We're doing no such thing! You boys are crazy! Why would we want to peek at you getting dressed?"

It was an argument that Verna Riedel heard about every other morning. There was one stove pipe leading upstairs, and it provided the only warmth for the two bedrooms the children shared. They always huddled around that pipe to stay warm while they dressed. She and Wooster *had* to find a bigger house. She grabbed a broom and bumped the handle against the kitchen ceiling several times.

"Settle it up there and get down here for breakfast, or you'll be late for school!"

Virgil was the first boy down the stairs. "Mom, Cora and Marjorie were looking at us getting dressed. I saw them peeking through their fingers."

Verna sighed. "Virgil, I highly doubt that the girls were peeking. What earthly interest could they have in watching you boys dress?"

Virgil sat down in his chair at the table, sullen. "Well, they *were*. You just ask Robert. I bet he saw them, too."

Before long, the rest of the boys descended on the small kitchen. Robert joined Virgil at the table. He reached for a piece of toast, casual. Having dropped out in the eighth grade to help on the farm, he was already done with school and would be working with his Grandpa that day. No need to rush. Ross, on the other hand, was frantic.

"Mom, we're gonna be late for school!" Ross said.

"Yes, I *know*," Verna said. "That's why I was banging on the ceiling. You and Virgil will drive me to distraction." A favorite saying of Verna's, Robert had been accused of the same thing many times.

The girls soon arrived at the table, little Marjorie being pulled along by Cora. Marjorie adored her big sister.

"Mother, I am eighteen years old now, and I have no desire whatsoever to look at these boys getting dressed! And Marjorie is too little to care about such things. We can't even have a peaceful morning with these scallywags getting so worked up over nothing."

Verna ignored the complaint, chucked Marjorie under the chin and sat her in a highchair. "Sit down, Cora, and eat. You and Robert are going to help me get stores in the basement this morning. We've got to move some things around down there, so let's get going."

Cora ignored Verna, focused on something entirely different. "Mom, do you think Pop would let Beau Jacobs come courting Sunday afternoon?" Cora said.

"Maybe Beau Jacobs should come ask your Pop himself," Verna answered. She knew Cora was sweet on Beau, and the idea that Beau should come ask Wooster himself made Cora uncomfortable. It probably made *Beau* uncomfortable, truth be known.

On cue, Cora shifted in her seat. "I'll tell him to do that, but you know he's kind of shy."

"He better get *un*-shy if he's to go out with you. Your father likes a strong man, one who's not afraid of his own shadow." She gave Marjorie a bite of oatmeal. "That's a good little girl," she cooed to her baby. "What happened to Dale Swerline? He seems like a nice young man."

"Oh, I haven't decided between the two of them," Cora said.

"Criminy, Cora. You're practically an old maid. Eighteen! You better figure it out pretty soon," Robert said.

"Robert Riedel! I am *not* an old maid. What's wrong with you boys this morning?" Cora pushed herself away from the table. "Mother, I'm not hungry. I'm going on downstairs and start working."

"Not before you read your Bible, you're not. Go on, now. And besides, I don't want you moving things around in the basement till I'm down there and can see what's going to end up where."

Cora disappeared into the parlor, muttering under her breath.

"And stop your grumbling," Verna called after her.

"Mom, can't Cora help you with the basement? Grandpa wanted me to come over this week, and I think this might be the best day," Robert said. "Do you have heavy things to move?"

"Kinda. It's all the canned goods, the potatoes, apples, and so forth. Oh, and those gallon jugs of cider…well, I s'pose you could go on to Grandpa's. Cora and I can take care of it while the boys are at school. We'll just take Marjorie down there with us."

"Thanks, Mom. I think Grandpa wants me to help him clean the chicken coop."

"Oh, brother. Are you sure you wouldn't rather be in the basement?"

"No, Mom, I don't mind helping with the chicken coop. I'll be home before supper, all right?"

"All right, son. I'd tell you to have fun, but I'm pretty sure you won't."

Verna didn't know why Robert was so anxious to help with such a repugnant job, but there must be something attractive about it for the young man to so readily volunteer.

What Verna didn't realize was that the work *was* fun to Robert because of the horses. They were important to the task ahead because of their strength in hauling away the chicken excrement. Robert loved his Grandpa's horses more than just about anything. He learned how to properly care for horses from Grandpa, who loved them almost as much as he loved his children.

By the time Robert got to his grandparents' house, Grandpa was already out back, preparing for work that most people would think of as disgusting. But not Grandpa. To him it was just another chore that had to be done to maintain an orderly farm. He was whistling an old tune to himself. Robert didn't recognize the song.

"Hey, Grandpa! I'm here!" Robert hollered as he approached. "What do you want me to do first?"

"Finish that cookie in your hand, that's what I want you to do first," Grandpa said, laughing. "You don't want to drop it in this muck, that's for sure. Got into Grandma's cookie jar, did ya?"

"Well, she offered, and I didn't resist. She's the best cookie baker in Wyandot County." Robert had eaten a lot of cookies in his lifetime, and no one could beat his Grandma yet. He popped the last of the molasses gem in his mouth.

"Tell you what," Grandpa started. "Why don't you go ahead

and get the team hooked up to the low wagon. We'll shovel the manure into it and take it out back to dry a little. I'll put it on the fields once it's good and dry. Won't be so smelly, either."

"Which horses should I use?"

"Take Old Beulah and Bud. They're the oldest, and this won't be such a heavy load for them. But they've gotta have *some* kind of job to do so they'll feel like they're still useful. Horses need to feel useful." Grandpa attributed lots of human traits to his horses.

Smiling to himself, Robert did as he was told. Old Beulah and Bud were compliant. Because of their age, they were used to work routines and were easy to harness. He brought the wagon out of the barn, leading the horses to the shady area near the chicken coop.

"Gonna be a hot one today," Grandpa said. "We're better off to get this done this morning. This afternoon will be miserable. The smell will get strong, too."

Robert agreed. He kicked off his shoes, rolled up his pantlegs, and waded barefoot into the slimy chicken manure, just as his Grandpa had done. There was no other way…they couldn't ruin their only pair of shoes, or in Grandpa's case, boots. The two men worked together, lifting shovel after shovel of chicken manure into the low wagon. Bud and Old Beulah stood still, swatting the occasional fly with their long tails.

Because Grandpa was so fastidious and completed this onerous job on a regular schedule, there was only one wagon full of manure to shovel, and the men were finished with their job before noon. They took the wagon farther out on the property behind one of the big white barns. They climbed into the wagon, pushed the manure around so that it was in a layer instead of in piles. It would dry faster that way. They unhitched the horses, took them back to the horse barn, and gave them water and oats.

"Let's go wash our feet," Grandpa said.

They headed for the hand pump in the barnyard. Robert pumped first, allowing Grandpa to stick his feet under the faucet while water ran freely over them. Then it was Robert's turn. He never minded that the job included getting his feet covered in chicken dung. It was easy to wash off. He was always clean before it was time to return home.

"Let's go see if Grandma has some lunch for us."

Robert walked side-by-side with his grandfather, a man he

admired. Grandpa was a hard worker and ran a good farm. A true horseman, he also liked to run selected horses in sulky races at the Wyandot County fair. As they walked, Robert hoped out loud that someday he'd get to be a driver for one of the races.

"I know these horses pretty well, now, Grandpa. I'd like to drive Palding Boy in a race. He's my favorite."

Grandpa had a picture of Palding Boy painted on the barn where all eight horses were stabled. Palding Boy was the favorite of all his horses. Robert remembered his Grandpa once telling him that the other horses might have been a little jealous about the picture. Robert personally thought *that* might be carrying the human traits a little too far. Nevertheless, Palding Boy was a good trotter and Robert loved him. If he ever got a choice about which horse to race, Palding Boy would be his first pick.

"Son, there's more to racing than just getting on the sulky and driving the horse. I'd want you to have some lessons from one of the boys who've been doing it for years. People *can* get hurt racing, you know."

Robert had seen a few crashes in his life. That was part of the excitement. Unless the horse got hurt, of course.

"That's not a bad idea, Grandpa. Who should I talk to?"

"I'll see if Frank Reilly could work with you. You better talk it over with your mother and dad first, though."

Robert knew his mother would have a fit. He was still a boy— in her mind, anyway.

"I'll be sure to do that. I think Pop would be fine with it, but Mom…."

"That's what I mean," Grandpa said, raising his eyebrows.

Grandma had turkey sandwiches with cheddar cheese and apple slices waiting for the hungry men. "I assume you both washed your hands good?"

The men looked at each other and laughed. "We near 'bout had to take a bath!" Grandpa said. "I almost waited too long to get that job done this time," he confessed.

"Well, sit down and eat. Robert, the cookie jar is over on the counter. I moved it to where it was easier for you to get at."

Robert grinned. "You know me so well, Grandma."

"I sure know that sweet tooth!"

Lunch was over in a matter of minutes. "Robert, will you put the horses out to pasture? I'll be out in just a couple of minutes," Grandpa said.

"Sure. Be glad to."

Robert let all eight horses out so they could graze in one of the fenced pastures, around which, Grandpa had a practice track for Palding Boy and the other three racers. All eight horses were beautiful—even Old Beulah and Bud. Robert stood at the fence and admired how they interacted with each other, the swoop of their necks, the brush of their tails. How they could bear all their weight on those skinny legs was a mystery to Robert. *God's handiwork*, he thought.

Back at the house, Grandma and Grandpa had taken up a seat under a shady oak. There, they would rest for a few minutes before starting any other chores. Robert joined the couple, recovering from a full morning of physical labor. They stayed quiet, enjoying a breeze that had kicked up out of nowhere. Grandpa scanned the sky.

"As hot and humid as it is, we might get a thunderstorm today."

"We could use the relief. I'll go open the rain barrel just in case," Robert said.

"Thank you, boy." Grandma appreciated what a helper her grandson could be. He didn't have to be told every single thing that needed to be done—he just saw it and accomplished it. He was smart that way.

By the time Robert returned to the oak tree, Grandpa was snoring, and Grandma wasn't far behind. Robert moved his chair a little closer to Grandma and put his feet up on a tree stump, whispering to her.

"Grandma, how old is Grandpa now?"

"Seventy-seven."

"Wow. He's sixty years older than me."

"And he feels every bit of it. Look how tired he is."

"How old are *you* now?"

Grandma smiled. "Now Robert, don't you know it's impertinent to ask a lady her age?"

He blushed, but he was hot, and his face was so red he didn't think Grandma noticed.

"I'm sorry, Grandma."

Then she laughed. "Boy, I'm teasing you! I'm not too proud to tell you I'm seventy-three."

"You don't look it."

"You're just saying that to make up to me," she laughed again.

A strong, cool breeze reached them again. Robert noticed that the sky had grown dark with ominous clouds on the horizon.

"Grandma, I think it's fixin' to rain. I better go get the horses in before it starts up. It could get bad fast."

"Lands, yes. I think you're right. I better get your *Grandpa* in," she said, joking.

While Grandma tried to rouse Grandpa, Robert trotted out to the horse paddock. "Bud! Old Beulah! C'mon! Giddup!"

The horses, lazy with full bellies, slowly walked towards him. He reined them up and walked them to the barn. Then he returned to the field. He saw lightning in the distance, and the thunder was so loud it hurt his ears.

"Jamie! Miss Sally! C'mon! Giddup!" Jamie and Miss Sally were younger, and maybe sensing a change in the weather, trotted over to Robert. He repeated the procedure he had carried out with the other two horses. Just as they arrived at the barn, it began to pour.

As quickly as he could, Robert stabled the two horses and began a dead run back to the field. The four remaining horses had huddled under an oak, which branched out like a green umbrella, and at first, they seemed nonplussed about the rain. As he got closer, Robert saw they were pawing at the ground with their hooves. Out of the corner of his eye, Robert caught a glimpse of his Grandpa trying to get out to the field, too. Robert picked up his stride.

Neither man was close enough to make a difference in the fate of those horses. The storm had come up too fast. Lightning struck that tall, tall oak tree, lighting it up like fireworks. The horses dropped over onto the ground almost as a group, one quickly following the other. Robert was sure he felt each thud. He was sick at his stomach, knowing the horses had been electrocuted. They were all dead, sure as anything.

"No! No!" Grandpa hollered, trying to run out to the field. Another loud crack of thunder—lightning struck again, this time, between the tree and the fence.

"Grandpa, go back to the house!" Robert yelled. "Go back to the house!" Now he ran in the direction of his grandfather, who was still headed for the field. He caught up with him just as the old man was getting ready to climb over the fence. Grabbing the back of his jacket, he kept him from making it over.

"Grandpa, let's go to the house. You can't help those animals."

"Palding Boy! Palding Boy!" Grandpa was grief-stricken.

"You can't help Palding Boy, either! C'mon! We'll be the next ones killed!"

The old man looked at the younger. In the pouring rain, his face was the saddest sight Robert had ever seen. He turned and began a shuffling walk back toward the house.

"Grandpa, we can't dawdle out here. It's not safe. C'mon, now." The rain continued in a steady downpour. Robert put his arm around his grandfather's back and urged him forward at a quicker pace. Lightning crackled every few seconds, raising hairs on the back of Robert's neck.

They arrived at the house, drenched and depressed. Grandma brought them towels and tried to help them get dried off as best they could.

"Grandma, the horses…" Robert began.

"I already saw the whole thing from the back porch, boy. You go get one of Grandpa's old shirts and pairs of dungarees. I'll work on him."

Robert did as he was told, and when he returned to the kitchen, he saw his grandfather still wet, sitting in a chair by the table, hunched over, head in his hands. Robert walked over and put a hand on his shoulder.

"Grandpa, I tried to get the horses in the barn. I tried."

His grandfather looked up at him. Robert thought he saw tears in his eyes, but he wasn't sure. He had never seen Grandpa cry—ever.

"Boy, I know you did. That storm just come up too fast for us. Four horses gone in one fell swoop…."

Grandma busied herself with some activity. Robert didn't know for sure what she was doing, but he heard her sniffling and knew she was trying to hide the fact that she was crying. The rain continued to come down, though the thunder and lightning had subsided. Now, it was just another summer shower.

"I better head for home, but I'll come over and help you bury the horses, Grandpa. It'll be an awful lot of work digging the holes."

"Yes, boy, we'll need more'n you and me. I don't want to talk about it now. You come over tomorrow and we'll talk about it then."

Grandpa stood up and strode from the kitchen. Robert went over to where Grandma was puttering at the sink.

"Grandma, I sure am sorry. I promise to come back tomorrow to help, okay?" He put his arm around her shoulders.

His grandmother turned and hugged him tight. "Be careful out there. In fact, why don't you wait up a bit before you go out again?" He knew she was worried about more lightning.

Robert looked out the window. "It might be as good as it's gonna get for a while, Grandma. I'm gonna go." He shook his head. "I sure am sorry," he repeated.

He walked to the door, gave one more look into the living room, but Grandpa wasn't there. *Probably wanted some privacy,* he thought.

"I'll be back tomorrow," he said to Grandma one more time as he left the house.

Just like that, Robert's racing career was over.

5
LATE FALL 1927 – THE WAGNERS

"Dad, won't you come to church with us? You haven't been in such a long time."

"No, Edith. You all go on." William Wagner had taken the children to Mt. Zion church regularly after Alverta's death in 1920 but stopped attending not many months later.

Edith moved close to her father's side. "Dad, I miss singing hymns with you. You helped keep me in the right key, you know." Her father wasn't really a strong singer, but she hoped to kid him into a brighter mood. He gave her a sideways glance.

"I know better than that. You all go on, now. I'll see you when you get home."

Discouraged, Edith called to her younger brothers. It was just her, Claude, Del, and Ricky at home now—all the other kids had married and started families of their own.

"Boys, come on! We'll be late!"

She heard a rumble coming down the stairs. The boys—probably all vying to be first down the steps, jostling each other as they raced.

It's a wonder they don't break their necks! "You boys settle down. Time to get going." Edith led the pack out the front door and began the mile walk to Mt. Zion. She knew the walk would do her good. Her brothers fell in behind, still elbowing each other and kidding around as they half-walked, half-wrestled their way to church.

"If you boys don't straighten up, you're going to wind up falling on this wet road. You'll be a mess before we ever get to church!"

"Who made you the Queen of England?" Del spouted.

"I'm the oldest. *Someone* has to keep you three in line!"

"Well, whoop-dee-doo for you!" Ricky barked.

Edith had passed her sixteenth birthday on November 8. Sweet sixteen, William called her, displaying one of the smiles that were so rare these days. She made herself a small cake, upon which she placed one candle. Her older brothers and sisters didn't make the party, but the younger boys sang to her as she blew out the candle and made a wish. *I wish my father would be happy again.* Nothing for herself. Her thoughts were only of the man whose ongoing sadness was a shadow over their home.

They arrived at church and ducked into a back row as the first hymn started up. Edith saw a few disapproving looks as the four Wagner children filed into the pew. She also caught a smile on Wade Eberle's face. Or was it more of a leer? She wasn't the least bit interested in Wade, and she turned her attention to her hymnal.

The boys never sang in church. Edith could see their lips moving, but no sound came out of their mouths. *Those fakes!* Edith loved to sing. If she ever had children, she decided, they would *all* sing. She would teach them four-part harmony. *Homes should be full of music.*

When they had finished "Oh God Our Help in Ages Past" and listened to readings from the Gospel, they settled back into their pews for the sermon. Pastor DeWalt came to the lectern wearing his black Sunday suit. He was unsmiling, severe in his countenance. Edith hoped the boys could behave just for the next forty minutes so as not to invoke the minister's ire. Without William there to give them a chastising look, they could be ornery, even in a solemn place like the church.

"Thanksgiving!" boomed the pastor's voice, shocking Edith back to attention. "What do we have to be thankful for?"

"Good question," muttered Claude under his breath.

Edith narrowed her eyes and placed a finger over her lips to shush her brother.

"This Thursday, we will be remembering to give thanks to God, will we not? We will be thanking him for another year of his love and provision. For food on the table and a roof over our heads. We will thank him for our good health. And even when our health is not so good, we will thank him for continuing to cover us in his benevolent protection.

"We will thank God for our families," the minister continued. "Parents, say thank you for your children, and children, take time to thank God for your parents who nurture and strengthen you, not only with food and care, but with the knowledge of God's love for you."

Edith found herself tuning out. The minister's voice droned in the background as she thought of Mama and how much she missed her smile and laughter throughout every corner of their home. She wanted to emulate her mother in all ways possible. She was tired, though. She worked so hard to take on the role her mother would have played in her brothers' lives. After her sisters married, she was solely responsible as the only woman in the house. She kept their home clean and orderly so that it might be a source of cheer for her father. She cooked and baked, did laundry, and helped with all the chores her mother had taught her to complete. Make butter. Mend clothes. Can fruit and vegetables. Beat the rugs every spring and fall. Refresh the straw ticks after threshing. Every job was important to her own preparation for marriage and a family, but it was most important to maintaining some sense of normalcy in a family where 'normal' would never mean the same thing again. Her brothers didn't require a heavy hand, thankfully—just the occasional correction when they got too full of themselves. Her father seemed to need peace, and everything she did was with that goal in mind. But she realized again, she was just plain tired. Some days, it felt like too much.

She snapped back to attention when she heard Pastor DeWalt winding up his sermon.

"In every single day, be grateful for what God has done for you," the minister intoned. "No matter what situation you find yourself in, no matter how hard times might be for you, God has a way of using that circumstance to make you stronger. If the road was easy, we might never seek his face. He uses the difficult times to pull us closer to him so that he can teach us to be patient, to persevere. It is in the hard times that he molds our hearts and brings us closer into a relationship with him. So no matter what, we have plenty to be thankful for this Thanksgiving. Carry that with you this week as you celebrate the holiday with your families."

Pastor DeWalt walked over to a big oak throne chair where he sat in silence as his congregation contemplated his words. Edith looked at the ornately carved chair thinking, *he looks like a king up there.* After a few minutes, the minister stood up and directed the congregation in singing "Now Thank We All Our God." Edith did not sing. She wanted to memorize the pastor's words, and so, focused on them.

Repeating the words to herself many times helped her remember…

No matter what situation you find yourself in, no matter how hard times might be for you, God has a way of using that circumstance to make you stronger. He uses the difficult times to pull us closer to him so that he can teach us to be patient, to persevere. Edith knew it was true. She straightened her shoulders.

As she and her brothers walked down the steps outside the front of the church, Edith felt someone grab her elbow. She turned. Wade Eberle.

"What are you doing after church today, cutie?"

"I'm going home to make lunch for my dad and my brothers." Edith was as matter of fact as possible. She didn't want to encourage Wade, who had a reputation for being 'fast' with the girls.

"What are you doing after that? Would you like to go for a ride? My dad just got a new Pontiac Coupe."

"And just exactly where is it that we would go in this Pontiac Coupe?" Edith asked.

"Oh…just around the countryside." Wade had a familiar smirk on his face. "Maybe we could find a nice place to park and…read the Bible."

Edith snorted. "I'm sure!" She pulled her arm away, stiffened her spine, and pulled herself up to her full height. "No thank you, Mr. Eberle, for your offer, but I'll be occupied at home today." With that, she moved away to catch up with her brothers, turning back to see Wade still staring after her with that unsettling grin on his face. For one second, she thought about how fun it would be to take a ride in a brand-new car, something her family could never afford. Then she shivered and remembered it was *Wade*.

Edith was used to being ogled. Though she never thought highly of her own looks, most of the older boys in town thought that she had grown into a beautiful young woman. With thick, dark, curly hair, a good figure, and laughing eyes, lots of young men wanted to court her. But she still hadn't met a boy with whom she would ever be more than friends. She knew God had already chosen one special man for her, and she would wait.

As they walked home, Edith left thoughts of Wade behind and concentrated again on what Pastor DeWalt had said about making the best of every circumstance, about growing closer to God. She thought again about the truth of his words. God gave her the strength to get through her mother's death and help her family. God was giving her perseverance, and even if she didn't understand why it had to be this way, she knew she needed to trust God for the ability to carry on. He was preparing her for something.

***

Thanksgiving Day, November 24, 1927. Edith had cooked a small turkey from their own flock, which Claude had slaughtered and Ricky had de-feathered after much complaining.

"Isn't this woman's work?" Ricky whined.

"It's *family* work," Edith answered. "Do you want turkey for Thanksgiving or not?"

Having successfully quieted the protests, she also fixed mashed potatoes, carrots, green beans, homemade rolls, and pumpkin pie with fresh whipped cream. It was a feast.

Her father worked in the barn all morning. It was hard for him to face holidays without Alverta. He avoided contact with the children until it was time to sit down and eat.

"Dad, come in! Soup's on!" Del called to him while Edith brought each steaming dish to the table. She placed the food on a crisp, freshly pressed white linen tablecloth. The table looked beautiful— almost like a wealthy family.

William knocked the mud off his boots at the door, entered the kitchen, and crossed over to wash his hands. Edith waited for some comment on the food. No mention was forthcoming.

"Let's pray, Dad," she said, encouraging the head of the household to lead them.

"You say the prayer this year," he answered.

She tried to explore his face, but he had already bowed his head. She felt the sting of tears beginning to well up, then cleared her throat. "All right. Everyone ready? Lord, we thank you for another year of your loving providence. We're grateful that you continue to watch over our family—those here at this table and those who are in their own homes today. We thank you for this food—bless it for its intended use, to strengthen us in body and mind. And we humbly ask you to continue to guide us closer to you every day. Amen."

She had barely gotten the blessing out of her mouth before the boys were grabbing for the food she had worked so hard to prepare. William concentrated on his meal, wordless, while his sons babbled about school and hunting and basketball. It seemed that in a matter of minutes, the meal was over.

William rose, said "thank you" and went back out to the barn. The boys scattered.

Edith looked around the kitchen and sighed. She knew Christmas would be much the same. Holidays just weren't as joyful as they had once been. Oh, they'd go over to Grandpa Hufford's and have a big meal with the entire family—despite not exchanging gifts, they always had fun. But then they'd come home, do their chores, and retire to the oppressive quiet of a home without a mother.

Perseverance. Yes. Edith knew God was preparing her. For what, she could never have guessed.

6
A NEW BEGINNING
1928

"Who are you staring at?"

His trance minimally interrupted by Ed Jones, Robert never moved his eyes. "What do you mean, who am I staring at? I'm not staring at anyone."

"The heck you aren't. If I didn't know better, I'd say you were staring at Doris Wagner's little sister."

Had it been that obvious? "I was looking at Doris. You know I went out with her a couple of times."

"Yeah, but Doris is by the punch bowl, and you're looking at the cake table."

"All right, all right. Leave me alone, will ya? Nothin' wrong with a fella looking, is there?"

"Not a thing. Just so you know, she's only sixteen."

"I said leave me alone, will ya!"

A quiet minute passed, and having processed Ed's last statement, Robert turned to face him. "Sixteen you say? Are you sure about that?"

"Yup. Just turned sixteen not that long ago, too."

"Brother. You'd never know it. She looks like she's about twenty."

"Oh, she's a looker all right. Say, her dad's mighty strict, isn't he? I mean, didn't you have to practically beg him to go out with Doris?"

"Not exactly. But yeah—he's cautious, I guess. He's such a quiet man it's hard to tell with him."

The two young men sipped their punch, backs against the wall, surveying the other young people waiting to go into the auditorium and take their seats for a band concert. Like ponies let out of a paddock on a warm spring day, the crowd was restless from being cooped up through the cold winter. The room was full of lively chatter and occasional outbursts of loud laughter. Girls in bright dresses floated from conversation to conversation. Young men did their best to gain their attention. Robert and Ed continued in quiet surveillance for several minutes.

"You s'pose she'd think I was too old for her?" Robert began again.

"How should I know?" Ed said.

"Well, for criminy sake…you knew she just turned sixteen! I thought maybe you talked to her or something."

"Well, I haven't. I just know she had a birthday. I must have heard Doris or Ralph Wagner talking about it, you know, at church or some such thing. Gees, I can't believe you didn't meet her when you were out there courting Doris."

"I might remember seeing her around, but…" he trailed off. He didn't remember seeing her as the girl he saw before him now.

The men continued watching the activity. Robert saw Evelyn Geary walk over to where Doris' little sister was standing and begin a conversation. This was his opportunity. Evelyn was a friend. He made his way toward the cake table.

The girls were chatting, animated, cheeks flushed bright pink. Robert overheard them talking about the concert that was to start in only a few minutes. There was no time to waste.

"Hi, Evelyn," Robert opened. "How are you?"

"Oh, hi, Robert!" she answered, a wide smile on her face. "Gosh, it's nice to see you. I saw you over there with Ed Jones a minute ago. Where'd he go?"

"He went to find his brother. How have you been?" Out of the corner of his eye, he could see Edith was paying little attention to the conversation he was having with Evelyn.

"I'm good, I'm good. Robert, have you ever met Edith Wagner?"

At this, Edith spun and turned her full attention to Robert. She was stunning. Dark brown, curly hair. Deep, deep chocolate brown eyes. *So deep a man could drown in them.* He flushed at the thought and turned his head away, hoping she wouldn't see.

"You dated my sister, didn't you?" Edith said.

"Uh, yes, I did. We went out a couple of times." Why did she have to bring *that* up?

"Didn't you like her?"

"Well, I think it might have been more that she didn't like *me*."

Edith laughed—a hearty, full-throated, head-thrown-back laugh.

"I don't see what's so funny about it," Robert said.

"Oh, don't grouse, now! I just thought your answer was funny."

There was an uncomfortable silence. Evelyn had wandered off to the other side of the room. Edith looked around and pretended to pay no attention to the young man standing beside her, taking only an occasional peek out of the corner of her eye to gauge his demeanor. Finally, he spoke again.

"Who are you sitting with during the concert?"

"Evelyn. We came together."

"Would you mind if me and Ed sat with you girls?"

"Why would you want to do that?"

"Criminetly! I was just askin'."

Edith hid a playful smirk, put her hands behind her back and began raising up and down on her toes, then her heels, considering this proposal.

"I suppose it would be fine. You can sit with us." The queen had issued a proclamation.

"You don't have to do me any favors."

Then she put one small, warm hand on his forearm. She looked him in the eye, her face open, honest, and kind. "I was just joshing with you. I'm sorry. I'd be happy to have you boys accompany us. I'm sure Evelyn would say the same."

When Robert recovered from the unexpected show of intimacy, he offered her his arm. "Then let's go on in and find a good seat up front."

Edith took his arm. "We ought to find Ed and Evelyn first." She smiled, and though she had no idea, Robert was hooked—hopelessly and eternally hooked.

***

"Mr. Wagner, I'd like your permission to court Edith."

William narrowed his eyes and looked over the top of his newspaper at the slender, ramrod-straight young man in front of him. "Didn't you go out with Doris before?"

Is everyone going to bother me about that? "Yes sir, I did. We went out a couple of times. I think she found another beau, didn't she?"

"Yes, she did. And she's betrothed to him. Riley Puterbaugh."

"Well good for her. I hope she's very happy. Riley's a good man," Robert said.

"Yes, he is. Now what's this again about Edith?"

"I'd like your permission to go out with her, Mr. Wagner."

William folded his newspaper and placed it on the table next to his chair. "Sit down, son. Let's talk about this a little." He waved his hand to indicate where Robert should sit.

Robert sat down, felt a nervous tickle in his throat and coughed.

"You need some water, son?"

"No sir. I'm fine. Just a little dry throat, I guess. What I'd like to talk to you about…."

"Let's start with what I'd like to talk to *you* about," William interrupted. "First of all, how old are you, son?"

"I just turned 21 last December," Robert began.

"I thought you looked a little older than Edith. You know her age?" William leaned forward in his chair, his gaze steady.

"Yes, sir. I know she's only sixteen. Do you view that as a problem?"

William leaned back, put his fingertips together and sat quiet for a minute.

"She's legal, I suppose. But legal or not, sixteen is mighty young," William finally said.

Robert sat very straight in his chair, wanting to appear mature and determined. "Well, Mr. Wagner, I can tell you this—I already admire Edith most highly, even though we've only had occasion to speak to each other a few times. I could tell right off the kind of girl she is—how she's been raised. If I may speak forthrightly, I believe she is the girl I'm meant to marry."

William's eyes opened wide. *These young people, always in such a hurry to move life along.* He sat back in his chair.

"I don't know how in tarnation you could believe such a thing when you haven't even begun a courtship yet. Setting that aside, I see

41

no good reason why the two of you shouldn't be allowed to go out. Tell me, what do you do for a living?"

"Right now, I work on our farm and my grandpap's farm. I also shear sheep, and I paint houses in the summer. I make a decent living."

"Have you ever been in any kind of trouble?"

"No sir. My pop would tan my hide if I ever embarrassed the family name."

"Do you go to church?"

"Yes sir. We go to the United Brethren church every Sunday. The only time I've ever missed was when I was sick. Oh, and a few times during the harvest."

"Well, I suppose you could escort Edith to church to start with, but you need to know we go to Mt. Zion."

Had he heard William correctly? He could start dating Edith? Robert could barely contain his excitement, swallowing several times before he spoke again.

"Would it be all right with you if I ask her today?" Robert said.

"Sure, sure. She's upstairs cleaning. I'll call her down."

William got up from his chair. It wasn't easy for him to stand on his skinny legs. Robert wondered if there was something wrong with him, his legs were so thin. He watched the older gentleman hobble off to find his daughter. Only after he was out of the room did Robert allow himself to smile.

He heard them returning and quickly stood up to greet them. "Here she is. You young people talk. Edith, I'm going out to the barn for a while." William left the room.

Edith indicated that Robert should sit down again, and she sat in the chair where William had conducted his interrogation.

"Well, Robert. Hello. What brings you here?"

As if she didn't know. "I came to ask your dad if I could call on you. He's given his permission."

"He has, has he? So now are you planning to ask *me* about *my* feelings on the subject?"

She didn't smile and held her hands folded in her lap, prim and proper—formal.

"Of course," Robert began. "Courtship requires two interested parties, doesn't it?"

"Oh, so it's a courtship," Edith said. "I s'pose that would be all right, but I'll have to let a couple of other boys know that I'll be seeing them less."

Was she toying with him? She had a sparkle in her eye, mischievous and playful.

"Other boys? Are you going out steady with them?" Robert said.

"Oh, no, but they've been coming around for a little longer than I've known you, and it wouldn't be fair to just leave them hanging, now would it?"

"No, I guess not." He was dejected.

Then she smiled.

"I wasn't that interested in them, anyway. I've been waiting for just the right boy to come around," she said, taking a deep breath before adding, "and now he might be here."

He felt his heart beating in his throat. He didn't know if he could croak out the next words.

"I'll pick you up for church on Sunday. What time do your services start?"

"We try to be there by 9:15 because the service starts at 9:30," Edith said. "I don't like getting stuck sitting in the very front pew or the very last pew. Can you be here a little after 9:00?"

"You bet. It'll be chilly, so I'll bring a blanket for us."

"Oh, my brothers will appreciate that, too!"

Brothers? Oh, brother. He forced a smile. "All right, then. I'll see you Sunday morning."

"I'm looking forward to it." She had such a sweet way of saying things and smiling her wide smile. He badly wanted to kiss her.

"Good-bye, Edith." He turned away before he could embarrass himself.

"Good-bye, Robert. Don't forget your hat."

He turned back and saw she was holding his hat out to him. As he took it from her, their hands brushed against each other.

"Thanks," he said, his voice raspy. "G'bye now."

He closed the door behind him and headed toward where his horse was tied up. He looked back at the house for a second, and while he couldn't be sure, but he thought he saw his very pretty Edith peeking at him from behind a lace curtain. He tipped his hat and the curtains were quickly closed.

"She's the one. Thank you, God. You sent me *the one*."

***

"Uncle Wesley, can I borrow $25 from you?"

"$25! That's not exactly pocket change, Robert. I already loaned you $50 to buy that Roadster you got." Wesley Riedel was sitting at his kitchen table with a cup of coffee. He eyed his nephew up and down. *The boy has moxie.*

"I paid it back, didn't I? I worked hard to get you paid back in just a couple of months."

"Well, you *did* do that. So, then…another loan, eh? What do you need it for?"

"A wedding band."

"What? Did you just say a 'wedding band'?"

Robert grinned. "Yes, sir. I'm getting married. Didn't think anyone would have me, huh?"

His uncle laughed. "I was thinking more that you'd never settle down. A wife might hamper your hunting and fishing time. Who's the lucky girl?"

"Edith Wagner."

"William Wagner's girl?" Now Wesley knit his eyebrows together and leaned forward. "Isn't she a little young for you?"

"That's what Pop and Mom said, but when they met her, they saw how mature she is. And of course, her dad brought the subject up, but over the last few months, I won him over." Without arrogant intention, Robert puffed his chest out.

"Well, draw up a chair and tell me about her."

"All right." Robert sat down in a ladder-back chair and thought about where to start. "I met her at a concert. I had seen her before, of course, because I dated her sister, Doris, a couple of times. But me and Doris would never work out—she wasn't really my type."

"I didn't know you had a 'type'," Wesley said.

"To be honest, I don't think *I* knew I had a 'type' till I met Edith. She's the only girl I've ever even considered being married to. She's beautiful, first of all, but then…." He stopped, not knowing if he could put into words the way he felt about Edith.

"Better be more to it than beauty, boy."

"There is." Robert took a second to pull his thoughts together. "She's funny. She's got the best sense of humor of any girl I ever met. And she's funny partly because she's always so cheerful. She has a joyful spirit. You know—an optimistic outlook about life. But she's not silly, like so many girls her age. She's got her head on straight. She knows how to work. She's *had* to work since her mom died when she was young. She's the answer to what has kept that family together, the way it looks to me. She can work around the house, can cook better than my own mom, but she also knows how to handle horses and work a garden—she's just smart. And she's got *energy* about life. I've never met anyone like her." He stopped talking. He was out of breath.

"Hmm…" Wesley leaned back in his chair. "And you think she's worth $25?" he said, a roguish look in his eye, a half-grin on his face.

"Heck all Friday, she's worth a *million* dollars, but all I need right now is $25." Robert grinned back at his uncle's joking.

Wesley considered this for a brief second. "Hold on, son. I'll be right back."

His uncle disappeared for a minute. Robert could hear him unlocking something, fiddling around in some papers and re-locking whatever it was. Probably where Uncle Wesley hid his money.

"Here you go, boy. I assume I'll get an invitation to the wedding?"

"You bet. We're going to get married in August, have a big feast at her dad's house."

"How long have you been courting? Aren't you going to have a little more of an engagement than a couple of months?" Uncle Wesley put a hand on Robert's shoulder. "You want to make sure of these things, you know. Marriage isn't anything to trifle with."

"Uncle Wes, I've never been so sure of anything in my life, and when you get to be around her more, you'll know why I say that."

Wesley smiled. "I'll look forward to it."

Robert smiled, too, and shook Wesley's hand. "Till you're better paid, I thank you." He turned for the door and ran for the car. He was on an important mission. He had a ring to buy.

7
OCTOBER 1929

"Edith, Jim Sowers and some of the fellas say there's a run on the bank uptown. They're going to pull out their money. I better go pull out some of our money, too, I s'pose."

"What did you say, Robert? A run on the bank?" Edith wasn't familiar with the term, but something about Robert's tone worried her. His words were clipped, anxious. "What exactly does that mean?"

"They told me the stock market crashed, and the banks are closing their doors right now—shutting down for the day, maybe even longer." Robert grabbed his hat and started for the front door.

"*What?* My lands, I never heard of such a thing! How can they close? People need to be able to get their own money!" Edith held their son, Bobby, a little closer. He was barely six months old.

"That's exactly why they call it a run. Everyone's 'running' to the bank to get their money out before they can't get their hands on it anymore. I'm going to go up to First National and get us some extra cash to have on hand. I'll be back in a few minutes." Robert came back for a quick kiss, then hurried out the door.

Extra cash. There was little cash to begin with, let alone extra. She had grown up knowing what it was like to be poor, and she wondered what this 'crash' might mean for taking care of her new son. He was the most beautiful baby she had ever seen, with dark, curly hair and green eyes. "We'll be all right, Bobby," she said. "Just you wait and see."

She realized she was trying to convince herself. Bobby was too little to know the difference.

There was work to do. She put Bobby in his playpen with his rattle and teddy bear, then began baking bread. She proofed the yeast, mixed the ingredients, and began kneading the dough. The pounding, pushing, and pulling took all her strength and concentration. It was a satisfactory job to do when anxiety cast its heavy cloud, and as she had been the bread maker for her father, brothers and sisters, she was skillful at the task. Her breads turned out light, yet hearty, with a "good chew," as her father always put it. Breadmaking was therapy at a stressful time, and this wasn't the first time she had used it as such.

An hour passed. *Robert should be home by now.* As minutes continued to tick by, she tried to push away her tension. While the bread rose, she swept the kitchen with an old cornhusk broom. *I wish I had one made of straw.* Straw brooms seemed to pick up the dirt better. A straw broom might be considered a luxury now.

She dusted the living room, using linseed oil to polish the wood with such vigor that it shone. She plumped the pillows at the ends of the sofa. She changed Bobby's diaper, fed him, and sang a song to him. She went back to the bread and kneaded it for the second time, putting it into greased loaf pans to rise once more. Still no Robert. She sat down at the kitchen table with a cup of coffee.

Her thoughts were consumed with how much things cost...things they would need. A first-class stamp cost 2 cents and a 10-pound bag of sugar was 59 cents. A pound of butter was 43 cents. A pound of cheese...28 or 29 cents. A roll of toilet paper, 5 cents.

She thought back to her childhood and the hard work they learned to do after her mother died. *We had to keep body and soul together...how did we do it?* She rested her head on her hand for a minute and remembered. Planting a huge garden so they could preserve vegetables for the winter—washing clothes by hand on a washboard in the kitchen—separating the cream from milk the cows provided in order to make butter. *What a job that was!* She chuckled to herself about how the kids each took turns cranking the handle on the cream separator. It had to be spun so fast that not one person could complete the job alone. And butchering day—slaughtering the hogs, grinding and stuffing the sausage. They had worked hard in order to survive.

Edith realized she should stop reminiscing and worrying and instead, start planning. She was a master at saving. *I know how to stretch a dime!* She started writing a list of the things she would be responsible for. Each word increased her resolve.

I can make my own butter...I did it all the time as a child. Sugar...we just won't eat as many sweets. Eggs...we can raise our own chickens. And bread is a dime a loaf. Maybe I could sell some of what I make. I know how to can vegetables and fruit…we'll have supplies all winter long. And I know how to sew. I can make little Bobby's shirts and pants and my own clothes, too. She thought of herself as a partner to her husband, helping support their family by being careful and smart about expenditures. As she listed her ideas, she also prayed. From early in life, she had found that prayer always helped.

God, we're just getting started with our family. I don't understand everything that's going on right now, but I know we're in your hands and that you're going to guide us through this. Help me to be a smart wife, a loving mother, a good money saver so that I can take care of my precious baby. He's everything to me, Lord, and I thank you for his good health. Oh, Heavenly Father! Help us through this crisis, whatever it turns out to be.

As she whispered her "amen," she heard the front door open…Robert's slow steps into the living room…the quiet 'click' of the door being closed. She knew from his hesitant pace that the news must be bad.

He was removing his hat and jacket when she got to the living room. His face was pale, and his eyes were downcast. It took many long seconds for him to finally raise his face to meet her gaze.

"Edith," he began, "it's not good. There's a limit on what we can withdraw from the bank right now. I was able to get $25. How much cash do we have around the house?"

Edith took a step back, clutching her apron, shocked by the news. "I'm not sure. I'll check my purse. And you've got some money in the shoebox under the bed."

"Yeah, I'll go check that. I'll put this cash with whatever's in there."

Robert went to their bedroom, and Edith grabbed her purse. Three ones and some change. That was it. She went to the bedroom where Robert was seated on the bed, counting the money he found in the shoebox.

"$7 and change," he said, not looking up. "That plus our $25 from the bank…$32."

"I have $3 in my purse, plus some change," Edith said. "That's $35, plus. We'll be okay. I've thought of some ways to save…"

Bobby's crying stopped her mid-sentence.

"I'll be right back."

She went out to the kitchen and picked up her baby from the playpen where he had been sleeping. She rocked him in her arms and cooed to him all the way back to the bedroom. Robert had not moved, continuing to look at the money in the shoebox, his brow wrinkled in worry.

She stood in the bedroom doorway and bounced Bobby in her arms. "What I was starting to say, Robert, is that I've already thought about some ways we can save money, things that I can make instead of buying. I'm used to it. I made everything after Mama died—made enough for Dad and the seven kids who were still home. I know how to manage on a few cents!" She smiled, hoping he'd look up and see how confident she was, even if she didn't feel as confident on the inside. What *did* she feel? *Determined*, she thought. *I'm determined.*

"I haven't told you the worst of it. The money situation is so bad that a lot of those fellas up on Wall Street are jumpin' outta windows. At least, that's what I was told. They're committing suicide." Robert shook his head back and forth. "They've lost so much money in the stock market, they don't even see that life is worth living."

Edith's jaw dropped. "Robert! That can't be! Would people really take their own lives over money?"

"I s'pose if they've been used to living the high life and suddenly they're in the poor house, they might consider it."

"Well, that's just about the saddest thing I think I've ever heard. To be so hopeless…" she trailed off. "Look at us. We don't have a lot of money. I've *never* had a lot of money. I'm not ready to die over it."

"That's the difference," Robert said. "We've never been used to having lots of money, so it's not as upsetting to us to do without. I know my family didn't have it as bad as your family did, but neither of us were ever rich. When I heard people were killing themselves, I felt kind of glad we *aren't* rich, to tell you the truth. At least we know how to work and take care of ourselves."

He walked over to Edith, enveloped her and their baby son in his arms. "I'll do some extra trapping and try to get as many minks as I can—their hides are more valuable. And I'll see if I can find a job that pays a little more. I heard the glass factory was hiring. I'll go there first." He started to walk away, then turned back to face her. "No one knows how long this is gonna last. We just need to get ourselves ready for the worst." He squeezed her tight, then headed outside to the small barn behind their house.

Edith walked back into the kitchen. Bobby seemed contented,

so she put him in his playpen. She remembered her own childhood and what it meant to be poor. *We never realized we were poor because we didn't count on material things for our joy.* As she put more wood in the stove to bake their bread that day, she silently thanked God again for the blessings of a good husband and a healthy baby.

8
March 1930

"Robert, come on in and wash up for supper! We're going to have birthday cake for Bobby!"

Edith pulled the screen door closed and turned toward the kitchen. She had to dodge some laundry hanging on the back porch—it was still too cold to hang it outside. *I sure will be glad to see spring,* she thought as she pushed her hair back from her forehead. She looked forward to crocuses and daffodils…it wouldn't be long.

She smiled at her baby boy, exactly one year old today. He got cuter with every passing minute, it seemed, and smarter, too. He knew how to twist her around his little finger. Currently using a rattle to bang on a small truck in his playpen, he cooed and babbled as if every sound meant something. *It probably does mean something to him,* she decided. She walked over and tousled his curly hair, then turned her attention to her cooking.

She had potato soup boiling on the stove. Robert would need a hot, stout meal after working all day at the pottery, a job he took soon after the depression started. The pottery paid better than the glass factory, where he had worked when the Great Depression hit, and they counted themselves lucky that he had been able to obtain a position there. Even after the hot work he did all day, there was still plenty to be done at home. He was in the barn caring for their one cow and the sheep.

The scent of homemade bread filled the kitchen. She heard Robert knocking the snow off his boots on the back porch.

"It sure smells good in here," he hollered. "I'm hungry as a horse!"

"Come and get it—it's ready," she hollered back. She picked Bobby up and put him in his highchair. "There you go, son. Are you hungry, too? You want mama to feed you some soup?"

"Dada," he answered.

"Well, I like that! Calling for your dada when I'm the one who's about to feed you!" She chuckled. *How could anyone be any happier?* Even with the whole country in a depression—even with their own spare finances—she found joy in every day.

Robert entered the kitchen and went straight to the sink to wash his hands. "Honey, I'm half-starved. Boy, it smells good in here."

"You said that," Edith laughed. "It's nothing special, Robert…just potato soup and bread. And of course, Bobby's cake."

"What kind did you make?" he asked.

"Chocolate with caramel frosting."

"You're kidding. Where'd you get the brown sugar for the frosting?"

"I traded Elmira Higgins for it. I gave her a loaf of bread."

Robert picked up a towel to dry his hands, turned and stared at her. "A whole loaf of bread? For brown sugar?"

Suddenly, Edith felt as if she were being scolded. "Well, yes. I wanted to make a nice cake for a change. We haven't had a cake in quite a while, and I was out of sugar stamps. It's Bobby's birthday, after all." She turned and smiled at her son. "He has to have a cake on his first birthday."

Robert walked over and put a hand on her shoulder. "I'm sorry. I didn't mean to sound cross. I was just surprised. You know, we can make a loaf of bread last all week. I was just thinking about how we've had to stretch things."

"You're right, but I think we deserve to splurge a little on such a special day." She looked at Bobby, who was banging a spoon on the table of his highchair. "We've both worked awful hard to make our pennies go farther since the depression started."

"Very true. Well, I appreciate you making a good cake and that's the end of it. I'm sorry I even said anything. We'll enjoy supper and singing 'Happy Birthday' to our boy, and we'll have a piece of his father's favorite dessert. Can't ask for a better evening than that!"

Edith stood up, pecked him on the cheek and said, "Sit down. I'll bring your soup." She walked over to the stove, dished up a bowl of thick, steaming potato soup and brought it back to the table. "Don't add salt—it's got enough already," she warned Robert. "Here's the pepper, though. I'll bring the bread."

She retrieved butter, the bread and a good knife and sat them down on a cutting board in front of her husband. "There you go, honey. It's still warm. Slice some for me, too, will you?"

Robert began cutting the bread while Edith got soup for herself and for Bobby. She sat where she could lean in close to Bobby's highchair, spooning up some soup and softly blowing on it to cool it down before she fed it to her baby. He opened his mouth like a little bird.

"You must be hungry, too, big boy!" she exclaimed, and both parents laughed. Bobby was growing fast and had a big appetite.

"I can't believe he's a year old today," Robert said.

"I can't either," Edith said. "He's such a good little fella, the time has flown by. And I might have a surprise for you. I think I'm pregnant right now."

Robert stopped with a spoonful of soup halfway to his mouth. He put the spoon back down in the bowl and stirred slowly. "You're not fooling with me, are you?"

She continued calmly feeding the baby. "No. I wouldn't kid you about something like this. I'm late, and I feel kind of like I did with Bobby, so I'm pretty sure...." She trailed off, not certain how Robert was receiving the news.

"Edith, I don't know what to say. This isn't the best time to be having another child," he began, rubbing his forehead. "You know this job at the pottery doesn't pay that well. It's better than nothing, which is what a lot of people have—nothing—but this scares me a little bit."

"Me, too, but there's nothing we can do about it if I'm pregnant. I'll go see the doctor tomorrow and have him run a test to make sure, but I'm almost positive."

Robert stirred his soup slowly. "How did this...?" He knew the answer, stopped himself mid-question, and began eating again. "Listen, we wanted another baby. I just didn't think it would happen so fast. I'll try to find a better-paying job again."

"We're in this together. Maybe I should try to find work, too," Edith said.

Robert shook his head back and forth. "That doesn't make sense to me, Edith. You should be here at home with the children. Think of it this way...if you work, you may be taking a job away from a man that needs to support his family. How would *that* make you feel?"

Edith clenched her jaw and grit her teeth so that she didn't say what she was thinking. *I need to help support our own family.* But she knew Robert was right about one thing—who would care for the children if she worked?

"I s'pose that's true. Well, no need to worry till we find out for sure, right?" She smiled and wiped Bobby's mouth. "Now it's time for Mommy to eat, little buddy."

She gave Bobby a crustless piece of bread to gnaw on and turned to her own supper. "If I'm not working elsewhere, I can make a bigger garden. That will help a lot, don't you think?"

"Sure will. You're the most industrious girl I've ever known. There's not a lazy bone in your body. I appreciate you thinking of trying to go to work, but honestly, I think we're better off for you to stay right here at the house. Just concentrate on things a woman is good at, like gardening and preserving. At least we'll have a roof over our heads and food in our stomachs."

Edith wanted to say they might find out she was good at other things, too, when they heard a knock on the front door. "I'll get it," she said.

A frighteningly slender man with a long, scraggly beard was standing outside the front door. Despite the cold day, he had on only a ragged, thin-looking jacket. His boots looked worn, and Edith could tell his pants had seen better days. He held a frayed gray hat in his hands. She opened the door slightly to the stranger.

"Hello, ma'am. I'm A.C. Cewalt. I wonder if you might have some odd jobs I could do in trade for food?"

She took a step back, shocked. This was the first time a destitute person had showed up at their door, though she had heard of these things happening in other towns and in big cities.

"Robert, could you come out here?" she called. "Mr. Cewalt, please come in out of the cold and warm up." She opened the door wider to allow the man to come in.

His face turned bright red, and he looked down at the ground, shuffling his feet. "Oh, no, ma'am. I don't mean to be any bother. I just haven't eaten in a couple of days and wondered if you might have some work in exchange for a meal."

Robert entered the living room and began mentally assessing this stranger. He looked harmless enough. "Hello sir," he said, extending his hand.

"My name is Robert Riedel, and you've met my wife, Edith. How did you say we could help you, now?"

"I was just telling your wife that I haven't eaten in a couple of days, and I wondered if there might be some work here at your place that I could do to earn a meal."

Robert and Edith looked at each other. There were tears in Edith's eyes. "His name is A.C. Cewalt, honey. I think he could sit down and have some soup with us, don't you? Please come on in, Mr. Cewalt. I have a big pot of potato soup on the stove. There's plenty for you, too."

"Yes, man, come on in. Don't stand out there in the cold!" Robert said.

Mr. Cewalt hobbled in. He didn't walk like a man who was able to do much work. Robert tried to figure his age. He looked like he might be in his sixties, at least.

"I appreciate this, folks, but I can't take no charity. If I'm to eat, you'll have to give me something to do." Mr. Cewalt was insistent.

"I'll tell you what. After you eat, you can help me put some more fresh hay out in the cow's stall. It's supposed to get colder tonight," Robert said. "I've been working all day and I'm getting tired, so that would be a big help."

"All right. I'll gladly do it." Mr. Cewalt seemed relieved at the idea that he could 'pay' for his meal, Robert thought. *A man has his pride, even at the worst of times.*

"Come sit down," Edith said. She picked Bobby up out of his highchair and put him in his playpen. "It's our little boy's birthday today. You came on just the right day because we have cake for dessert." She cut a slice of bread and offered it to Mr. Cewalt, who bit into it before he was fully seated. She went to the stove and brought back another bowl of soup.

"You got a real nice-lookin' young'un, there," he said with his mouth full. "Ma'am, I don't know when I've ever tasted better bread. You made this yourself?"

"Yes. I learned when I was young, and it's a good thing with times being what they are. Where you from, Mr. Cewalt?"

"I come from over at Tymochtee."

"And you walked all the way to Sycamore on a cold day like today?"

"Man's gotta find work some way," he said, putting a spoonful of soup in his mouth. "I got no other way to get around."

Edith and Robert looked at each other, knowing that the other was thinking about the distance between Sycamore and Tymochtee. It had to be at least five miles—maybe closer to six. In this weather.

"Mr. Cewalt, are you going to try to walk back home tonight?" Robert asked. "That's a pretty good distance at this time of the day and in this cold and snow."

"No choice. No choice." He continued eating as if he were ravenous. Edith cut another slice of bread and looked at Robert.

"Well, sir, if you would like, you could stay here overnight," Robert offered. "We've got an extra room. It's nothing fancy, of course, but at least you'd be warm."

Mr. Cewalt stopped eating, considering this offer. He wiped his mouth on his sleeve and said, "No folks, I couldn't do that. You're kind to make the suggestion, but this here is what I really needed—a hot meal. I couldn't impose any further."

"What about if I find some other work for you to do? Would you feel better about it then?" Robert asked.

Mr. Cewalt sat back in his chair and scratched his head. "I tell ya what. After I eat, we'll go out to the barn and do whatever work needs to be done. Maybe I could just sleep out there with the cattle."

"Well, it's not *cattle*—it's one cow and a sheep. It wouldn't be a very warm or comfortable place to sleep," Robert said.

"Better'n what I've had." Mr. Cewalt began eating again.

Edith could feel her eyes filling with tears once more. *Better'n what I've had.* Horrible. The depression was making beggars out of honest, hard-working people. And if it was doing this to adults, what was happening to the children?

"Mr. Cewalt, the offer stands. You are welcome to stay right in this house. We have work you can help with, so you deserve to have a bed to sleep in...not just a pile of hay."

He finished his soup without speaking further. When he had pushed his bowl away, he said, "I'll take a look at the barn and see what I think. How 'bout that?"

"If you insist," Robert said. "C'mon out and I'll show you what needs to be done."

Mr. Cewalt followed Robert out to the barn. Edith watched from the back porch, pulling her sweater close around her. It was cold.

That poor man can't sleep in the barn, she thought. *He'll freeze to death out there.*

She went to the kitchen and began to clean up. Bobby had fallen asleep in his playpen. She had hardly thought about him since the stranger came to the door. And she realized she hadn't finished her own soup. It was cold now, so she gathered up the dishes, boiling water on the wood stove to wash and rinse them. When she was finished, she got out cake plates and forks, and put a pot of coffee on the stove. It wasn't long before the men came in. Robert quickly kicked his boots off, but Mr. Cewalt took a little time at the task, having trouble bending to untie his well-weathered boots.

"Edith, Mr. Cewalt is sure he can sleep in the barn tonight. It really isn't too bad out there—I put down a lot of fresh hay—and he just doesn't seem to feel comfortable coming in the house," Robert whispered to her before Mr. Cewalt could enter the room.

"If you think he'll be all right..." she whispered, uncertain.

Mr. Cewalt peered in through the doorway to the kitchen and smiled for the first time since he'd arrived. "That barn will seem like a palace compared to a couple of places I've stayed. It's built tight. No air whistling through. I thank you folks for your help."

"Well, you're working for it, so no thanks are necessary," Robert reassured him. "Come have a piece of cake and a cup of coffee before you bed down for the night."

Bobby had awakened and was trying to pull himself up in his playpen. He was at the age where he was just starting to take a few steps on his own.

"Happy birthday, little buddy," his father said as he lifted him out of the playpen and into his highchair. "Time for some cake for you!"

Edith brought out the cake with one small candle in the center. The adults sang 'Happy Birthday,' Mr. Cewalt's voice a surprising, mellow baritone. Bobby clapped his chubby hands and laughed. When they were done, Edith sat a small piece of cake in front of him and showed him how to eat it with his hands. It wasn't long before he was a mess.

Mr. Cewalt laughed. "What a blessed day this has turned out to be!"

Edith handed him a piece of cake and poured a cup of hot coffee. *It really is simple things that make us happiest,* she thought. *A full stomach, a warm place to stay, a happy family. If only it could be that easy for everyone.*

After Mr. Cewalt had retired to the barn with one of Edith's warmest quilts, she and Robert sat and talked in front of the fireplace. Robert was rocking his sleepy son. Edith read a few verses aloud from Psalms. "'Blessed be the Lord, who daily loadeth us with benefits, even the God of our salvation. Selah. He that is our God is the God of salvation; and unto God the Lord belong the issues from death.'" She looked up. "Robert, how long do you suppose this depression is going to last?"

"I honestly have no idea," he said. "All I know is that there are a lot of people who don't have it as good as us, and we're just making it."

"Yeah, Mr. Cewalt's not the only man struggling out there," Edith replied.

"And if we have another child to feed, we won't be able to help everyone," Robert cautioned, "but we'll do what we can."

9
October 1930

"Honey, I think I'm going into labor. Can you let Dr. Montgomery know so he has time to get here?"

"Sure. When did it start up?" Robert looked across the kitchen at his wife, standing at the stove, stirring a pot of chili that was slated to be their supper. "Are you all right? Should you be cooking right now?"

"Oh, it started this morning, but the contractions are coming pretty regular, so it won't be terribly long, I don't think. I feel fine right now. I just want to get this chili done, and then I'll go lie down. It'll start to get worse pretty soon."

Labor and delivery had been normal with Bobby, at least as well as Edith could remember, comparing her own delivery to her mother's. She was a young girl when her last three brothers were born but remembered what her mother went through. There were several hours of occasional pains, followed by several hours of intense pain. Edith could still hear the moaning and groaning as if her mother were in the room with her. She also remembered that during her own labor with Bobby Jr., she had felt very much alone, as if everything about the birth depended on her. *Robert and dear Dr. Mockimer, God rest his soul, were right with me, but it's really all on the woman*, she thought. She mentally prepared herself for what was ahead as she stirred the chili, making sure it didn't burn on the bottom of the pot. At least Robert would have something to eat while she carried on the hard mental and physical work of giving birth.

Robert picked up the phone. As usual, the party line was busy.

"Mrs. Armatrout," he said. "This is Robert Riedel. Can I have the line for a minute to call the doctor?"

"Oh, is Edith in labor?" Mrs. Armatrout said. "Do you need any help over there? You know, I've helped birth many babies in my day! Have you got plenty of clean rags? Are you boiling some water?"

"Thank you, but we don't really need any help right now. I just need to call Dr. Montgomery," Robert told the busybody. The last thing he needed was Mrs. Armatrout coming to his aid. Or at least that's how she would portray it to the entire village—like she had completed the delivery herself.

He heard Essie Miller's voice in the receiver.

"Mary Armatrout, hang up! Let Robert have the phone. Good luck Robert! Give Edith my love."

He heard the click of Essie's receiver back in its cradle. "Mrs. Armatrout...?" he said.

"Oh, I'm hanging up right now! I'll come over after the baby is born and bring you some stew." Good ol' Mrs. Armatrout—always saving the day.

"All right. Thank you. G'bye, now." Robert was anxious to get the line free. He heard another click.

He dialed two numbers—3-8—Doc Montgomery's number.

"Hello. Dr. Montgomery speaking."

"Doc, this is Robert Riedel."

"Well, hello, Robert. What can I do for you?"

"Edith's in labor. She says it started this morning, but now her pains are coming more regular. Can you come over to see her?"

"I'm headed over to Ralph Baer's to check his oldest boy right now. Seems he fell out of the hay loft and maybe broke his arm. I might have to set it, then I'll call you and see how Edith's doing. If she started this morning, she'll have a little time yet. Tell me your phone number again."

"It's 4-5. I appreciate your help, Doc." Robert was anxious that the doctor might get caught up in another emergency before he could attend Edith. "Just give me a call as soon as you can."

"Robert, till I can call you back, keep an eye on how frequent Edith's contractions are and how long they last, all right? I'll call you as soon as I possibly can. I promise."

"Thanks, Doc." The men hung up. Robert walked back out to the kitchen, where Edith was still stirring her chili, but bent over. He knew she was in pain. He looked at the clock. It said 2:30.

"You all right?" he said, not sure if he wanted the answer without the doctor being available.

Edith straightened up. "I'm fine, Robert. My back just hurts a little and it felt good to stretch."

"Well, Dr. Montgomery is on his way to the Baer place, most likely gonna have to set Ralph's boy's arm. He'll call to see how you're doin' when he gets done. Why don't you sit down? I can stir the chili."

"It's done, really. We can let the fire burn down and just keep it warm. You should stir it once in a while, though. I'll go lay on the couch." Edith put the lid on the pot. "Pretty soon we'll have another little one. Are you happy?"

Robert gave her a hug. "I am. Where's Bobby?"

"Taking his nap. He'll be awake before long, though."

"All right. I'll try to keep him out of your hair. Go rest."

Edith left the kitchen and stretched out on the sofa. Robert tended the chili and waited for his firstborn to wake up. It wasn't long before he heard, "Dada? Dada?"

Robert was proud that his son had learned to call out "Dada" before he figured out how to form the word "Mama" and was relentless in teasing his wife about it. He went to Bobby's room and picked him up from his crib.

"Hey there, little fella! You're going to have a baby brother or sister before long. Criminy, your pants are soaked. C'mon—let's get you changed."

Robert got the baby cleaned up and walked into the living room where Edith now lay on her side.

"How're you doing?" he asked, bringing Bobby closer.

"All right, honey. I just had another pain, but it didn't last too long. How's my little boy?" she cooed to Bobby, who held his arms out to his mother.

Robert put the little boy down to stand at Edith's side. "You can't lay on Mommy right now, son. She's going to have another baby pretty soon."

"Beebee?" Bobby asked. "No," he added, shaking his head.

Edith laughed. "Too late, Bobby. Too late." Then she

grimaced slightly. "Ooh, here comes another one." She raised her hand to her forehead and concentrated on getting through the contraction.

"When was the last one? I'm supposed to be watching how often they come."

Edith didn't answer right away, preoccupied with breathing. When the contraction was over, she said, "Oh, maybe about fifteen minutes ago."

Fifteen minutes! Robert was concerned. It seemed like contractions every fifteen minutes indicated a need for the presence of a doctor. As he completed the thought, he heard a knock at the front door. "Oh, good! That's probably Doc Montgomery," he said, reassured by the interruption.

He opened the door to Mrs. Armatrout. She bustled right past him into the living room.

"Oh, Edith, you dear, dear thing. I've come to help you. Robert, did you check on the rags? Did you put water on to boil? Oh, little Bobby...you shouldn't be in here!" She tried to hug Bobby, who wriggled his way free of her embrace.

Robert strode to Edith's bedside. "Mrs. Armatrout, we're doing fine. Doc Montgomery will be here shortly." He picked up Bobby and took him to his crib.

"Here buddy. Play with this." He handed Bobby his ball, a well-loved teddy bear, and a wooden truck before returning to the living room.

"I can assist the doctor. I've done it many times, you know," Mrs. Armatrout said.

"So you told me. What do you need boiling water for anyway?" Robert was slightly annoyed at the intrusion of this overbearing woman.

"Why, so the doctor can sterilize his scissors, of course! Now you go get that ready and I'll stay with Edith."

Robert did as he was told. It would be easier to comply than incur further lectures on childbirth.

"And get some clean towels or something to wrap the baby in...."

Robert resisted the urge to tell Mrs. Armatrout what she could do with her towels and busied himself with those duties a husband could help with. And he didn't forget to stir the chili.

I shouldn't grouse. She'll be a good helper for Doc, he thought, calming his own nerves. He found several clean, relatively new towels and brought them to the living room. The towels were stiff and scratchy from having been hung on the clothesline to dry. Fine for drying off after a bath, but not so good for a baby.

"Oh, Robert. Surely you don't think she'll have the baby in here!" Mrs. Armatrout laughed. "Help me get her into your bedroom."

They helped Edith stand up, then began a halting walk to the bedroom. They had no more than entered the room when Edith's water broke.

"Uh-oh," Edith said.

"Uh-oh is right!" Mrs. Armatrout said. "Robert, you better call the doctor again."

"Holy cow! Holy cow! Edith, lay down." Robert was starting to feel a little frantic. "What if he can't come?"

"Just tell him Edith's water broke. I'm sure he'll get here on the double."

Edith cried out just then. "Ow, ow, ow! My back! Oh, Lord in Heaven, help me," she prayed out loud.

"Robert, go!" Mrs. Armatrout yelled.

Robert rushed out to the phone and dialed the Baer family's number, thankful no one was on the line.

"Hello."

"Eunice, it's Robert Riedel. Is Doc still out there?"

"Why yes he is."

"Please let me talk to him."

Eunice Baer must have heard the desperation in his voice. Robert heard the receiver drop, in in just a few seconds, he heard the familiar voice.

"Robert, what's happening?"

"Edith's water just broke. She's having pains about every fifteen minutes or maybe even a little less."

"Okay, I just finished up here. I'll come right over. Don't worry. We still have time. Is anyone there with you?"

"Yes. Mrs. Armatrout."

"Good. She's very helpful with childbirth."

Robert said, "She's been most reassuring." He was glad Doc couldn't see him rolling his eyes over the phone.

"I'll be there soon." Click. The doctor was gone.

Robert returned to the bedroom where Edith was beginning to sweat. Her face was pale, and she clutched the sheets in her hands. Meanwhile, Mrs. Armatrout fussed and fluffed the towels. "These are too stiff for a newborn baby!"

"Edith, Dr. Montgomery is on his way," he said, trying to comfort his wife. "He won't be long."

Edith didn't answer but offered a wan smile.

"Robert Riedel! Don't you have any softer cloths than this?" Mrs. Armatrout demanded. "How can I wrap a newborn baby up with these?"

"I'll see what we have," Robert said. He was tired of her already. *She's here to help*, he reminded himself. *She's here to help*.

Robert found older-but-softer towels and a few of Bobby's old baby blankets. As he made his way back to the bedroom, he heard another knock, but this time, the door opened without him having to answer it.

"Robert?" called a voice. "I'm here!"

"Come on in, Doc," he answered. "We're in the bedroom."

The physician made his way to the bedroom. He looked at his patient and smiled. "I'd say we have more of a labor room, here, than a bedroom. How're you doing, Edith?"

"I'm okay. I'm getting tired, though."

"Ha! Just wait. You'll be exhausted before it's over, but you're young and you're strong. You're going to do just fine. Robert, why don't you step out for a minute while I check to see how far along Edith is. Mrs. Armatrout, will you stand by, please?"

"Oh yes, Doctor," she gushed, sidling up to the physician.

Robert didn't have to be asked twice. Whatever it was that doctors did, he wanted no part of it. He had no desire to see his wife in any more pain than she was already experiencing.

Dr. Montgomery finished his exam and called Robert back into the room. "She's almost there, Robert. I'll just stay around because I don't think it will be long. Why don't you sit with her for a bit? Mrs. Armatrout, come with me and we'll get a few things ready."

"Of course, Doctor." Chest puffed out, she bustled out behind the physician.

"Robert?" Edith pulled his attention to her bedside. "Come hold my hand. I feel another contraction coming, and they're getting hard."

He sat dutifully at his young wife's side and let her squeeze his fingers till he thought they'd break. It was hard watching Edith go through labor pains.

"You're doing great, Edith. Just rest in between," he tried to comfort her.

"I'll be glad when it's over. We still haven't thought of any names, you know," Edith said.

"We'll figure that out after we see if it's a boy or a girl," Robert said. "For now, just rest, okay? You need all your strength for these contractions."

Edith closed her eyes and Robert could see her lips moving. He knew she was praying. She prayed with their boy every night and told him Bible stories that Robert doubted little Bobby could understand. But he knew Edith wanted to set their child on the right path from early in his life. She was a good mother—patient and loving.

"Oh, here comes another one. Robert, I feel like I need to push. Get the doctor!" Edith said.

He jumped up from his chair and hurried out to the kitchen, where Dr. Montgomery was showing Mrs. Armatrout some type of unpleasant-looking instrument.

"Doc, come quick. She's gotta push," he blurted out.

Both the physician and would-be midwife jumped up from the table. Mrs. Armatrout took off while the physician stayed behind to address the young father. "You wait here, Robert. It's likely time for her to deliver," the doctor said. He took the instrument he had been demonstrating along with his doctor bag to the bedroom.

Robert sat down at the table. He knew Edith was in good hands and would be fine, but it was hard to wait. He remembered Bobby's birth and prayed that this labor would soon be over for his wife. He was glad that God had seen fit to give women the job of having babies.

He could hear Edith crying out at times, and the sound of her cries stabbed at his heart. He stood up and paced around the kitchen. Bobby would be waking up from his nap soon. He went to the boy's bedroom and found him standing up in his crib with a smile on his face.

"Dada!"

Bobby was a cheerful little guy. Robert went to his crib and checked his diaper.

"Young man, you're soaked *again*. Let's get those britches changed." He began the task of changing Bobby's diaper. "You know, son, you're going to have to learn how to go to the bathroom like a big man pretty soon. Mommy's having another baby right now!"

"Dada!"

"Yes, yes, Dada. Dada and you are going to help Mommy, right? You're going to be a good boy and I'm going to help her around the house."

"Wawa."

"You want some water? Okay. I guess you just got rid of all you had, didn't you?" Robert chuckled and picked up his boy. "C'mon. Let's go get some wawa."

Just as he got to the kitchen with the toddler, Robert heard the cry of a newborn.

"Here, Bobby. Take a drink. That's right. Good boy. Now let's go see Mommy."

As they reached the bedroom door, Dr. Montgomery looked up and said, "C'mon in, fellas. We have a beautiful baby girl to meet you." Mrs. Armatrout was cleaning up the infant, grinning as if the baby were her own.

Robert looked at Edith first. She was very pale but smiling. "Robert, wait till you see her. She's beautiful. Hey, Bobby. You have a new sister." She tried to prop herself up on her elbow.

"Edith, lie back down. You're not quite ready to sit upright. Give yourself a few minutes." Dr. Montgomery was kind but firm. "Let me check your uterus before you go trying to hug that boy of yours."

Edith did as she was told. "Well, now I have *two* cute little children. I'm going to be busy."

"As if you weren't already," Mrs. Armatrout chirped. "Children keep you on the run, even when it's only one or two of them."

"Thank you for your help," Robert said to the woman, sincere. "I'm glad you were here."

Mrs. Armatrout blushed. "I'll stay for a while after the doctor has gone to make sure everything goes all right."

"That's not a bad idea, Mary—that is, if you're able to stay," Dr. Montgomery said. "Edith, you don't need to be getting up and hustling around this house. Stay put for a little while and let Mary help you and Robert with Bobby and with cooking and so forth."

"I already have supper cooked out there. In fact, you're welcome to stay and have a bowl of chili, Doctor," Edith said.

"I should have known you'd be all prepared," the physician laughed. "I can't stay, my dear, but I appreciate the offer. Your uterus feels nice and firm. Mary, do you know how to check the patient's uterus?"

"Yes sir, I sure do. How often should I check, though?"

"I'd say once an hour for a couple or three hours. Are you able to stay that long?"

"I'll be happy to stay that long," she said. "Robert, do you want to see your baby?"

Mrs. Armatrout wrapped the baby in a receiving blanket, and she approached Robert with her arms out, as if she were presenting a trophy. "She's a beauty."

Robert looked at the tiny face squinting up at him. She *was* beautiful...a headful of dark hair, perfect little features. Five fingers on each hand. He'd check her toes later.

"What are you naming her?" Mrs. Armatrout asked.

"Golly, I don't know yet. Edith, what do you think about this girl's name?"

"How about Clara?" Edith said.

"That's my wife's name!" Dr. Montgomery said.

"And that's why I chose it," Edith replied. "I'm so grateful for your help, Dr. Montgomery."

"Well, that's a high honor! Wait till I tell *my* Clara." Dr. Montgomery squeezed Edith's hand. "You take care now and listen to what Mary tells you to do. I want to see you in the office in a week, so when you're up and around, call the office and make an appointment, all right? And if anything seems out of line, don't be afraid to call me." He turned and headed for the door, stopping just long enough to shake Robert's hand.

"Now you've got one of each, Robert. A wonderful family."

"Thanks, Doc. I sure appreciate everything you did," Robert said. "We'll call the office and find out how much we owe you."

"That's fine, but it's not the important thing at this very minute. Right now, just worry about your wife and your children. We can talk about money matters later," he said as he walked out of the bedroom, leaving with a big smile. *Another baby born*, he thought, as he walked to his Plymouth. *Another new life in this old world.* It always seemed like a miracle to the country doctor.

In the house, baby Clara began crying.

"Maybe she needs to eat?" Robert said, carrying the baby over to his wife.

"Probably. It's a lot of work, being born," Edith said.

She put the baby to her breast, and as natural as can be, little Clara began suckling. Before long, though, she stopped and started crying again. Edith looked up at her midwife.

"What's wrong with her?" she asked, alarmed at Clara's wailing.

"Let's see your milk," Mrs. Armatrout said.

Edith expressed some of her breast milk.

"Why, your milk looks no good! Too thin! That baby will starve if we don't do something different." Mrs. Armatrout was adamant. "Robert, do you have any milk in the icebox?"

"Yes, I believe so. At least a little."

"Do you have a bottle I can warm some in?"

"Sure. Edith, honey, where are the bottles?"

"I have some in the cupboard above the sink. They're all washed up and ready to go, but I didn't think we'd need them this soon," Edith said.

"I'll go get one." Mrs. Armatrout left the young couple alone.

"Robert, if my milk is no good, we've got to give Clara something else. She's so little!"

"Yeah, she's kind of a runt. Don't you worry, honey. She'll grow. We'll take care of her," Robert reassured Edith. Nevertheless, he was worried. They had counted on Edith being able to breast feed the baby for quite a while.

"I think I'll get us another cow," Robert said. "It's about time I did that, anyway."

"Oh, Robert, what in the world will you buy a cow with?" Edith said. "We're already strapped." She stroked her baby's face and tried to comfort the fussy little infant.

"You let me figure that out. Why don't you try feeding Clara again?"

Edith put the baby back to her breast, and once again, she began taking nutrition from her mother.

"At least she's not crying now," Edith said.

Mrs. Armatrout came back into the room. "I mixed up a tiny bit of cream of wheat with mostly milk. Let's see how she takes this."

Edith handed her baby to the midwife, though she felt unsure about giving such a tiny infant cream of wheat. "Do you really think she can have that so soon?"

"Oh, yes. Trust me. Babies are tougher than you think, and it's a very thin mixture." She offered the bottle to the baby and at first, Clara struggled with the unnatural nipple. Then she began to suck hungrily.

"See? She's going to be fine." Mrs. Armatrout smiled down at the baby.

"Maybe we should talk to the doctor about it?" Edith sat straight up, hesitant about the new feeding plan.

"I'm sure he'll say it's fine," the would-be midwife said. "You want her to get enough nutrition so she can grow. You just don't have it, Edith. I can tell by looking at your milk."

Edith reluctantly backed down. This woman had been so helpful with the labor and delivery, she surely knew what she was talking about.

"Why don't you rest now, Edith? I'll take the baby out and finish feeding her so you can sleep. Then we'll get you up and try to start walking a bit." Mrs. Armatrout left, with Clara in her arms.

"All right, if you think that's best." Edith turned on her side and closed her eyes.

Robert kissed her on the forehead. "Everything's good, honey. Get some sleep. I'll take Bobby out and feed him some supper."

"Mash his chili beans up a little bit, Robert," Edith answered. "And don't let him have the spoon or he'll have chili everywhere."

Robert laughed. "Don't you worry about that. I've seen him in action before, you know." He left his wife, whose eyelids were already fluttering.

In the kitchen, Mrs. Armatrout was burping Clara. "She ate well, Robert. She was a starving little thing." Mrs. Armatrout stood up, lightly bouncing the baby up and down in her arms. "I'm just going to walk her around a little bit till I can get a good burp out of her."

She was a starving little thing. The words stung him. Well, they weren't starving, but Robert knew the road ahead had just gotten a little bumpier and a little less certain for his growing family.

10
April 1931

There was loud banging on the front door. Busy in the kitchen, Edith was startled by the noise and worried that it would wake up her babies. She wiped her hands on a towel and went to see who was making all the racket, but before she could get there, Robert's younger brother, Virgil came in through the screen door. He was pale, and his face was taut.

"Where's Robert?" he asked, somber. "Anna Lee is sick—very sick. Doc says she might die. She's got spinal meningitis."

Edith stopped in her tracks. "Meningitis—oh, no." Tears immediately filled her eyes. One of the most frightening diagnoses that could be made. Not Anna Lee! She was only five. "Virgil, he's out with the sheep. Go right on out there."

Virgil said nothing more, exiting through the door he had come in. Edith saw him running for the barn. She dried her tears and went to the babies' room, trying to decide what to do. Wake them up to take them over to Wooster and Verna's? Robert would surely be going to his little sister's bedside. *Wait...meningitis is contagious. I can't take the babies over there.* Edith was scared. Anna Lee was so young she seemed more like one of their own children than Robert's baby sister. Anna Lee had been a precious surprise addition to the Riedel family. Edith couldn't fathom staying away at such a time.

Bobby, now two, was stirring in his crib. He would be awake soon. Clara had just turned six months old. She was likely to stay asleep a little longer. Edith got a clean diaper ready for when Clara woke up, then headed back out to the kitchen to finish the breakfast dishes. There was no telling what the rest of the day would entail.

Robert and Virgil were coming through the back door as she entered the kitchen.

"Edith, I gotta get over to Plankton. Don't come right now. Stay here with the kids. I'll come home when we know what's happening," Robert said.

"Or call me. Please call me, Robert," Edith said, giving him a long, hard hug. "Okay—go on. Call me, *please!*" she repeated.

"I will, hon," he called back over his shoulder as he made a run for their Roadster. Virgil was already in his parents' Model A, throwing stones as he pulled out of the driveway.

Edith stood and watched as the vehicles disappeared. She was in shock. Anna Lee—such a sweet, beautiful child. She washed the dishes from breakfast, her mind spinning with worry about the little girl. *Worry does no good*, she thought. *Pray.*

Pray she did. She talked to God non-stop while she dried the dishes and put them away. She called on Jesus for protection of Anna Lee, for strength for Verna and Wooster, and for God's wisdom and guidance of the doctor's helping hands.

"Mommy? Mommy?" She heard Bobby's voice calling her. She stopped her work and her prayer and walked in to find her young son standing up in his crib, one leg up over the rail, a huge grin on his face.

"Mommy!" he said, his cheerful voice causing Edith to cry. Grateful for her healthy children more than ever, she thought how awful to have a sick child, especially with something as serious as meningitis. She crossed the room and picked Bobby up, holding him tight. He wriggled around.

"Down. Down," he mumbled against her chest. Then she had to laugh.

"You are always on the go, aren't you? Are your pants dry? Let me check." She held on to him with one hand, felt his pants with the other. All the while, Bobby tried to pull away.

"Me pway wif Daddy." He loved roughhousing with his father.

"Daddy had to go away, son. He went over to Grandpa's. He won't be home for a little while."

"Weed me a stowy?"

"What a wonderful idea," she said, with more enthusiasm than she felt, but it would be a distraction from her worry. "Are you thirsty? You want something to drink first?"

"Milk."

"All right, buddy. Let's go. Now be quiet so we don't wake your sister up."

They left the kids' room and went to the kitchen. Bobby drank his milk so fast Edith thought he would choke. *Now I'm being paranoid.*

"You were very thirsty! Let's go read. You pick out the book you want."

"Babah!" Bobby was speaking more clearly every day, but he still didn't have the hang of 'The Story of Babar,' his favorite book.

Edith held Bobby on her lap and read aloud. The minutes moved along without her being aware of how much time had passed until the jangling of the phone pulled her from quiet time with her son. She jumped at the sound.

"Bobby, be a good boy and look at the pictures while Mommy talks on the telephone."

He sat on the floor, turning the pages of his book while Edith rushed to answer the phone. ·

"Hello?"

There was momentary silence on the other end for a few seconds. Then, a quiet voice.

"It's me. Anna Lee is in serious shape. It's meningitis for sure. She's not speaking to anyone at this point. I mean she doesn't talk at *all.* She doesn't move. It seems like she's barely even breathing."

"Oh…oh…." Temporarily speechless, Edith was filled with grief. "Robert, what happened?"

"Mom's so distraught she hardly says anything, but from what I gather, Anna Lee went out to pick some flowers for her early this morning. Violets. She came home with a fist full of violets."

Edith heard Robert choke up momentarily. Hot tears filled her own eyes once again. She wiped them away and waited while he gathered himself and continued. "Not long after she got home, she complained to Mom about her head hurting. Mom had her lie down, thinking she'd just go to sleep and be all right when she woke up. That was it. She hasn't opened her eyes since then. Doc's here right now, but he's been plain-spoken about it. It doesn't look good."

Edith cried openly. "Oh, I'm so sorry. What can I do?"

"Nothing right now. Doc says this stuff is contagious. Don't come over here. Stay home with the kids. I'm gonna stay with Mom and Dad and help with whatever I can help with."

"What about you? Are you at risk?"

"Doc doesn't think so—I mean, we're all older and healthy. He's not letting us run in and out of her room willy-nilly, though."

"Well, be careful, and call me when you can. Let me know if she wakes up."

"I will. 'Bye."

"Good-bye."

Edith put the receiver back on the hook gently. She didn't want any loud noises. She wanted everything to be quiet. Somehow in that moment, quiet meant calm.

She went back to Bobby, still looking at his book.

"You're such a good boy, Bobby. Let's put your book away for now, okay? Let's pray for your cousin Anna Lee."

"Anna Wee," he repeated back to her.

"Yes, Anna Wee," she said, using Bobby's name for her. "Anna Wee is sick, son."

He made a face. "Did she fro up?"

"No, but she's very sick, just the same. Let's pray for her."

"Ahwight." He bowed his head and folded his hands as she had taught him.

She knew Bobby probably didn't understand much of her prayer. When they were done, she took Bobby out to the kitchen for a snack and waited. And waited.

***

At 12:30 on Sunday morning, Edith heard the front door open and close with a quiet 'click.' She rose up on one elbow. Robert didn't speak but crossed the bedroom and sat on the edge of the bed. He reached down to untie his boots, taking his time. When the boots were off, he stretched out on the bed and stared up at the ceiling.

"She's gone."

Edith began to cry. She thought she had run out of tears by now. She leaned over to wrap one arm around Robert. "I can't believe it. She was just a little child."

Robert turned his head to look at her. "It was all peaceful at the end. She just slipped away."

"Still!" Edith said. "It's just too much! How are Mom and Pop doing?"

"Mom is in rough shape. Pop is trying to keep her together. I think he's doing a little better with it than Mom is at this point."

Edith dried her eyes on the sleeve of her nightgown and rolled to her back. "I'll get some food put together tomorrow to take over. I'll make a big pot of soup. They can eat some of that and then have leftovers, too. And I can make a pie to take. And...."

Robert cut her off. "You don't have to do it all yourself, honey. Remember, we've got lots of family and friends from church, too. They'll all be bringing food over. You've got two little kids to take care of. Mom and Pop will be all right after a time. I can't think about it anymore. Let's try to get some sleep."

Edith closed her eyes, but Anna Lee's face floated before her.

Little children should not die. It was another topic to talk to God about, but for now, she had to get some sleep. Her own children would be up early, and now, more than ever, she wanted to savor every minute of every day with them.

11

1933

"Mama! Mama! There's tigers in the woodshed!"

Edith looked up from her sewing. She heard Bobby before she saw him but waited to make another stitch until he and Clara entered the house. One-year-old Mary was sound asleep in the same playpen Bobby and Clara had both used, and she hoped her four-year-old's shouting wouldn't awaken the babe.

Bobby and Clara came bursting in the back door, causing a clatter. Mary stirred, her eyelids fluttering briefly. As her two toddlers entered the room, Edith put a finger over her lips and said, "Shhh. Your baby sister is asleep."

Bobby and Clara temporarily forgot the tigers and tiptoed over to see their little sister. Clara, still small, stood on her toes to peer over the rail of the playpen. Not satisfied with her view, she sat down on the floor and gazed at the baby through the bars of the playpen while her brother told their harrowing tale in more hushed tones.

"Mama, me and Clara were outside. We wanted to play in the woodshed, but when I opened the door, there were tigers in there!"

It was hard not to laugh. The young mother had to concentrate to put on a serious face. "My goodness! Tigers! I wonder where they came from. Can you show me?"

"We better wait for Daddy."

"Why, son?"

"He might have to get his gun and kill them!"

"Oh, I bet Daddy wouldn't want to kill the tigers. If anything, he might want to call the zoo up in Toledo and ask them to come get the tigers, don't you think? The zoo could use some tigers, I'll bet."

Bobby seemed to consider this, rocking back and forth on his feet. "Maybe."

Clara spoke up. "They were pretty."

"Oh, were they? Well, maybe they aren't so scary. Why don't we go look while Mary is still asleep?" Edith put aside the shirt she was mending. "Come on, kids. Let's go out and see the tigers. Wonder what those wild animals are doing in our woodshed!" She was still struggling not to laugh.

Bobby and Clara followed as Edith, six months pregnant again, waddled out to the woodshed. When they got close, Bobby and Clara slowed their steps, holding hands, staying several feet behind their mother.

"Be careful, Mama," Clara said.

Edith rotated the wooden door latch and slowly opened the door just a crack. She looked in, then opened the door wide. "Oh, my goodness!" She turned back to the kids with a smile on her face.

"Come here, you two. We don't have tigers. We have kittens!" Edith walked into the woodshed, and in seconds, the children joined her. The kittens were mewing. Clara immediately went towards the kittens, hands out as if to pick one up. "No, no, Clara, we must leave them alone. Their mama doesn't want any people like us fooling around with her kitties. See, they're still little, like Mary."

Clara backed off. "But I want to play with them."

Edith took hold of her children's hands and walked back outside, closing and securing the woodshed door. "Let's sit down here for a minute," she said.

The children sat cross-legged on the ground, and Edith joined them, knowing how difficult it would be for her to stand back up. She shook her head, disgusted with her own short-sighted decision. Too late now.

"Kids, you know how you always wanted to hold Mary and carry her around when she was first born? It's because you loved her and were so proud to be a big brother and a big sister. But remember how I told you 'no'? *You* were too little, and *she* was too little." The children shook their heads, remembering their restrictions around the baby.

Edith continued. "The same thing is true for new kittens. The kittens' mama doesn't want humans carrying her babies around.

They're too little, and she has to take care of them for a while so they can grow strong. When they get bigger, she won't mind at all if you play with them. Can you be good children and wait?"

"Yes, mama," both children said in unison. Then Bobby added, "Will they get to live with us? Can we keep them?"

"I'm sure your daddy will be glad to have them around. Did you know that kitties catch mice?"

"What do they do with the mice?" Clara asked.

Oh, brother, Edith thought. *I set myself up for a question I don't want to answer.* "Well, they scare the mice away, so they don't get in our corncrib." *Talk about a fast one!*

"Yeah, but what do they do when they *catch* them?" Bobby said.

Caught in her own fib, Edith decided to continue embellishing—the kids could learn about the circle of life later.

"They play with them awhile, then they tell them, 'Get lost! Stay out of our corn!' Then the mice run away and go find some cookies to eat instead."

She could see this whopper turning over and over in Bobby's mind. His brow was wrinkled as he scratched his head and thought about what his mother had said.

"Mice like cookies?"

"You bet they do. Mice love to eat all kinds of things that we like, too. Hey, how about if we go have a cookie right now?" Distraction was often the key to peace.

"Yeah!" Bobby shouted. He grabbed Clara's hand. "C'mon, Clara!"

The kids ran for the house with Edith lagging well behind. "Lord, forgive me for lying to my own children, but I just don't have it in me to tell them all about cats killing and eating mice. I promise I'll tell them the truth when they're older." Satisfied that the Lord understood, she tried jogging just enough to catch up with the kids and settle them down before they entered the house...she was hoping Mary was still asleep so she could finish her mending before Robert got home from the pottery.

***

"Hey, honey, where are the kids?"

"Gosh, I don't know. I thought they went out back to play."

It was a beautiful, sunny Saturday, July 22. Edith was more than ready for her child to be born, but in the meantime, there were three others to worry about.

"They had lunch about a half hour ago and ran out the back door, but now that I think about it, I haven't heard them since," she said as she headed for the back door. "I'll go take a look around."

"All right, Edith. I'm going to sit down and look at the paper for a minute."

Robert had been working all morning, too. Edith knew he was about worn out, working at the pottery all day, working around the homestead every evening, and catching up on everything else on the weekends. That usually included some time fishing or hunting or checking his traps. Fishing and hunting meant food on the table. Trapping meant extra income.

As she walked through the backyard towards the woodshed, she noticed Robert's roses. He grew beautiful roses and took great pride in manicuring them to perfection. It was not unusual for Edith to find one flawless rose in front of her seat at the table at least once a week. He was still romantic, even after three kids and one more on the way.

There was no sign of the kids. She expected them to be playing 'house' in the woodshed, as they often did, much to Bobby's protest.

"I don't want to play house! I want to play cowboys and Indians!" was his usual gripe. He rarely won the battle because he loved his little sister and caved in to her requests.

Edith opened the woodshed door, expecting to find Clara serving water to her brother in one of her little teacups. To Edith's surprise, there was no sign of the children there, either.

She backed out of the woodshed and closed the door. She went behind the woodshed to look—nothing. She felt her heartbeat quicken. She went to the corncrib, the barn, the sheep pen. Nothing. Now her heart was racing, and dark thoughts clouded her mind.

She really couldn't run anymore, but she walked as quickly as she could to the house.

"Robert, I can't find the kids anywhere!" she called as soon as she hit the back porch.

She heard him fold the paper and by the time she got to the living room, he was standing.

"I'll start at the neighbors' houses," he said. "You catch your breath, sit down, and stay here in case those two come home."

She didn't want to sit down, but knew he was right. Someone should stay at the house, and since labor and delivery were somewhat imminent, it made sense for her to stay put. She paced. How could they have disappeared so fast? What if someone had driven by and kidnapped them? What if they had gone down to Sycamore Creek and fallen in? Then she prayed. She felt sure God would protect her children, so she decided to say thank you for that protection, as if she could will it into being.

An hour passed, and Robert returned home. "No one has seen them. I went a mile in each direction, and I can't believe they could go farther than that. I'm kind of worried now. I went everywhere I could think of. Think I'll just run up to the sheriff's office and check in with them."

"Oh, Robert!" Edith couldn't help but tear up now. He wrapped his arms around her.

"Edith, I'm sure they're fine. I just have a feeling they're sitting at someone's table somewhere, eating cookies and drinking milk. You know those two. I'll be back in a few minutes. Try not to worry. I know we're going to find them, and worrying is no good for you in your current condition, my dear." He smiled and left.

Once again, Edith prayed. "God, please keep an eye on Bobby and Clara. Those two can get into such mischief, and they're too little to know if they're getting close to harm. I try to be a good mother and not let them get hurt. Let Robert be right—let them just be somewhere having milk and cookies…." Her head popped up. Cookies! Cookies! She might know where her children were, after all.

She wrote a quick note to Robert, left it on the table, put Mary in the stroller and headed out for a two-mile walk to the Ratliff residence. The day was hot, but she walked as fast as she could, unconcerned with how Mary bounced in the stroller. Nine months pregnant, the walk would take her an hour. Frustrated, for the entire walk she blamed herself for the incident and prayed for forgiveness, feeling like a bad mother, but as she got close to the Ratliff place, she saw the front screen door push open. Two little children walked out, hand-in-hand. *Her* children!

"Hi, Mommy!" Bobby called.

"Hi, Mama!" Clara echoed.

"Oh, children!" Edith said. As best she could, she squatted down, and the children ran into her arms.

She hugged them so tight that Bobby complained.

"Mom, let me go!"

Edith laughed in relief, then became stern. "I want to know what you two were doing. Who gave you permission to come over to the Ratliff's?"

Both children stood silent and wide-eyed.

"Who gave you permission to come see Mrs. Ratliff?" Edith repeated, her tone more ominous to the little ones.

"No one," Bobby finally said.

"Come with me. You two hold hands." Edith pushed the stroller, and the whole crew marched up to the Ratliff's front door. She knocked and waited for Mrs. Ratliff to appear.

"Edith, come right in," Mrs. Ratliff said as she answered and opened the door. "Good grief, you're sweating to death! Come in and have some iced tea."

Edith left the stroller outside, picked up Mary and stepped into the coolness of the house. "Thank you so much, but it appears the Riedel family has been enough bother for one day."

Mrs. Ratliff laughed. "Bother? Good heavens, no. These two are no bother. In fact, I was happy to see them. We don't see you all as much since Mary was born. May I hold her?"

"Of course." Edith handed the baby to Mrs. Ratliff.

"She's as cute as a button!" the older woman exclaimed. "And you're soon to have another?"

"Yes, any old day now, actually. And I don't mind telling you, I'm ready."

Mrs. Ratliff laughed. "Sit down for a minute, Edith. You can stay just a minute, can't you?"

"All right. I suppose I can. Bobby—Clara—sit down."

The kids sat on floor at her feet, sheepish.

"I'll bring you some tea." Mrs. Ratliff disappeared into her kitchen, still holding Mary on her hip like a woman who had lots of practice. She reappeared with one glass of iced tea. Edith took a long swallow.

"That *does* taste good. Thank you. It took me almost an hour to get here. I'm a little slower than usual."

"Well I can imagine. You look like you're ready to pop right now! Let me guess—you came over about the kids."

"You guessed right!" She looked at Bobby and Clara, who

continued looking sheepish. They knew they were in trouble.

"I fed the kids lunch and they asked to go out to play. I was busy with Mary and cleaning up after lunch and lost track of how much time had passed. About a half hour later when I checked on them, there was no sign of them anywhere. I felt awful—like a failure as a mother. Then Robert started checking in with neighbors without luck and went up to the sheriff's office. I was actually praying when something hit me…they love your cookies."

Mrs. Ratliff began laughing. "You know your children well, my dear! Yes, we've had sugar cookies and tea this afternoon, haven't we kids?"

Both children looked up at Edith, trying to gauge her reaction before answering.

"Yes ma'am," Bobby finally said. "And they were really good!"

Mrs. Ratliff laughed again, but Edith maintained a stern posture. Mrs. Ratliff tried to stifle her amusement.

"What do you children know about asking people for cookies when you go to their house?" Edith asked the toddlers.

"Not to." Bobby's answer was simple.

"That's right. What in the world would make you think you had permission to come down and beg cookies off Mrs. Ratliff?"

Tears filled Bobby's eyes. "I don't know."

Clara provided the plain details. "We wanted a cookie." Guileless.

"I want you two to apologize to Mrs. Ratliff for coming to her house without her even expecting you and for asking for cookies."

Bobby and Clara stood up and walked over to Mrs. Ratliff's side. Mary cooed at her brother and sister. Clara started to reach for her little sister, then dropped her hands to her side where Bobby took hold of one.

"I'm sorry, Mrs. Ratliff," the little boy began.

"I'm sorry too, Mrs. Ratliff," Clara added.

"Well, children, as happy as I was to see you, your mama is right. You should never, ever go anywhere without asking her permission, and if your mama doesn't want you to ask people for cookies when you visit, you shouldn't. You should always listen to your mom, right?"

Bobby was swiping at his eyes, and Clara remained apologetic. "We'll never do that again," she said. "Not ever!"

"All right, then. Maybe instead of you two sneaking down here, after your new baby brother or sister is born, I can come pick you up and bring you to my house for lunch and to play. Then we could have some cookies for dessert. What do you think about that idea?"

Bobby and Clara looked at Edith. "That would be all right, children, because Mrs. Ratliff has *invited* you."

Both kids smiled, and the tears began to dry up.

"We've got to go. Robert will wonder where *I've* gotten to." Edith stood up and reached for Mary.

"I'm so glad you came by," Mrs. Ratliff said, adding in a whisper, "even if it was to catch up with two ornery little kids!" She laughed again.

The quartet started for home, this time at an even slower pace. "While we're walking home, I want you two to think about what you did. I was worried about you when I couldn't find you, and your daddy was terribly worried! You must never, ever do such a thing again."

They walked in silence. About a half mile from home, Bobby spoke up.

"Mommy, when Mrs. Ratliff comes to get us, will we have a baby brother or a baby sister?"

"I don't know, Bobby. Only God knows that."

"I hope it's a baby brother," the little boy groused.

Three days later, Phyllis Corrine Riedel was born.

12

December 1933

The Great Depression hung on, making middle class out of upper crust, poor out of the middle class, and leaving the poor destitute. Robert worked every day at the pottery—long, hot hours spent making bowls and vases and all manner of earthenware he could never afford to buy for his own family. He trapped in the early mornings before work. Once the traps were set, he had to check them for captured prey. Rising before the sun came up (*when* it came up—Ohio winters included little sunshine) he dressed in long johns, wool shirts, thick overalls, woolen socks and heavy boots, trying to defeat the bitter cold while he removed muskrats, minks, raccoons and rabbits from the traps. After his day job, he skinned the small animals, taking care to leave the hides undamaged so that they could be sold for the highest possible price. The evenings and weekends meant more hard work in caring for the few animals they owned—the cows and sheep. Even with so much of his time spent in hard labor on behalf of his family, there was little money for anything but the bare necessities.

Edith kept the household running in the smoothest manner possible, all to support the family in her own way. Now with four small children, day-to-day life was busier than ever. She sometimes worried about the lack of fresh fruit for her little ones. Of course, they had plenty of apples—apples from their orchard were abundant, saved in cold storage for eating throughout the winter. But the children rarely had an orange or a banana. If it didn't grow in Ohio, chances were it could not be obtained, especially in needier families. She sometimes wondered if this was the reason they were all suffering from colds.

Edith had a cough. The kids had a cough. The only person who didn't have a cough was Robert, and for that, the young couple was thankful. He needed to work. There were mouths to feed.

All four kids recovered from their sniffles, but Edith's cough continued unabated. She had been coughing for three weeks. She felt weak and tired all the time but didn't want to complain. Then on a Saturday afternoon, while Robert played with Bobby and Clara on the floor, Edith fainted. Even her usual strength of will couldn't stop it.

When she came to, Robert was cradling her in his arms as he knelt beside her. Bobby and Clara were standing at his side, eyes wide in fright and puzzlement.

"What happened?" Edith started to try to rise.

"Wait, wait just a minute," Robert said, preventing her from getting up. "You just fainted and fell right down on the floor. There wasn't a second to catch you. Just stay put."

"Fainted? I fainted?" Edith was foggy in thought and understanding of her current predicament.

"Yes, honey. Just be quiet for a minute and get your mind together. Bobby, do you think you can get a drink of water for Mommy?"

"Yes, Daddy." Bobby took off for the kitchen.

"Mama, are you sick?" Clara asked.

Edith didn't answer. She was still cloudy.

"Mama might be a little sicker than she thought," Robert said. "Clara, you go check on your little sisters, all right? Can you do that for Daddy?"

"Yes, Daddy." Clara disappeared to check on her sisters, both of whom were napping. Just about that time, Bobby showed up with his own child's cup, filled to the brim.

"Thank you, son." Robert took a sip off the top—the cup was too full to give to a recumbent person—then he helped Edith raise up enough to take a sip herself.

"Oh, that does taste good," she said. "Maybe I'm a little dehydrated."

"That could be. You hardly ever have time to *think*, let alone drink enough water." Robert was concerned. Edith was a strong woman. He had never seen her laid low like this.

"C'mon. I'll help you up to the couch." He assisted Edith to her feet, walking with her the few steps to their sofa. He sat her down saying, "Listen, you need to rest. I'm sure you're getting down because of this cold. You got the kids well, but you didn't get yourself well. You're on the go all the time. Lie down for a while. I'll take care of the kids."

"Oh, I'm fine, honestly. I just passed out. In a minute, I'll be ready to start supper."

"No, Edith. I'm insisting. I want you to stay right on this couch for a while. I can get something around for supper. I used to help my mom all the time, remember? I was pert' near as good a cook as she was. Listen to me, now…you've got to get well."

Edith leaned against the back of the couch. She knew he was right. She was weak and could feel that she was starting to run a fever, but she would not say that to Robert—he would worry. He made it easy to relent. "All right. Thanks. I'll rest for a while." She stretched out and closed her eyes.

"C'mon, Bobby. Let's go see what your sisters are doing while Mommy rests." He took the boy's hand and went to find out what Clara and her sisters might be up to.

When they got to the children's room, they found that Clara had climbed into Phyllis's crib and was sound asleep with her little sister. She loved that baby! Mary, now one and half years old, was awake, standing in her crib.

"Daddy, out!" she said, arms outstretched, a smile on her face. She was daddy's girl.

"All right, you little rascal," Robert said. "But be quiet now…don't wake your sisters."

Robert took Bobby and Mary to the kitchen with him. "Bobby, you play with Mary and help watch out for her while I figure out what to make for supper. Don't let her wake your mama, okay?"

"Yes, Daddy. Why is Mommy sleeping in the day?"

"Son, your mom is sick. She needs to sleep so she can get well."

"Does she need some medicine?" Bobby asked.

"She might, son…she might. We'll see how she's doing when she wakes up."

Robert set about planning and preparing a supper Edith would be proud of. He fried venison hamburgers, made gravy to go over them, peeled and cooked potatoes to mash, and got green beans ready. He opened a jar of applesauce—a kid favorite. They would have sugar cookies for dessert. He checked on Edith occasionally. She was asleep, but something about her breathing was off. He was certain he could hear some rasping sound with each breath. He put his hand on her forehead. She felt warmer than normal. *But she's sleeping okay.* He went back to his work. Now, Clara had awakened and joined the other kids in the kitchen.

"Bobby, can you get forks and spoons for you and your sisters? Then help Clara get up to the table, all right? I'll put Mary in her highchair after I look in on your mom."

Bobby did as he was asked while Robert checked on Edith one more time. By the time he got back, Clara was seated, while Bobby was trying his best to get Mary into her highchair.

"I was trying to help, Daddy," Bobby said, "but she's too little."

Robert laughed. "Here. I'll get her. She's too little to step up but she's too big for you to lift now." All the children were growing fast, even though Edith frequently worried about their health. *She should be worried about her own health,* he thought as he spooned food onto each child's plate.

He heard Edith coughing. "I'll be right back. Bobby, you say the prayer and then you kids can go ahead and eat."

Bobby bowed his head and started, "God is great, God is good…" as Robert went into the living room where Edith was sitting straight up on the couch. She couldn't stop coughing. He sat behind her to support her until the hacking stopped. It was then he realized how thin she had become—he could feel her vertebrae through her dress. How had he not noticed this before?

"Edith, I think you should see Doc Montgomery Monday. This is getting out of hand."

"Oh, Robert, I'll be fine. I'm just coughing more because I was laying down. I'll get a good night's rest tonight and you'll see. I'll be fine by Monday. Maybe I won't go to church tomorrow. I'll just rest."

Robert had been worried, but now he was truly alarmed. Edith never missed church. If she was suggesting it, she was sicker than he had realized.

"Let's see how you are tomorrow, but my feeling is that you should go see Doc on Monday. That's my two cents. Do you feel like you can eat something?"

"I'm not really hungry, but I'll try a bite or two. I know I should at least try. What did you make?"

"Come see for yourself. It's a regular feast." He smiled and helped her to her feet, relieved that she seemed more steady.

They walked to the kitchen where the kids were almost finished with their own supper. "Mommy!" they each yelled, excited to see her.

"Oh my! Well I'm happy to see all of you, too," Edith laughed. "Gosh, you'd think I'd been sleeping for a week. Supper looks good, honey. Where's Phyllis?"

"She's still asleep. I'll get her in a minute. Let me put some food on a plate for you," Robert said. "Just sit down and let me wait on you for a change."

"Don't get too much…I'm just not that hungry today," Edith said.

Robert looked at her face again. She was pale. The color around her mouth was gray-ish, and he was more worried than ever. He retrieved supper for his wife.

"You kids go play," he instructed the children. "I hear the baby fussing now." He went in to Phyllis, changed her diaper and returned with her to the kitchen. He put her in the playpen while he warmed a bottle of milk.

Edith was picking at her food. As instructed, Robert had not put much on her plate to begin with, and when she was done, the amounts he had given her were changed little.

"All right. I'll clean up. Why don't you go in the living room with the kids."

"I believe I will. Maybe I can go ahead and read them their Bible story."

"You want me to walk with you?" Robert asked.

"No, no. I promise you I'm just fine."

He watched after her as she headed in to where the children were playing. As he cleared the table, he heard her gathering them around her chair and beginning the story of Moses. Her recitation was interrupted by coughing every few sentences. He knew she *must* see the doctor.

***

Edith was restless in her sleep. Robert woke up at daylight to find her sweating, mumbling, coughing. He felt her forehead. She was burning up.

"Edith, Edith…honey, wake up. You've got to take some aspirin and drink something. You've got a fever."

Edith stirred, opened and closed her eyes. She turned over on her side. Immediately, she began to cough, a harsh, jagged sound. She choked, causing her to sit up. Robert clapped her on the back, hoping to dislodge the mucous she needed to cough up. When she finally gagged up the mucous, he caught it in a handkerchief he grabbed off the table by their bed. He looked at it the contents of the handkerchief—blood.

Robert knew what blood meant. Edith was catching her breath. He jumped out of bed and said, "I'm calling Doc. You don't you move an inch. I'll be back."

He was grateful it was early enough in the morning that the party line wasn't in use. Of course—Sunday—everyone would be getting ready for church. He dialed Dr. Montgomery.

"Hello. Dr. Montgomery here." The phone had not rung many times before it was answered.

"Dr. Montgomery, it's Robert Riedel. I'm sorry to bother you on a Sunday morning, but I'm worried about Edith, and I think you better come over if you can."

"What's going on, Robert? You sound upset."

"I am. It's Edith's cough—she's coughing up blood."

The physician cleared his throat. "All right. Listen, is she breathing okay at this minute?"

"Yes. I mean, she coughs an awful lot and then it's hard for her to catch her breath, but in between, she seems to be breathing all right."

"Good. Keep her resting. I've got to get a cup of coffee in me, then I'll be right over unless you think I need to skip the coffee."

"No, Doc—get yourself awake, but I appreciate you coming as soon as you can."

"I'll see you in just a few minutes then." Robert started to hang up, but he heard Doc calling his name in the receiver. "Robert! Robert!"

"Yes, Doc?" Robert said, placing the receiver back to his ear.

"Till I get there, don't let the kids in around Edith, and if you handle any of her sputum—her spit—make sure you throw away whatever she coughs the mucous into and wash your hands very, very well. Whatever she has could be infectious."

The men hung up. Robert got a glass of water and went back to his wife.

"Dr. Montgomery is coming over to see you in just a bit."

Edith tried to get out of bed. "That's ridiculous. You call him right back and tell him to stay home or go on to church. I'm…." She couldn't finish her sentence. She was coughing again. Robert stayed with her till the spasm passed. She collapsed back against her pillow.

"Maybe I should just stay in bed."

"You absolutely should stay in bed. Doc says the kids shouldn't be around you right now. You may have an infection they could get. I'm going to get a box of tissues and a trash can in here. Whatever you cough up, you have to cough it into a tissue and then throw it away."

"What? All right." She was too fatigued to argue.

"I'm going to check on the kids. Hopefully, they're still conked out."

Robert walked to the children's room. All four were sleeping, but he knew it wouldn't be long till they were up and ready to go. He thought about what they had handy that he could give them for breakfast—it needed to be something quick and easy this morning. He checked the icebox. They had milk. He checked the cupboard—corn flakes would have to do.

Doc Montgomery was knocking at the door. Robert was surprised and relieved that he was already there. He let the physician in.

"Where's our girl?"

"In bed, Doc."

"Good. Now, before I go examine her, tell me what's been going on."

"Sure. She's had a cold for about three weeks now. The kids got it first, then Edith started up. Even after the kids got better, she was still coughing her head off. I didn't notice till yesterday that she's lost some weight. I felt every one of her ribs. Yesterday she passed out. I told her she was coming to see you Monday but last night, she started with a fever. She was hot as heck. Sweating, even. She was real restless all night. The final straw was this morning. She started coughing up blood. She tried to get up a little bit ago, but she's way too weak."

"All right. Let me go in and examine her. Have the kids been around her?"

"Well, sure, right up till they went to bed last night. They're still asleep, so they haven't been 'round her this morning."

"Let's keep them out of her room for now. When they wake up, make sure they don't come running down to her room first thing."

"Gotcha, Doc. I might call my sister to see if she can come over and help me with them for now. I'm sure she would come."

Doc rubbed his unshaved face. "That might not be a bad idea, Robert." He was calm, but his voice conveyed his concern.

While Doc headed to the room where Edith rested, Robert called Cora.

"Cora, it's Robert. If there's any way you can, I need you to come over and help me with the babies. Edith's sick—really sick."

"Oh lands! What's wrong with her?"

"Not sure yet. Please just come on over, and I'll tell you all about it when you get here."

"I'll be there in just a little bit, brother. I'll pray all the way."

Robert knew she would. He headed for the bedroom when he heard Bobby coming down the hall. He was holding hands with Mary.

"Daddy, we're hungry."

"Okay. Let's go get some cereal."

"Where's Mommy?"

"Mommy is sick today, buddy. You and I are going to have to keep the girls away from her. Do you think you can help me with that?"

"Sure, Daddy. Does she still have a cold?"

"Yes, son. I think your mama has a very bad cold."

Clara was coming down the hall by this time, rubbing her eyes. Robert directed her into the kitchen where he poured three bowls of corn flakes and milk. He knew it wouldn't be long before Phyllis would wake up.

"You kids say your prayer and eat all your breakfast. I'm going to check on your mom."

Robert finally made it back to the bedroom where the physician was listening to Edith's lungs through her nightgown, a troubled look on his face. Robert saw another bloody tissue in the trash can.

When Doc finished his exam, he turned to Robert and said, "Sit down over there. You and Edith need to hear this together."

Robert knew what was coming. He had seen this before.

"Edith, I think you might have tuberculosis." She started to speak, pushing herself up on her hands. "No, now, settle down. I don't know for sure until we do an X-ray, but based on the symptoms Robert told me about, and based on you coughing up this blood and how your lungs sound, I'm highly suspicious. *Highly* suspicious. Robert, you're going to have to get her over to Mercy Hospital in Tiffin and get a chest X-ray. I'll write the order to send over there with you."

Robert was processing all that had just been thrown at him when he heard his sister come in the front door.

"Robert? I'm here...."

"Don't come back here, Cora. The kids are in the kitchen." Robert got up and went out to meet his sister. He was most definitely going to need her help now.

Cora was hugging each of the children when he got to the kitchen. She set her purse down and took off her coat while Robert poured her a cup of coffee.

"How's Edith?"

"It's not good, Cora. Doc thinks she has TB."

Cora plopped down on a chair. "Oh, Robert...."

"What's TB, Daddy?" Bobby asked.

"I'll explain it in a little while, son, all right? Let me talk to Aunt Cora for a minute." He turned back to his sister. He spoke in a quieter tone, trying not to alarm his children. "She's been sick for at least three weeks—maybe four. The kids had a cold, and we thought she just had a cold, too. But hers kept hanging on. She's tired a lot, but of course, we just thought that was because she's so busy with these kids all the time. She's getting thin because she hasn't been eating that well. She's been coughing her head off. Now she has a fever and she's coughing up blood."

"What happens next?" Cora asked.

"Doc says take her to Tiffin to get an X-ray, just to make sure. What happens after that, I don't know. Cora, I need help with these kids. Can you stay with them till I get Edith back home?"

"Of course, of course. Just get her to the hospital and I'll pray that the doctor is wrong."

"I've known him a long time and I've never known him to be wrong about anything yet," Robert said.

"Me either," Cora said, glum.

***

Doc's diagnostic skills had not failed him. The treatment included a stay in the sanatorium at Mt. Vernon. Robert was devastated but held it in check. Edith was distraught, crying all the way to the facility.

"How will you manage? How will you take care of these

91

children when you have to work?" Her crying made her even more short of breath, causing her to cough twice as much.

"Edith, don't worry about that. Cora has the kids at her place right now and she'll take care of them till she and I can get it all figured out. I know all four of them can't stay with her. We've got lots of family and friends that will help, though. The last thing you need right now is to be so upset and worrying. Mt. Vernon is the best place to get the treatment you need."

She tried to stop her tears. Looking down at her hands, she said, "What if the treatment doesn't work? A lot of people do *not* get well from this, Robert."

He knew it was true, but he said, "You're not going to be one of those. You're going to get well and come back home to us. Don't even think like that. You've got to keep the positive attitude you always have about everything—keep your chin up. And you've got to pray like you always do, too. I know that's what *I'll* be doing."

They pulled into the parking lot at the sanitorium, an imposing brick building.

"Christmas. What are you going to do about Christmas?" Edith said.

"Well, we've got those doll babies for Clara and Mary, and I got Bobby that little farm set. Didn't you make some dresses for the dolls?"

"Yes. They're in the closet up high. Nothing is wrapped. You'll have to play Santa Claus all by yourself." Edith began to cry again. "I hate missing Christmas with the kids."

"If you're not in the hospital this Christmas, you might not be around for any *other* Christmases. You have to think of it that way, Edith. The kids will miss you—heck, *I'll* miss you—but we can miss you for one Christmas a lot better than we can miss you for all the rest of the Christmases in our lives."

They entered the facility. Edith went through the admission process, coughing through most of the questions they asked her. Then she and Robert were taken to the ward where Edith's bed had been assigned. They sat on her bed together to say their goodbyes.

"I don't want to stay here without you and my babies."

Robert hung his head. He didn't want to leave her there, either, but he had to. He lifted her chin so that her eyes met his.

"I love you more now than I did on the day we got married. I don't want anything to happen that takes you away from me. That means that I have to give you up for now. It's temporary. Do you understand me? I'm going to tell myself that every day. That's what I want *you* to remember, too. It's temporary."

She blinked and swallowed. "It's temporary." She began coughing again. "You best get out of here, Robert. I hope and pray none of you have it already."

"You know me. I never get sick. But I'll keep a close eye on the kids for a while. Try not to worry. I'll be back to see you as soon as I can. I'll let you know what's happening with the children, so don't fret over them. Worrying will only make you sicker." He kissed her on the forehead. "I'll call down here and see how you're doing till I can get back."

Once more, tears filled Edith's eyes. "I love you so much." She put her arms around him, careful to keep her face away from his.

He hugged his thin wife. "Do everything they tell you so you can get well as fast as possible. Try to eat. Rest all you can. Do whatever they tell you."

"I will. I will."

"Good-bye, Edith." He turned towards the door. He couldn't look back. He needed to clear the tears from his own eyes before he began the nearly seventy-mile drive back to Sycamore.

13
January 1934

"Well, I think we've got it figured out, Robert. Bobby will stay with Mabel and Virgil, Clara will go with Bertha and Hallace, and the two little ones will go to Mrs. Dawson's house." Cora had organized and written a list of who was going where and what they would need. Robert was grateful.

"Cora, I'd have been in a mess with all this if you hadn't helped me."

"Don't think a thing of it. If I was in the same boat, you'd help me." She was right. The brother and sister had always been close. "They could stay with me, but our house is already full."

"It sure is," Robert chuckled. "Well, now all I have to do is pack up the kids' clothes and toys and deliver them where they're supposed to go. I'm going to try to take them to Mt. Vernon with me sometimes. Even if they can't go in, they can wave at their mother while she's in the sunroom. She'll be able to see them from there. It'll do her good to see them even if it's from a distance."

"I couldn't agree more. It will be good for the kids, too. They're so little they might not remember her if you don't take them to see her, even if it's from a distance."

Robert hadn't thought about that—that the children might not remember their mother. It strengthened his resolve to make sure he took the kids with him to see her whenever he could.

Cora headed home, and while the kids slept, he started packing clothing and other belongings they would need. He knew that some of their toys would help them feel better about having to live with other families—they needed something of their own to remind them that they would be coming back home. While he packed, he thought about how he was going to explain all this. The two littlest girls weren't old enough to understand much at all, but Bobby and Clara might grasp some of it.

Bobby was the first to awaken. His naps were growing shorter as he got older.

"Daddy, what are you doing?" The first words out of his mouth caused Robert to stop packing and sit down.

"Come over here, buddy, and sit down with me for a minute. I need to talk to you man-to-man. Do you know what that means?"

"No."

"It means like a grown-up."

Bobby smiled. "Like a big man?"

"That's pretty much it. Son, you know that your mom is very sick, right? That she has tuberculosis, which is a very bad disease that makes it hard for her to breathe. She has to stay in a special hospital. You understand all that, right?"

"Yes, Daddy. You told us about it—that Mom might have to stay at the hospital for a long time."

"You know that I have to work. I have to work at the pottery, and I have to keep up with my traps and take care of the animals."

"Yes, I know. You have to work hard every day."

I'm glad he recognizes that, Robert thought. "Bobby, I can't be gone at work all day long every day and have you children here by yourselves. With Mommy in the hospital, there's no one to take care of you, and I've gotta work to pay the bills for Mommy being in that hospital, plus buy food and gasoline for the car—all that costs a lot of money. I *have* to work."

Bobby didn't respond, but kept his eyes glued to his father's face. The little boy moved his eyes toward the small valise his father had been packing for him, then back to his father. He looked confused.

"Buddy, you and the girls are going to go stay with some of your aunts and uncles for a while. You are going to stay with Aunt Mabel and Uncle Virgil. Clara is going to stay with Aunt Bertha and Uncle Hallace. Mary and Phyllis are going to stay with a lady your Aunt Cora knows, Mrs. Dawson. You'll all have to stay in these different places only till Mommy comes back home."

"But Mommy might not come home for a long time, right?"

Robert put his arm around Bobby's shoulder and pulled the boy close. "Yes. We just don't know how long it will take for her to get well, son. I need you to be a good boy and help Aunt Mabel and Uncle Virgil around the house. I also need you to be brave until our family can be back together. Do you understand?"

"Yes, sir." Bobby went over to his suitcase and looked inside, moving articles around. "My clothes and toothbrush are in there and my teddy bear. Can I take my truck?"

"You bet, son. We'll pack that right in with your other things." He was surprised at the little guy's resilience. He only hoped the girls could be so brave.

Clara was the next one up. Since she was barely past her third birthday, the explanation to her was a little more difficult. When the tears began, Robert reminded her of the fun she had at Aunt Bertha's. "Aunt Bertha always lets you help her bake cookies, doesn't she? And doesn't she make pretty dresses for your dollies?"

"Yes, Daddy. But I want to stay with you."

It broke his heart. But the worst was yet to come. Mary and Phyllis. They were babies. How could they ever begin to understand? And they were going to a complete stranger's home. He and Cora had debated it...which child should go where?

"Robert, the girls are so little that they won't even remember this situation. Keep them together and let them go to Mrs. Dawson's house. She's one of the kindest people I know, and she's excited about having the girls with her."

"Cora, Mary is so sensitive. She's not quite two, but I think she *will* remember all this. Phyllis probably won't. Are you sure about this idea?"

"What do you remember from age two?" Cora said.

Robert had to admit that he remembered little before the age of five. "All right, we'll go with this plan."

Now he was confronted with having to try to explain it to Mary.

"Mary," he started, the tiny thing sitting beside him on the couch. "You are going to go on a fun trip. You are going to stay with a very kind lady named Mrs. Dawson. You will sleep at her house, and eat at her house, and play at her house, too. Phyllis will be there with you. What do you think of that?"

"Okay, Daddy." Mary jumped off the sofa to go play.

Robert knew she didn't have a clue about what he had just told her, but he had to keep moving. Time was not on his side. He couldn't afford to miss work, so kids had to be delivered to their temporary homes.

The phone rang. "Hello," Robert answered.

"Robert, this is Virgil."

"Oh, hi, Virgil."

"How are you doing over there?"

"As well as can be expected, I guess. I just broke the news to the kids about going away for a while. Bobby and Mary took it pretty good. Clara took it the hardest."

"That's what I'm calling about. You've got all these children to deliver. Why don't you let us just come pick Bobby up? That's one less trip you'd have to make."

"If you can, I'd sure appreciate it. I've got to take Clara to Fostoria and the other girls to Marion, then get back home. Heck, all together I guess I've got about a hundred miles of driving around to do today."

"That's what I told Mabel. All right. Give me a half hour or so and I'll be there."

"Thanks, Virgil."

Robert hung up. He was suddenly overcome with the sadness of his situation—of Edith's situation. The whole thing felt too heavy to carry. He swiped at his eyes, grateful that he had a family who cared.

"Heavenly Father," he prayed, "I don't understand your ways all the time, but I'm going to try to remember that we're all in your care and that you're watching out for my wife and children. Thank you."

He raised his head. Clara was standing in the doorway, holding her little red cardboard suitcase. "I'm ready to go, Daddy." Her tiny jaw was set. She was a little soldier. He felt the sting of tears welling up again, and he blinked hard.

"Come here, you stinker." Clara ran to him. He wrapped his arms around her. "You're a good girl, Clara. You make me proud while you're at Aunt Bertha's, all right?"

"I will, Daddy."

He squeezed her tight. "Good girl. Now can you help me get things ready for Mary and Phyllis? Can you pick out some favorite toys to take with them?"

She didn't answer but ran off towards their room. Robert didn't immediately follow, thinking to himself, *I'm going to miss my children. I can hardly stand the thought of them not being here.* He slumped, held his head in his hands for a minute, then straightened up. *The kids are acting braver than I am!* It was the last time he would allow himself to feel sad.

14
June 1934

"Robert, have you gone to see Mary and Phyllis lately?" Cora called him just as he came in from the barn. It was almost 8:00 in the evening, and Robert was exhausted.

"No, I haven't seen them for about a month. Why, Cora? Is something wrong?"

"Not really *wrong*, but I think Mrs. Dawson might have taken on more than she's able to do. You know, she's up there in years, and I think she forgot how busy two little ones can keep a person, especially now that Phyllis is walking. I talked to her this morning, and she sounded very, very tired."

Robert rubbed his forehead. Now what? He himself was so tired he could barely think.

"I'm not sure what to do, Cora."

"Well, I have an idea. Remember the Koehler's?"

Robert knew the family. They lived in Upper Sandusky. Their parents and his parents had been good friends.

"Sure, I remember them. What about 'em?"

"I think they'd take the girls. They have an older daughter, themselves—Janice Louise. I think Janice would help care for Mary and Phyllis. Would you like me to talk to Frances?"

"I didn't know you were still in contact with them, but if you think they might be willing…."

"I'll call Frances tomorrow. I'll let you know what she says."

Robert hung up. Mrs. Dawson probably *was* a little too old for such young children. Mary had just turned three and Phyllis would soon be a year old. *At those ages, kids are a handful.*

Thinking about it all was dispiriting. His wife seventy miles away…his children scattered across central Ohio. He couldn't help but feel a little depressed.

He recalled his promise to himself—he would *not* be sad.

Robert thought back on the Koehler family as he readied himself for bed. Aaron and Frances had three children of their own: Rita, Janice Louise, and Jacob. Rita was married, but the younger two were still at home—teenagers. He wondered how the family would respond to the idea of having two very little children in the house again. Tired and ready for sleep, he could only hope for the best, praying as he drifted off.

After another long day of labor at the pottery, Robert was making a bite of supper for himself when the phone rang. Once again, it was Cora, and she had good news.

"Brother, not only will the Koehler family take Mary and Phyllis, but if you want, they'll take Clara, too."

"What? Well, that's certainly wonderful news. I can hardly believe it."

"I wasn't surprised when they said they'd take Mary and Phyllis, but I was surprised when they said they'd take Clara. That's three. That seems like a lot to me," Cora said. "I'll leave that up to you. I think Clara's been fine at Hallace and Bertha's hasn't she?"

"Yes. In fact, she's getting spoiled—*that's* how she's doing." Robert laughed. "Bertha does love that child! I think let's just leave it at the two little ones. They'll be plenty of work for the Koehlers, I'm sure."

"I agree with you. To overload one family might mean they wear out faster, don't you think? Listen, I can call Mrs. Dawson for you…."

Robert interrupted. "No Cora, I'll call her myself. It will give me a chance to thank her for all she's done. And I appreciate your help, too, in case I haven't said it lately."

"Oh, pshaw, I haven't done anything but make a couple of phone calls."

"Ha! You're my moral support, too, you know." In his mind's eye, Robert could see his sister beaming on the other end of the phone.

"I'll talk to you tomorrow. If you want someone to ride down to Marion with you to pick up the kids, I'll go along."

"That'd be nice, sis. I'll take you up on it. See you tomorrow."

Robert ate a ham sandwich and thought about what to say to

Mrs. Dawson—how to tell her the girls they were going to another home. Their lives had already been disrupted once. He knew Mrs. Dawson was kind to them. Would they be scared all over again? No matter. It had to be done. He finished his sandwich and picked up the phone.

"Jenny, I need long distance. Marion 5-2."

"All right, Robert. One moment please...."

He waited while the local operator made the connection he needed. It wasn't long before he heard, "Go ahead."

"Mrs. Dawson?"

"Yes, hello?"

"This is Robert Riedel."

"Oh, Robert, how good to hear your voice." Cora was right. She sounded tired.

"How are the girls doing?"

"They're lovely, Robert. I couldn't ask for two sweeter babies to care for."

Now he wondered if she would be disappointed that he was calling to take them away from her. He chose his words carefully.

"You have been tremendously kind. It's been such a relief to know my two girls were in good hands, but I've been worried about the toll it's taking on you."

Mrs. Dawson laughed. "Well, I didn't remember how busy little ones keep you, that's for sure. Oh, don't get me wrong. I enjoy the children very much. But I'll put it this way—I'm not having any trouble getting to sleep at night." She laughed again.

"I'm sure of it. You know, I miss those two so much. It's hard for me to get to Marion to see them as often as I'd like. Mrs. Dawson, I have another family in Upper Sandusky willing to take the girls. They have a teenage daughter who can help care for them, and I'd be able to see them a little more often. I would never want you to think I didn't appreciate what you've done for us, but I'm going to come get the girls and bring them back to Upper."

"Oh, Robert. I take no offense at that! You need to have these children closer to home if that's possible. I'm happy for you. Who is this family? Would I know them?"

"Aaron and Frances Koehler. Does that sound familiar to you?"

"No...let's see...no, I don't believe I know them. Well, just the same, it sounds like a good opportunity to get the girls closer to home, so I'll start getting things ready for them. When do you think you'll come get them?"

"Not till Saturday. That's the first day I'm not working."

"All right, then. I'll have all their clothes laundered and packed Saturday morning."

"Mrs. Dawson, Edith and I can never repay you for the kindness you've shown us. There's nothing more precious to us than our children, and you've provided them loving care just like you were their mother."

"I like to think of myself as their replacement grandma." She laughed once more. Robert knew she had not been offended by the change.

"I'll see you on Saturday, probably around noon. Cora is coming with me, so I'll have to pick her up before I start for Marion."

"I'll see you then," the older lady said.

As they hung up, Robert realized how happy—how excited— he was at the thought of his two youngest daughters being closer to home. Upper Sandusky was half the distance of Marion. He'd be able to get all the kids together a little more often, maybe take them *all* to see their mother. That would cheer up Edith. She needed it more than ever.

***

Over a Saturday morning breakfast, Aaron and Frances Koehler explained to their own children what was soon taking place in their home.

"A man named Robert Riedel has four little children and his wife has become very ill. She has tuberculosis." Aaron was matter of fact.

The older of the Koehler's two children, Janice Louise, took in a deep breath. "That's awful! That can kill you!"

"Yes, it certainly can, but Mr. Riedel's wife is in a sanitorium and is getting a little better, so everyone hopes she'll be completely healed and get to come home before long. That said, Mr. Riedel has to work practically day and night to pay for her care, and he has no one to watch his children. The oldest two are already with relatives, and the youngest two are going to stay with us."

Janice looked at her brother, Jacob, two years her junior.

"Are there any boys?" Jacob asked.

"No, son, I'm afraid not."

"How old are these kids?"

"Three and one."

"Oh, for criminy sake!" Jacob got up to leave.

Aaron glared at his son. "Jacob John Koehler, you sit right back down. There'll be none of that."

Jacob knew his father's look well enough to know that he'd better comply. He plopped down, arms folded across his chest, a dour look on his face. "Well, if at least one of them was a boy..." he started to complain.

"Son, I'm going out to the barn. Why don't you join me when you're done with breakfast? Maybe a little work will help you get over your poor attitude." Aaron left the room.

Frances spoke, taking a softer approach. "Son, can you try to imagine what it would be like if I got so sick I had to be sent away? You all are old enough to cook and clean and do laundry on your own. It wouldn't be impossible for you to manage, but you'd still miss me, wouldn't you?"

Jacob nodded his agreement. "Yeah, ma. I know what you're getting ready to say. These kids are little, so we have to help them."

"Yes, son, that's exactly right. And we *are* going to help. They need a family to look after them. You can be like a big brother."

"Jacob, I bet it will be fun. Think of it like being around Amy and Lucas. I always get a kick out of our cousins, don't you?" Janice Louise loved her littler cousins and tended to be a 'mama hen' when they were at family gatherings.

"Don't forget that Lucas is a *boy*," Jacob groused. "But two little girls?"

"Oh, for Pete's sake! Don't be a baby!" Janice said. "Mom, where are they going to sleep? Rita's old room?"

"Yes. It's full of sunlight. That will be good for the girls."

"I'll go up and start dusting a little. I don't dust in there as often since Rita moved out."

"Wonder what Rita will think of two little kids tearing up her room," Jacob muttered.

"I think she'll be happy that her room is being used to help someone who's in a lot worse situation than she is, that's what I think." Frances was stern. "She would want us to do this."

"Okay, ma. I'm sorry. I'll get used to it, I guess. What do you need me to do? Can I help with something?"

"Nothing in the house, so why don't you go out with your dad to tend the animals?"

Aaron walked back into the kitchen in time to hear Frances volunteering her son's services to him. "We don't have much to do, Jake. Just finish mucking out the stalls. That's good for you…builds up your muscles."

"I'd rather do that than dust off the dolls in Rita's room."

Frances swatted at Jacob with a dish towel. "Get out, you two. Rita and I will get things ready for our guests."

For three hours, Frances and Rita cleaned and rearranged things in the room the Riedel girls would occupy. Frances was occasionally distracted by some old toy or school paper that Rita had written. She saved a few things that were precious to her and threw the rest out.

"Well, this was a good excuse for getting rid of a lot of things we don't need!" Frances said when they were finished.

"Look how good it all looks!" Janice added, satisfied. "The girls will have a really nice place to stay." She looked out the window and saw an older model car pulling into their driveway. "Not a moment too soon, Mom…look."

Frances crossed over to the window and saw a slender young man helping two tiny girls out of the car. The oldest held on to a small bag. *Might be all they have*, Frances thought.

"Let's go greet our little guests." Frances and Janice started down the hall to the stairs.

"I got some of the toys in the attic cleaned up, too, Mom."

Frances squeezed her arm. "Thanks, honey. We're going to do everything we can to make these children feel welcome. It won't be the same as their own family, but we'll make it as homey as we can—try to make it *like* family."

Janice opened the front door. Her father and Jacob were making their way towards the stranger walking to the front of their home. As she and her mother stepped out onto the porch, her father offered his hand to the gentleman. Then they came to the house. Two little girls straggled behind, holding hands, managing the bag, and looking around with wide eyes. The men reached the porch, where Mr. Riedel took off his hat and nodded to Frances.

"Fran, you remember Robert Riedel. Robert, this is our

daughter, Janice Louise," Aaron started. "And those two little cuties are Mary and Phyllis."

The girls stepped up to the porch. They never let go of each other's hand, nor did the older child let go of her bag. They didn't speak. The little girl holding the bag looked down at the ground, timid. The baby was wide-eyed, observing the Koehler family.

Frances squatted in front of the girls. She spoke softly. "Mary and Phyllis—I'm happy to meet you. We're so glad you're staying with us."

Both girls looked up at their father, uncertain. "Only till Mama gets well," Robert said. "Then we'll all be together again at our own house, right?"

Mary nodded, but still did not speak.

Frances stood, and now it was Janice's turn to squat. "Mary and Phyllis, I'm Janice. Why don't you come with me? I want to show you where you are going to sleep and show you the toy room, too."

At that, the little girls' eyes lit up. They looked at their father one more time, then followed Janice Louise into the house.

"Folks, until you're better paid, I sure appreciate this," Robert said. "It's been hard on all four kids, but these two youngest ones...." He shook his head. "They're just too little to understand. Mrs. Dawson took good care of them, but she's getting up there in years, and it was too much to ask of her. It's a lot to ask of you, too, but you're younger and have a little more help around...you know what I mean." He looked down at the hat in his hand. "Cora tells me you are good people, and I trust her word about you. Please take good care of my girls."

"Mr. Riedel, we'll treat them just like they were our own," Frances said.

"Now, don't go spoiling them," Robert said.

"You won't have to worry about that, sir," Jacob said.

Both Frances and Aaron laughed. "Jacob will be happy to tell you there's not much spoilin' that goes on around here," Aaron said. "Everyone has to pull their weight."

"That's good. That's what I want," Robert replied. "We don't really know what all we have to face. Times could get harder."

"Yes, I wondered...how is your wife, Mr. Riedel?" Frances said.

"She's a little better, but not even close to coming home. I don't think the doctors know what to expect either. Half the time I don't know if they graduated medical school. Everything's a guessing game, it seems."

"I'm sure they're doing all they can," Frances said. "It's a hard disease to cure."

"They told me they could end up taking out part of her lung."

Frances put a hand over her mouth, gasping, while young Jacob's eyes widened. "Holy mackerel! How would they do that?" he asked.

Aaron cast a stern glance at his son. "Jacob! Mrs. Riedel isn't even going to need that operation because we're all going to be praying for her, right?"

"Yes, dad."

"Well, thank you once again. I guess I better get going. It's been a long day. Cora went with me to get the girls, then I dropped her off back home and brought the girls over here. I still want to get home before it gets too dark."

"Smart idea. Do you want to tell the girls good-bye? I can go get them," Frances said, turning towards the door.

"Oh, no, no. I don't think that's a good idea. It'll just upset them," Robert said, putting his hat on his head and backing carefully down the porch steps. "Just tell them I love them, and I'll see them soon." He got into his car and backed out of the driveway. Frances and Aaron watched his car till it disappeared around a curve.

"I'm surprised he didn't want to say good-bye. I think the girls will be more upset by that than if he'd have waited for them," Frances said.

Aaron pondered this before answering. "I think he was more concerned about how upsetting a good-bye would be for *him*."

They walked through the door to hear squeals and giggles upstairs. Jacob, already roughhousing with the little ones—just like family.

15
December 1934

Bobby Riedel looked forward to Christmas. Aunt Mabel and Uncle Virgil reassured him that Santa Claus knew he was living with them and would make a stop at their farm.

"I hope I get a new truck," Bobby said on a snowy afternoon. "A red one."

"Let's write Santa a letter and make sure he knows that," Mabel said.

They sat together at the kitchen table and wrote a brief, heartfelt letter to Santa. Bobby dictated while Mabel wrote.

> *"Dear Santa,*
> *I have been a good boy this year. I helped pick up chicken eggs and pull weeds. I want a new truck for Christmas. Red, please. Can you help my mama get well? She is sick and I miss her. I love you Santa."*

"Should we sign it 'Love, Bobby' or should we say 'thank you' to Santa?" Mabel asked.

"Say thank you so he knows I have good manners like Mama taught me."

"Oh, I'm sure he knows that. You're a *very* good boy." Mabel tousled his hair. Her voice was tender.

"Bobby, I know you miss your mom. I wish she would get well fast, too. I like having you here, but I know you'd rather be at your own house."

"That's where my Dad is."

"Well, most of the time your dad is working so he can pay the doctors to take care of your mama and pay for her medicine. But he comes to see you, right? You're always happy to see him."

"I like it when Daddy comes to see me. Can I go make a snowman with Uncle Virgil now?"

Mabel chuckled, not certain Virgil would be interested in making a snowman. "Sure, Bobby. You go get your Uncle and make him go outside with you. I'll fix some supper."

As her curly-headed ward ran out of the kitchen, she thought about what it must be liked for a five-year-old to be separated from his parents for so long. Bobby was too young to express his feelings about his situation. And the girls! Younger still. What were they going through?

She began her work, praying for her brother-in-law and his family. As she peeled potatoes, she glanced out the window over her kitchen sink and smiled at two figures in the snow wearing matching red hats, gray mittens, and wool coats. Their scarves were wrapped tight around their necks against the wind as they bent over rolling snowballs for a snowman. Just a normal day for a child in an abnormal circumstance.

***

"I'm not a squirt! I'm big!" Clara Riedel told her uncle as they hung the last of the tinsel on the Christmas tree Hallace had cut that morning. "Daddy always calls me that. But I'm big now."

"Well, one thing's for sure. You're spunky," Hallace laughed.

Clara scrunched her eyebrows together, quizzical, and put her hands on her hips, which made Hallace laugh even harder.

"C'mon, Squirt. Let's go see what your Aunt Bertha is doing. I'm getting hungry. How 'bout you?"

"Yes, Uncle Hallace."

Hallace took her hand. "Thank you for helping me decorate the Christmas tree."

"I like the Christmas tree. It looks pretty now."

"Yes, it does. I bet Aunt Bertha will like it a lot."

"Does Daddy have a Christmas tree at my house?"

Hallace stopped and looked down at the tot. A child's face—full of concern for her father. He sat on his heels so he could look directly into her cocoa eyes.

"Clara, I think your Daddy's working so hard that he hasn't thought too much about a Christmas tree."

Clara's expression gave no indication of her thoughts, and she didn't speak for a minute. After seeming to consider Hallace's words, she said, "Can we get him one?"

Hallace gave her a hug. "You bet. Tomorrow morning, why don't we go out and cut one down together? I know just the tree we should pick."

"Then we can put it at my house and decorate it for him!" The four-year-old ran off to find her aunt, leaving Hallace in the hallway, shaking his head at her determination.

***

Frances Koehler was full of ideas for how to make Christmas a happy time for her own family, but especially for little Mary and Phyllis. Two knitted sweaters were wrapped and hidden in the top of her closet. Two new dolls with patent leather shoes were stashed underneath Janice's bed. And stockings over the fireplace—those were waiting to be stuffed with oranges, apples, homemade bonbons and peppermint sticks. Frances hummed a Christmas carol to herself as she spent a late evening finishing the hem of a plaid wool skirt that would match Mary's new sweater.

Janice Louise, searching for her mother, called out, "Mom, I'm going to hit the sack!" Then she walked into the room. "Oh, Mom! That skirt is going to look so cute on Mary! It's darling."

"I've got to get one finished for Phyllis, too. I have it cut out. I just don't have any of it sewed together."

"I can help with that. I'll work on it tomorrow. Thank the heavens school is done for a while!"

"You're ready for Christmas vacation, I take it?"

"I sure am. School has been hard so far this year."

"Your grades are good, though. I'm proud of you. *And* I'm proud of how you've helped with these two little ones. I think they look on you as their big sister."

"How is Mrs. Riedel doing, anyway?"

"She's having a rough go. Still coughing up blood. I guess she's gained a little weight, though. Mr. Riedel said they feed the patients a lot of protein. They even raise their own cows and pigs on a farm close by, so they have plenty of meat."

"How long do you think she's gonna have to be there?"

"Nobody knows. Simple as that. It's up to God, Janice Louise."

"Don't they have any medicine that will help?" Janice sat down and fiddled with the sewing implements in her mother's large sewing box.

"I guess not. The patients have to sit out in the sun a lot, and they have to rest a lot. That's about it."

"Good grief! That would drive me bonkers!" Janice watched her mother, whose head was bowed, intent on her task. Frances was so dedicated to her family, to helping others, and especially to making Christmas as 'normal' as possible for Mary and Phyllis. How could anyone stand to be away from their mother for so long?

"Mom, don't ever get sick, okay?"

Frances raised her head and smiled at her daughter. "Janice Louise, in about six months, you'll be sick of living under this roof. You'll be graduating. You'll be itching to get the heck out of this house and move on with your life." She laughed so hard she dropped her thimble and had to dig around under her chair to retrieve it. When she looked back up, Janice had tears in her eyes.

"Now what's all this?" Frances said, reaching over to pat her daughter's arm.

Janice swiped the tears away with the back of her hand. "It's just sad. You know, what these kids are going through, away from their parents. Mom, you're partly right and partly wrong. I'm excited about graduation, and I *do* want to 'move on,' as you put it, but I'll never be sick of being around you and Dad."

"Glad to hear it. We try not to be too embarrassing." Finished, Frances bit through her thread and stuck her needle in a red pincushion shaped like a tomato. "Hey, aren't you and Bart Gilson supposed to be going to the 'Snowball Dance' tomorrow night?"

"Oh, Mom, he's history. We don't jive anymore. I'll have plenty of time to help you sew that skirt for Phyllis." Janice stood. "At least until some other cat shows up." She winked, causing Frances to laugh out loud.

"Some other 'cat,' huh? The terms you kids have for each other!" She tucked Mary's skirt into a drawer and wrapped an arm around her daughter's waist. "C'mon. Let's call it a night. I'll be glad for your help as we get closer to Christmas. That is, unless some 'other cat' shows up."

* * *

Robert's eyes were heavy with fatigue. He squeezed them closed, and as usually happened when he had a minute to rest, Edith's face floated before him. He missed the way her eyes sparkled when she smiled. He missed the smell of her hair, the sound of her voice. He missed sitting by her on the sofa as she read stories to the kids each night before bed.

He forced his eyes open. *I'm being selfish. The kids...that's who I should be focused on.* He pulled his attention back to wrapping the few Christmas gifts he had been able to afford. Teddy bears with pink and yellow bowties for Mary and Phyllis. A new doll with blonde curls for Clara. A toy airplane for Bobby. The rest of the money had gone to Mt. Vernon for Edith's care.

Christmas wrapping had always been Edith's job. He fumbled with the tape and festive green paper with Santa's smiling face printed all over it. *Right now, I'd like to punch Santa in the nose.* Then he shook his head. *Can't ever let the kids see that attitude.*

He stuck the last piece of tape on the last present and went to bed.

16
August 1935

"Edith, your chest X-ray hasn't improved much, but you haven't been running a temperature every day anymore, and your cough is not as productive. I think we're on the right track."

Edith sat on the end of an exam table in her pajamas and robe. It was cold in the exam room and she could hardly wait to be out in the sunlight again. She spent most of her daylight hours in the sunroom with other patients. She had developed a few friends there.

"How long is this going to take?" she asked. "I've got little children at home."

"And you want to be around for those children for a long time, I assume. Edith, it takes as long as it takes. I can't give you date. Tuberculosis is not easy to cure. We don't have pills to give you to make it go away. Rest, nutrition, and sunlight. That's all we can offer. And then we monitor to see what kind of progress you're making."

"What if it never gets any better?" Edith was not one for *rest*. She was a girl who had worked hard all her life. Rest was for nighttime.

"As we've discussed, sometimes patients have the infected part of their lung removed. It's a last resort, and it is not a surgery I'd want you to have to go through. You're not even close to that, anyway. It's hard for young mothers such as yourself to be patient, but you must be exactly that." The physician walked behind his desk. "I'll see you next week."

The exam was over. Edith headed down the hall to her ward, Ward B. She was glad she didn't have any stairs to climb…stairs were still too much.

She sat in a chair by an open window. Maybe a breeze would kick up. It was stifling hot in the ward, though fans were strategically positioned to provide some small degree of relief from the heat..

She was isolated, quarantined from her own family. She was desperate to be part of their day-to-day lives again. Robert was working night and day. The children hadn't seen her in so long…would they even know her? *I've always been so healthy. How could this have happened?*

A few patients and staff were strolling the grounds. Did they miss their families like she missed hers? *This kind of separation is no help to anybody.* She watched the patients outside and wondered what effect the humidity might have on their condition. It didn't seem like anything good could come of extra moisture in an environment where infection already existed. *But I'm not a doctor.*

"Edith, what's the word from Dr. Phillips?"

Her favorite day nurse, Cindy Devereaux had entered the ward, crisp white uniform, starched white cap unblemished. A single, thin black stripe on the cap designated her as a registered nurse. Only Cindy's 'Clinic' shoes showed the wear and tear of hours on her feet.

"More of the same, I'm afraid. My X-ray looks no better. 'Rest, nutrition and sunlight.' That's the word of the day again, I guess."

"I'm sorry to hear it. How long has it been now?"

"A little over eight months."

Cindy sat down in a chair left of Edith and reached over to take her patient's hand.

"You know, sometimes patients are in here for years, Edith. *Years.* This is a very difficult disease to get rid of."

A thought occurred to Edith. "How is it you nurses don't have it? If you can protect yourselves, why can't I protect my children and husband?"

"We're not right next to you, kissing and hugging you. We're not sharing a bite of ice cream with you. We're not close enough to you to allow your cough or sneezes to hit us in our faces. Here, we can limit our exposure. That's harder for your family to accomplish. TB patients just have to be quarantined, more or less, and have very limited contact with other people. Except each other and us nurses, that is."

Edith turned back to the window. "Lepers. We're just like the lepers in the Bible."

Cindy stood up. "You kind of *are.* I hate to say it, but that's a pretty good comparison. I've got to get going on rounds. Chin up, Edith. Believe me, it could be worse for you."

"I know it. I don't mean to complain."

"You miss your kids. I understand it. But don't let it get you down too long. That's no good for you, either. A good outlook is so important to healing." The young nurse strode off on her rounds.

It could be worse for you. Edith opened her Bible and turned to Isaiah. She flipped the thin pages until she came to Chapter 40 and read a passage that had always been one of her favorites.

"But they that wait upon the LORD shall renew their strength; they shall mount up with wings as eagles; they shall run, and not be weary; and they shall walk, and not faint."

Reading aloud generated a cough that was harsh and nonproductive. She closed her Bible and her eyes. "All right, Lord, give me patience to wait on you. That's all I'll ask right now. Amen."

17

November 1935

"Mary, Phyllis—time for breakfast!"

Janice Louise moved around the kitchen gathering eating utensils and glasses for milk. Frances was at the stove scrambling eggs and frying bacon. Aaron and Jacob were out milking the cows but would soon be back at the house, ready for breakfast. As for Mary and Phyllis—well, they were in for a surprise. Janice smiled to herself, happy for their small guests.

The girls could be heard coming down the stairs one step at a time. They were just big enough to make it up and down the steps on their own.

"Mom, can I tell the girls about the trip?" Janice asked.

"Sure, honey. They're going to be thrilled. I can hardly wait to see their faces!" Frances was smiling, too. "They are so precious. I'd almost forgotten how fun it is to have little children in the house."

"I know! It seems like forever since Jacob was that little, and of course, I was little, too. I didn't have much appreciation for him back then."

Both women laughed, the older knowing it was true, the younger, embarrassed by her own admission.

Mary and Phyllis appeared in the kitchen. The two perpetually held hands, as if they were afraid to let go of the other—as if they might be lost without the sister. It was sweet and sad at the same time.

"Good morning, girls!" Frances said. "Have you washed up for breakfast?"

"Yes, Mama Koehler," they answered in unison. Frances had told the youngsters to call her 'Mama Koehler' early on, hoping it would help them feel like they had the security of a mother figure.

"Then go on and sit at the table. Your breakfast is almost ready."

"How about a good morning hug?" Janice Louise asked.

They both loved Janice Louise, who always said 'yes' to playing 'tea party' or 'house'. The girls ran to her and wrapped their arms around the teen. She lifted them off the floor a little. "Oooh, you girls are growing so fast! I can barely pick you up!" She set them back on their feet and took their hands, guiding them to the breakfast table and helping them climb up onto chairs that were too high for them to get on by themselves.

Jacob and Aaron walked into the kitchen, pulling off their heavy coats and work gloves.

"I hope you two are hungry," Frances said. "I've got a good breakfast for you."

"Starved," Jacob said, and Aaron nodded in agreement.

"Starved is right. It's getting cold out there in the barn. We need a good breakfast to help us stay warm when we go back out."

"Dad, it's Saturday. Don't we ever get a day off?" Jacob said.

"Jacob, when you work a farm, there's no such thing as a day off."

"Oh, pshaw."

"Son, quit complaining and sit down to eat," Frances said as she carried a large porcelain serving dish full of scrambled eggs to the table. "Go ahead and start serving up those eggs while I get the bacon and cinnamon rolls." She walked back to the stove.

"Cinnamon rolls? Wow! Why do we get cinnamon rolls today? It's not even Sunday," said Jacob.

"Oh, I just felt like making a treat," Frances said, opening the oven door. "Sounds good, doesn't it?"

"Heck yeah. I *love* cinnamon rolls." Jacob's mouth was watering at the smell now wafting over the kitchen.

Everyone took their place as Frances set the bacon and rolls in the middle of the table. Jacob started to reach for a roll, but his father shot him a look.

"Not till after your bacon and eggs, boy. And remember, in this family, we start meals with a prayer. Mary and Phyllis, will you say grace?"

The girls bowed their heads and said "God is great, God is good, let us thank him for our food. Amen." They raised their heads.

"That was a little short, but all right," Aaron laughed. "Everyone must be hungry. I have to say, it sure does smell good."

"Well, help yourself. I'll bring some coffee."

"Thanks, honey."

The table was quiet except for the musical clinking of silver against porcelain. When the rolls were passed around, an occasional "mmm" created a satisfied chorus.

Aaron pushed his chair back and sipped his coffee as the children and Frances finished their meal. "What's on the books for today, my dear? It seems to me that I remember something special going on today."

Frances wiped her hands on her apron. "Yes, I believe there *is* something special today. Let's see, now…what is it?"

Jacob, Mary, and Phyllis had stopped chewing and were looking back and forth between Frances and Aaron. "Well—what is it?" Jacob asked.

Janice Louise spoke up. "Mary and Phyllis, how would you like to go see your mama today?"

The girls looked at each other, puzzled by what they had heard. "Mama?" Mary asked.

"Yes, darlings. Your daddy is coming today to take you to see your mama. He'll take you and your brother, Bobby, and Clara, too! You're all riding in the car to see your mom!"

Four brown eyes welled up. Janice looked at her mother, startled by the reaction. Frances wasn't sure what might be going through their little minds, either.

"Girls, you are going to get dressed up and go see your mommy today. And guess what? I made you new dresses to wear!" She left the room, reappearing with two dresses made exactly alike—blue, with white collars and cuffs on short sleeves and a white belt at the waist.

"Oh, Mom! They remind me of 'Little Orphan Annie' except blue, of course," Janice said. "They're so cute!"

Mary and Phyllis jumped off their chairs, smiling, with tears now trickling down their cheeks.

"What do you say, girls?" Aaron asked.

"Thank you, Mama Koehler," they both answered.

"Oh, you're welcome, my little sweethearts. Now I'll tell you what. I want both of you to go brush your teeth and wash your faces and hands again. Then we'll get you dressed in your new dresses so you can be ready when your daddy comes to get you."

The two little girls hugged her, then took off for the bathroom.

Frances could hear them talking to each other. She still wasn't completely sure they understood what was going on, but she knew they liked their dresses. She followed so that she could help them get ready.

"Why didn't anyone tell me what was going on?" Jacob said.

"Because you can't keep a secret!" Janice kidded him.

"Aw, the heck you say. I can keep a secret."

"Oh yeah? Who told Mom what Dad got her for her birthday?"

"That was when I was just a kid."

"You're *still* just a kid. And you still have a big mouth."

Just as this debate was winding itself into a full-fledged argument, two little bluebirds walked into the kitchen, huge smiles on their faces, white bows in their hair.

Jacob walked over and swooped Mary up into his arms. "Aw, don't you look beautiful!"

Janice followed suit, picking up Phyllis and hugging her tight. "You, too, Phyllis! You look beautiful."

"Mama Koehler told us to sit down in the living room so we don't get messed up," Mary said. The little girl was quite solemn, and Janice had to stifle a laugh.

"Well, then, we better get you where you belong. You want to look your best for your daddy and especially for your mama," Janice said. She and Jacob took the girls into the living room and helped them get seated on the couch. The girls sat close to each other, holding hands as usual.

"Here, let's get the wrinkles out of your skirts," Janice said, smoothing each child's dress.

Jacob heard Aaron calling his name. He winked at the girls. "Little ladies, I have to go out to the barn, but I'll see you when you come home."

Frances and Janice Louise went to the kitchen to begin cleaning up the breakfast dishes. Mary and Phyllis sat very still on the sofa. They were afraid to mess up their dresses or mess up their hair, but they could talk to each other. For as loved as they were, the girls were timid, shy, and uncertain.

"Daddy will be here in a while," Mary told her little sister. "We have to be good so we can go see Mama." Three and a half, she was already her sister's protector and advisor.

Phyllis whispered back, shaking her head. "Be good."

The two sat, quiet and unmoving for a half hour. Then they

heard a car pull into the gravel driveway, and their excitement could no longer be contained. Frances beat them to the front door, where Robert was walking towards the house, a young boy on his right and another young girl on his left. Mary and Phyllis began jumping up and down.

"Daddy! Daddy!" they both called. "Bobby! Clara!" Once again, they began to cry.

"Hello, girls," Robert said, taking them both into his arms. Bobby and Clara stood behind him. "Don't you two look beautiful!"

"Daddy, we missed you," Mary said.

"I know, honey. I miss you and Phyllis, too. All the time." Robert hugged them both tight.

"What about me, Daddy?" Clara spoke up. She was still a tiny thing.

"Oh, Clara, I miss you and Bobby, too," Robert smiled. "I miss my whole family."

All four children draped themselves over him. Before it could turn into a wrestling match, Frances asked, "Robert, can I get you a cup of coffee before you get on the road?"

"No, Mrs. Koehler, but thank you. We've got quite a trip ahead of us and it's likely to be a long day for these little ones."

"How old is Bobby now?"

"I'm six!" the youngster said.

"And I'm five," Clara added, standing up straight. "My sisters are still little."

Robert laughed. "That's the pot calling the kettle black." Frances laughed, too. Such wonderful children! She felt herself hoping again that they would soon be able to be together.

"Before you go, how is Edith doing?"

"A little better, but the doctor keeps telling me that it's going to take some time, we just have to be patient. I'm growing tired of that word—patient."

"Well, I've always known it to be a difficult disease to beat, but we're continuing to pray for her and for you, too. I know it has to be hard to be separated from your whole family."

"It's just how it has to be for now," Robert said. "I almost think it's easier on me, in a way, because I'm busy working all the time. But for Edith it's rough. All she can do is sit around and think about her family and how she's stuck in that place. Like I say, it's just how it has to be. If she doesn't get completely over this, well...." He looked around at his children. "You know the consequences."

Frances closed her eyes. "Yes, I do. I do, indeed." She opened her eyes again. "Listen, I have some cookies for you to take. The kids might need a snack."

"Oh, golly, thank you very much. I packed up some sandwiches, so that will be a good dessert."

"Hang on. I'll go get them." She went to the kitchen and accompanied by Janice, returned with a box of cookies. She handed the cookies to Robert.

"Bye, little ones," Janice said. "See you when you get home. Be good for your daddy while he's driving."

"We will," Phyllis and Mary said.

"Let's go, kids," Robert said.

Bobby took Phyllis by the hand, and Mary latched onto Clara. Robert exited the home and headed for the Roadster, the children following in a row like pairs of ducklings.

"He's got a long day ahead of him," Janice said. "With those four stair steps, he'll have quite a trip."

"But they're good little kids," Frances said. "I have a feeling they'll get along just fine."

***

They arrived at Mt. Vernon before lunch. Robert was impressed at how well the four kids behaved on the drive down. For the biggest share of the trip, Bobby kept the girls entertained with snacks of popcorn and games of 'I Spy.' The four of them were just starting to get antsy when he pulled into the parking lot at the sanitorium, and they didn't take long getting out of the car, jostling each other to try to get out first.

"Come along, kids." He helped the girls down to the ground. All three had new dresses provided by their caregivers, and he wanted to avoid a fall. An inch of fresh snow had fallen overnight, but just enough had melted to form patches of muddy ground between the car and the building where Edith stayed. Their thin coats would not protect them much from a fall in the snowy mud. "Okay, everyone be careful. You don't want to get your new dresses dirty. Bobby, you hold on to one of your sister's hands, all right?"

Bobby did as he was told, taking Mary by the hand. Robert took hold of Clara and Phyllis, and they started for the over-sized white door of the ominous-looking red brick structure. Robert was beginning to feel that it resembled a prison, and he knew Edith felt that it *was* a prison. The children were quiet, trying to take in the enormity of the place. It was an impressive building to young eyes, and their amazement was obvious in the way they looked from one part of the building to another.

They entered the main door and came into a marble-floored lobby. Comfortable chairs were placed near windows overlooking the grounds. There was a table with a jigsaw puzzle, half completed. Robert walked his family over to a small play area he remembered seeing on his last trip to the facility. A sign in the space said, "CHILDREN'S AREA TOYS PROVIDED BY LOCAL CHURCHES."

"Kids, you can play here while I go see Mommy and talk to her doctor. I'll come back to get you when Mommy comes to the door so you can see her. Look—over here are some books you can look at and some dollies and toy cars. You be good and have fun till I come back to get you. Bobby is in charge, so you girls listen to him."

"Can we go see Mommy?" Bobby asked.

"No, son. You have to wait here, but before we leave, I'll bring Mommy over to the door so you can wave through the window and talk to her by the door, all right?"

"All right, Daddy."

Robert walked to the receptionist's desk. A young, blonde woman sitting behind the desk looked up from her work and asked, "May I help you?"

"This is a big favor, I guess, but I wonder if you'd mind just keeping an eye on my kids while I visit my wife? I s'pose it's not really your job, but…"

"I wouldn't mind at all, sir. I do it all the time for families who come to visit their loved ones."

"Thank you then. I promise I won't be gone long. I want to bring my wife to the door so the kids can see her."

"Which of our patients are you seeing today, sir? "Edith Riedel."

"Oh, of course. Ward B, right?"

"Right. Thanks, miss. I'll be back in a little bit."

Robert walked through heavy swinging doors. Each had a small window for restricted visits. It was enough of a window that the kids could see Edith if she might be allowed to walk that far. He went directly to Ward B and looked for his wife on the bed where she usually sat waiting for his arrivals. She wasn't there.

She knew I was coming. He went to the sunroom. Of the various locations that patients had permission to travel, the sunroom was her favorite because it was bright and warm. Even on a gray day like this, he could believe she might be there. There were several patients sitting on chaise lounges, but no sign of Edith.

She wouldn't be walking the grounds on a November day. Puzzled, he started back towards her ward. He saw several nurses scurrying around. They were in such a rush he wondered if there had been an emergency with one of the patients. *What if it's Edith?* Then he noticed a nurse he had never seen before. He waited till she was done charting, then approached her, his hat in his hand.

"Nurse, I'm looking for my wife—Edith Riedel."

"Oh, I believe Edith is still with Dr. Drake."

"Has she been in there long?"

The nurse, whose nametag said *Vera McLuckie, RN*, looked at her watch. "Now that you mention it, yes. She has been in there longer than usual. Would you like me to check on how long it might be before they're done?"

"I don't really want to interrupt, but I have our children downstairs in the lobby."

"Let me just go knock on the door. Why don't you come with me? Edith is one of my favorite patients, so let's see what's going on."

Robert followed the nurse down the hall to a door bearing the nameplate of Dr. Drake, where the young nurse knocked lightly.

"Come in," they heard from inside.

Nurse Vera opened the door slightly and stuck her head inside.

"Hi, Edith. Dr. Drake, please pardon the interruption. Mr. Riedel is here."

Robert could hear the answer. "Oh, have him come right in, Vera. We've got some news to share with him." The tone of the doctor's voice gave nothing away regarding the 'news'.

Robert entered, and Edith stood to hug him. Vera smiled and left.

"Hi, honey. Are the kids here?"

"Yeah. They're downstairs."

"Is someone with them?"

"Just the receptionist."

"Oh, gosh...." Edith sat back down. "Do you think they're all right down there?"

Impatient to move the conversation along, Robert answered, "Sure, hon. They're just playing. Now what's the news?"

The physician interrupted, saying, "I don't need to keep you long so you can get back to those children. Mr. Riedel, I was just telling Edith that I believe she's well enough that we can transfer her to a rehabilitation facility in Green Springs. Her chest X-ray is significantly improved, *finally*, and we don't feel she's infectious anymore, though she will need a lengthy rehabilitation effort to help her regain all the lung function she's lost. It'll be a good test of her lung capacity and a way to rebuild her strength. She's still got a long row to hoe, but she's making good progress now. Green Springs would be much closer to your home, wouldn't it?"

Robert sat silent. He had not been expecting such good news. Edith grabbed his hand. "Isn't it wonderful? Our prayers have been answered."

"Now Edith, don't get too riled up because your prayers *are* being answered, but they're not completely answered just *yet*. As I said, you still have a long way to go," the physician commented, serious.

"But I'm a lot closer than I was even a couple of months back. I'm ready to get going."

The doctor smiled. "I know you miss your kids and Robert, here. By the way, when you go home, who's going to help you with those kids? Will you be able to get enough rest? These are the things that must be planned before you go home, and you won't be *allowed* to go home till we are certain of what that plan *is*."

Robert squeezed Edith's hand. "I promise you this—by the time Edith gets to come home, I'll have it all figured out. How long will she need to be in Green Springs?"

"It really depends on a couple of things. First, will her lungs fully recover? The doctors there will continue to monitor that. Second, how soon will she get her strength back? We can't send her back to her family without those two issues being resolved—good lungs, good strength."

Edith stood up. "Thank you!. When will I be transferred?"

"You can go this week. We just have to call Green Springs and make the arrangements."

Robert shook the doctor's hand. "Thank you for all you've done caring for my wife."

"It's been my pleasure. Edith is a good patient. She's done everything we've asked her to do. I know you'll be glad to have her home, but the two of you remember—you can't rush TB. You've had to be patient, and you'll need to remain patient, or you'll be right back here, Edith. You understand?"

"Yes, sir, I do. I'm determined not to come back. I mean no offense, of course."

"None taken," the doctor chuckled. "You two go enjoy a little time together." He closed Edith's chart. "If I'm not mistaken, this is your birthday, isn't it?"

"Yes, it is."

"Since your children are here and you're not considered infectious anymore, you can go out and sit with them for a short time, but I mean a *short time*, all right?"

Robert wrapped an arm around her waist and squeezed. Edith's eyes lit up and her smile was wide. "Oh, thank you, Dr. Drake! It will be the first time I've hugged my babies in over a year!"

"I know. Happy birthday."

18
July 1936

Edith's patience was thinning. Counting back, she had been cooped up, away from her family for thirty months—two and a half years. Phyllis would soon be three. She had only been six months old when Edith was sent away.

"Every time I see the kids, they're almost unrecognizable because of how much they've grown since the visit before!" she complained to her roommate, Ruth Baggett. "I'm strong enough to get out of this place! I need to get home to my children and Robert."

"Ha! You *think* you're ready to conquer the world, but just wait till you get home and back into all the housework and laundry and cooking and running after children. You forget just how exhausting it all is when you've been out of commission for so long. You don't want to wind up back in the sanatorium, do you?" Ruth didn't hold back. "Edith, you've got four little kids. If that was the only thing you had to worry about, it'd *still* be exhausting. Why do you think they keep us in here so long? They know exactly what's waiting for us at home, and they know we could never keep up. These doctors see it all the time. They know everyone on the outside has to work like dogs these days just to keep body and soul together. You have to take all the time they recommend, or you'll end up right back here..." Ruth lowered her voice. "Or in a worse situation."

Edith directed her gaze toward the window. It was a bright, sunny Saturday. She thought about Robert, probably out in the garden, hoeing the peas or green beans. She could envision him standing up to give his back a break, wiping the sweat from his forehead with one of his red handkerchiefs, taking a swig of water out of his old canteen. Tears filled her eyes. *I should be there helping him.*

She turned back to face Ruth. "I know you're right. I've tried to be patient, but I'm about ready to explode. Robert needs me at home. The kids need their own mother to care for them. I've had it."

Ruth walked over and put her arm around her friend's shoulder. "Edith, we're both doing so much better, and you know as well as I do—we're among the lucky ones. I mean, I don't have any family to go home to like you do, but I'm anxious to bust out of here, too. Patience is a virtue, and no virtue comes easy. Why don't we go out and walk around the grounds? Get a break from these four walls?"

Edith sniffled. "You're right, of course. Okay, let's walk. I used to do that a lot when I was worried. It always helped. I'm sorry if I seemed cross with you."

Ruth grinned. "Oh, for Pete's sake. You don't owe me any apology. Everyone in here has an off day once in a while. You wouldn't be normal if you didn't."

"I don't feel anything like 'normal' today, that's for sure," Edith said. "Do you think we'll ever feel 'normal' again?"

"Sure, we will, Edith. I know you must be having a rough day 'cause you're usually the one holding *me* up. Did you not sleep well?"

"I haven't slept well since some time in December 1933." Edith laughed at her own comment. "C'mon. Let's go outside."

***

At age seven, Bobby was learning how to be a help to his Uncle Virgil and Aunt Mabel. They gave him the kind of chores that would make a seven-year-old feel useful and proud. He soaked up information like a sponge and asked a million questions about farm life, questions he would have liked to ask his own dad. How to plant the garden and the fields. How to hoe. How to know when the vegetables are ready. How to milk a cow. How bacon got made. How to make corn stalk teepees. It was endless. And the boy loved to read.

"He gets that from his mother," Mabel said. "Edith reads the Bible to these kids every night. Bobby can already read a lot of it himself."

"The way he covets learning, he can probably quote it all back to her, too," Virgil chuckled. "That kid's gonna be a professor or something."

"I don't know about all that, but he's a smart one, that's for sure."

They heard a car in the gravel driveway. Virgil went to the door.

"It's Robert. Wonder what he's doing here today." He walked out to greet his brother.

"How are you?" Robert called as he walked towards the house.

"How's that boy of mine?"

"He's doing fine, Robert—just fine. What are you doing here? I figured you'd be out in the garden while the weather's decent."

"I worked it all morning. You have to get it done before it gets so blamed hot. I figured I'd come over and see Bobby for a while."

"I think he's up playing in his room right now. I whittled him out some little cars and trucks that he seems to like a lot."

"Did he ask you to teach him how to whittle?" Robert laughed.

"Yeah, but I told him he's too young to mess around with a knife yet. That boy! I never saw a kid who asked so many questions."

"He's been that way since he was old enough to talk," Robert said. "I'm glad he's that way. He'll never be lazy as long as he's interested enough to keep learning."

"I s'pose. Well, come on in. I'll get him down here for ya."

The two men walked into the house and Mabel greeted Robert with a glass of lemonade. "I'm sure you've been out working all morning. Have you had anything to eat?"

"Oh, yeah. I know how to scramble up some eggs and make a piece of toast, you know."

"Well, that's good. Men should know how to take care of a few things around the house. Where was your brother Virgil when your mother was teaching you that stuff?" Mabel joked, giving Virgil a little shove. "This one barely knows how to boil water."

"We can't all be good at the same things...who would plow the fields and take care of the livestock?" Virgil kidded back.

Mabel shot him a look. "I believe I know how to do all that, too."

Virgil smiled, sheepish. "I'm pretty sure you do. I'll get Bobby." He started up the steps to the second floor.

"Robert, that brother of yours...honestly!"

Robert laughed. "Oh, he's a character all right. How've you two been doing with Bobby around? Have things been going okay?"

"Oh, heavens yes. He's a good boy, Robert. He's a *really* good boy. He does anything we ask him to do, and he loves to read. Did you know that? He can read parts of the Bible I can hardly read myself."

"He gets that from Edith, of course. She reads to the kids every single night without fail. Well, she did when she was home, anyway."

"Virgil and I were just talking about it. He's a smart one. He reads to our girls."

"Good. When Edith gets home, maybe he can read sometimes in the evening and give her a break."

"When will she get home? Do you know yet?"

Right then, Bobby came bounding down the steps and into the kitchen.

"Dad!" he cried, running towards his father with his arms out.

"Slow down, son!" Robert said. "And aren't you getting a little old for hugs? You look like a young man. How about a handshake?"

Bobby stood in front of his father, quiet, thinking about this change.

"I guess so," he said, extending his hand.

Robert shook the boy's hand, then gathered him up into a bear hug.

"I was just teasing you! C'mere, son. I miss you!"

Bobby and Robert play-wrestled each other for a minute before Robert set him back down, winded. He caught his breath.

"Son, I have an idea for you. How would you like to go fishing this afternoon?"

"That'd be swell, Dad!" Then the boy turned to look at Mabel. "Aunt Mabel, would that be all right? Did you have any chores for me?"

"Bobby, you go right on with your daddy and have fun." Virgil returned to the kitchen in time to catch the end of the conversation.

"Fishing? Did you say fishing? Well, Bobby, here's your chore…if you catch anything, you have to bring it back here and we'll have a fish fry." He looked at Mabel. "How does that sound, Mother?"

"Delicious, that's how it sounds. I'll make some slaw and fry up some potatoes to go with the fish."

"All right then. No chores this afternoon but catching a mess of fish. Oh—do you know how to gut and scale them?"

"No sir."

"All right. Well, there's another new thing you can learn."

"It sounds kind of yucky."

"It is, but no yuckier than some of the things you help me with around here."

Bobby didn't look convinced. "Well…okay. Let's go, Dad. Wait—I gotta get my hat." He bounded back up the stairs.

Robert and Virgil both laughed. "Well, he likes to learn new stuff. May as well be something useful. Gutting fish was never my favorite thing. Maybe we'll let him have a try at the knife after all," Virgil said.

"You two are quite a team, you know it?" Mabel said. "Getting a seven-year-old to gut your fish! Honestly!" But she smiled as she turned to her own work.

***

Robert and Bobby caught six nice smallmouth bass and a mess of bluegills. They brought them back to the house, and Bobby did, indeed, get his first 'try at the knife.' They all enjoyed fried fish and all the fixings, as well as family fellowship with Virgil, Mabel, and their daughters. When Robert was ready to leave, Bobby walked out to the car with him.

"Dad, when does Mom get to come home? I miss her," the boy said as his father opened the car door.

"I don't know for sure, but I hope it's soon. I miss her, too."

"I don't just miss *her*, you know—I miss you and our house and even my baby sisters. I want to go home."

"Now, Uncle Virgil and Aunt Mabel are awful good to you, right?"

The boy shook his head.

"They love you, son, and you know why you have to stay here for now, right?"

Again, Bobby nodded.

"Then you keep being a good boy while I work to pay for your mom's hospital bills. I have a feeling she's going to be able to come home pretty soon. She's getting stronger, son, but it just takes a long time. And when she *does* come home, we're *all* going to have to help her around the house, even your little sisters. Understand?"

"Yes sir."

"I'm very proud of you, Bobby. Aunt Mabel and Uncle Virgil both told me what a good helper you are, so I know you'll be a good helper for your mom, too. We have to keep praying for Mom so she gets well fast and can come home as soon as possible."

"I pray for her every day."

"That's good, Bobby. Now you go in and brush your teeth and get ready for bed. I'm sure your aunt and uncle are ready to call it a day." He got into the car and closed the door. Bobby stood with his hands on the edge of the open car window.

"I had fun today, Dad. I love you."

"I love you, too, buddy. Go on, now."

Robert watched as his son walked back to the house. Bobby stepped on to the porch, then turned to wave one more time.

"Bye!" he called.

Robert waved. He didn't trust his voice. It would give away how much he hated leaving his boy behind.

19

December 1936

Christmas Eve was cold, and snow fell, light and fluffy, easy to shovel. Robert was thankful for that as he headed out to start his car. It was early afternoon, and he was ready to pick up his children, excited that they would all be able to attend the Christmas Eve service at church together. He wanted his kids with him on this holy day of celebration.

He shoveled a path to the car, climbed in and started up the old Ford. He whispered a quick prayer of thanks that the car still ran relatively well, and he didn't have to worry about the expense of buying a newer model. The car sometimes sounded rough, and today was no exception, but after a minute, he could feel the heater beginning to warm up the interior.

He walked back to the house while the car continued to run. He took a couple of dollars out of the cookie jar where any extra cash was saved—he needed something for the offering plate. Then he checked to make sure he had turned off all the lights and closed the front door.

Driving to his brother's house to pick up Bobby first, he rehearsed what he would say to the children about their mom. *Mama has to stay at the hospital for just a while longer. She's a lot better, but she can't come home quite yet.* Another Christmas without Edith. He didn't look forward to it, and the kids would be heartbroken. Every time he visited or called, the older kids asked him if "mom will be home for Christmas." Mary and Phyllis were so little when Edith first became ill that he didn't know if they really understood that Edith was their *mother.* They called their surrogates "Mama and Daddy Koehler." Whenever the girls visited Edith, they seemed shy. Loving, but timid. They had a lot to overcome as a family. The only good surprise he had for the kids was that they would be spending the night in their own beds. They were coming home for a couple of days.

Robert arrived at Virgil's house, picked up his son, then headed for Bertha and Hallace's place to get Clara. As they drove, Bobby started his questions.

"Dad, when will Mom get home? I wanted her to be home for Christmas."

"Let's talk about all that when we get your sisters and I can tell everyone at once, okay?"

Bobby turned his face toward his window. He now knew the answer to his question.

They drove in silence till Robert got to his sister and brother-in-law's home.

"Stay in the car, Bobby. I'll go get Clara."

Continuing to look out the window, Bobby didn't say a word.

As Robert neared the house, the front door flew open, and Clara was standing in the doorway, dark eyes shining bright, a red wool coat with black buttons setting off her brunette hair.

"Oh, Daddy!" she said, tears filling her eyes. "I miss you!"

Robert picked up the tiny girl. "I miss you, too! Hey, when are you going to start growing, Squirt? Don't they feed you around here?"

A smile appeared through the tears. "You're silly, Daddy. I eat all the time!"

Bertha came to the door, greeting him with a peck on the cheek. "Robert, that's the truth. This little one has a good appetite, but she just doesn't gain weight. I even asked Doc about her not long ago."

"What did he say?" Robert said, concern in his voice.

"He said, 'Let her eat what she wants and eventually, she'll start growing.' I guess Doc ought to know what he's talking about."

"I guess he should. Clara, have you got everything you need?"

"I don't have my purse. I'll go get it."

"Goodness! You have a purse? Well, you might not be growing big, but you're certainly getting mature," Robert said.

"What does that mean, Daddy?"

Robert and Bertha laughed. "Never mind, Squirt. You go get your purse while I talk to Aunt Bertha, all right?"

Clara headed for her room.

"The kids don't know you're keeping them overnight, do they?" Bertha asked, keeping her voice low.

"Not yet. I'll tell them when all five of us are together. I've gotta break the news to them that their mother can't come home quite yet, so maybe that will be one little piece of good news for them. They get to be in their own home for a couple of days."

"A couple of days?"

"Yeah, I guess I didn't tell you. Since Christmas Day falls on Friday this year, they gave us a long weekend off from work. I'll bring her back on Sunday if that's all right with you."

"Well sure, but have you got food for tomorrow's meal? And I'm not trying to be nosy, but is Santa going to be able to bring presents for the kids? I know every extra penny you've got has been going for that hospital bill."

"I got some overtime the last couple of months, and I've done pretty well with my trapping, so I was able to pick up new doll babies for the girls, a baseball mitt for Bobby, and new pajamas for all four of them. I sure hope everything fits all right. Well, that's all they're getting, but yes, there are gifts. I have a smoked ham for dinner, and we can eat leftovers on Saturday and Sunday. We'll be fine."

"Hold on. Let me send some Christmas cookies with you. I know darn well you didn't make any of those." Bertha laughed and departed for the kitchen.

Hallace appeared with a newspaper in his hands and his reading glasses back on his head. "Well, Robert, how are you doing?"

"Fine, really, for not having my wife home."

"And when is that going to happen?"

"Still not sure."

"Good grief, man. This has been a long haul. Isn't my sister getting any better?"

"Sure she is, but the doctors are very cautious. They say it's easy to get just as sick or worse again."

"That makes sense, I guess." Hallace rubbed the rough stubble on his face. "Keep her there till she's really ready to come home. But your family—it'll be hard to get them back into a routine."

"I know. They barely know each other at this point. Hallace, I don't know how I'll ever repay you and Bertha for how good you've been to my little Squirt."

"Ha! You're kiddin' me, right? If it wasn't for Clara, Bertha would be making long lists of things for me to do. Clara keeps her out of my hair."

At this, Robert laughed.

"What are you two cackling about in here?" Bertha said, entering the room with a box of cookies in one hand and Clara in the other.

"Nothing important, dear," Hallace said.

"C'mon Clara. We've still got to get your little sisters and we don't want to be late for church. I see you have your purse now."

"Yes, Daddy, and Aunt Bertha gave me a nickel for the offering."

"I'm sure the Lord will be very grateful for that, honey." He looked from Clara to Bertha. "Thanks Bertha. And thanks for the cookies, too."

Bertha smiled. "Go on, now. Get going. You've still got the trip to Upper to make."

Robert took hold of Clara's hand and winked at Bertha. "Talk to you later."

Once Clara was in the car, Bobby's mood improved significantly, and he and his little sister talked about their many adventures with their aunts and uncles all the way to Upper Sandusky. When they arrived at the Koehler's home, Robert took Bobby and Clara to the door with him and knocked.

Frances Koehler answered the door, her cheeks flushed bright pink, her apron spotted with chocolate. She brushed her hair back from her face.

"Come in, come in. The girls are just upstairs putting on their dresses. We got a little behind while we were making some Christmas treats." She looked back and forth at the children standing on either side of Robert. "Hi there, Bobby and Clara. Guess what? Your sisters have a surprise for you! Just wait."

They heard little feet carefully coming downstairs, taking one step at a time. Then two happy girls, holding hands, walked into the room.

"Hi, girls," Robert said, walking over to hug them. "Merry Christmas Eve!"

"Merry Christmas Eve, Daddy," both girls replied, "We have a big surprise for you. You'll never guess what it is."

"So we heard. What do you say to your big brother and big sister?"

The little girls stared ahead, timid. "Merry Christmas Eve."

Bobby walked over to the girls and gave them a hug. "Hi, Mary. Hi, Phyllis."

Clara stood by herself, holding tightly onto her purse. Robert could see how much these children needed to spend time with each other.

"What's the surprise?" Bobby piped up.

The littler girls went into the kitchen and reappeared with a pine wreath, decked with a bright red velvet bow.

"It's a Merry Christmas wreath!" Mary said.

"Wow!" Bobby's eyes were wide. "Look Clara!"

Now Clara came forward. "That's pretty."

Mrs. Koehler took Robert aside. "I've got some homemade taffy in the kitchen for you to put in the kids' stockings."

Robert put his hand to his head. "I forgot stockings."

"That's no problem," Frances said. "Just tell the kids to put out one of their shoes for St. Nicholas. You can put the taffy in their shoes."

"Good idea. I don't think I ever heard of that before."

"It's a Catholic tradition. They do it early in the month, but it just popped in my head. I think you can get away with it." She handed him a small box full of taffy, each piece wrapped in wax paper. "I've got candy canes for you to hang on the wreath tonight, too." She handed him a brown paper bag.

"I don't know what to say…" Robert stuttered.

"Say 'Merry Christmas' and get on your way."

"Where's your family?"

"They're out in the woods finding a decent Christmas tree. Do you have one of those?"

"No, but we'll have a good Christmas just the same. That wreath will be enough. Listen, I'll be bringing the girls back on Sunday if that's still all right. Probably in the late afternoon, early evening."

"I remember you saying that during our last call. You've got clothes for the kids at home and so forth?"

"Yup. Enough for a few days, anyway."

"Okay. You all have a great Christmas. I keep praying for Edith, you know."

"I appreciate it. I'm still not sure when she's going to come home. I can't tell you how grateful I am for…." Robert trailed off, unable to continue.

"I know, I know. Now go on and enjoy your church service and your children."

"Thank you. I will." They both walked back out to where the children were waiting by the front door, chattering excitedly about their beautiful wreath and Santa Claus.

"Let's go, kids. 'Bye, Mrs. Koehler."

"Good-bye everyone, and Merry Christmas!"

Four replies of "Merry Christmas" rang out as Robert herded his brood out the door and into the car. When everyone was settled in their seat, he looked around, as contented as he could be without Edith there.

"Kids, I'm so happy to see you. Let's go to church."

The children were all smiling. Phyllis sang Christmas carols as they headed back to Sycamore to attend the church in which they had been baptized. Robert had no idea she knew these songs.

"Phyllis, how do you know these carols?"

"Mama Koehler taught us," Mary answered.

"Well, it sure sounds awful nice," Robert encouraged them.

"Daddy, when does Mommy get to come home?" Clara asked.

Robert hesitated. Tell them now before church and risk having them cry throughout the service? Wait till they got home, had their Christmas wreath hung and had eaten a cookie? He decided to get it over with.

"Kids, your mother is still too sick to come home."

He heard Clara moan, and Bobby, sitting in the front passenger seat, again looked out the window. Robert looked in the rearview mirror. Mary and Phyllis sat silent, displaying no emotion, each with lips pinched together.

"Try not to be too discouraged, kids. Your mama wouldn't want you to be sad because she's getting better, but the doctors say she can't come home just yet."

"I think the doctors are mean," Clara said.

"No, no, honey. You shouldn't talk like that. The doctors are not being mean. But your mama was very sick and it's taking a long time for her to get well. I don't think it will be too much longer, but if Mama comes home too soon, she could get even sicker again."

The car remained quiet until they arrived at church. When he had parked, Robert half-turned in his seat so that he could see all four of his children.

136

"Kids, listen to me. You're sad about Mom not being able to come home. I am too. But I promise you it won't be long, and right now, we're going to go into church and pray for Mom to get well a lot faster, all right? Can you do that?"

"Yes, Daddy," Clara said. "We'll all pray." Mary and Phyllis nodded their heads. Bobby said nothing. Robert knew that as the oldest, he was having the hardest time of any of the kids. After all, Bobby had more years to have a relationship with his mother.

"C'mon, Bobby. You help me with the girls. Take their hands."

The family trouped into church. Reverend Reinhart greeted them as they entered the sanctuary.

"Robert, I stopped down to see you this afternoon, but I see now what you were up to. Glad to see the children this evening."

Robert kept his response quiet. "They don't know it yet, but they're spending the whole weekend in their own home."

The Reverend looked surprised. "That's wonderful. Are you all set at home? Will you be needing anything? Anything we can help with as a congregation?"

"No, Pastor. We're all set."

Skeptical, the minister answered as cheerfully as he could. He knew the family's finances were tough.

"Well, all right then. Enjoy the service. I want you to know that the wife and I bought Christmas Seals this year. I hope the researchers find a cure for TB."

"Thank you, Reverend. They say every dollar helps."

As Robert and his children chose a pew, the minister signaled to another of the parishioners, Jim Farthing. They engaged in a quick, intense conversation, and Jim left.

The service was uplifting for Robert. The children were quiet and well-behaved. Phyllis sang her little heart out. Robert was astonished at her musical ability—she was only three. When it was time to go, the kids wasted no time getting their coats on. They walked through the vestibule, where Robert saw Reverend Reinhart and his wife talking to Jim and Helen Farthing, huge smiles on all four faces. He'd be smiling like that, too, if Edith was with them.

At home, the kids piled out while Robert retrieved treats from the back of the car. The front door was unlocked—no one locked their doors in Sycamore. "Go on in and warm up...pick out a good place to hang the wreath," he called to the children.

He was nearing the house himself when he heard squealing and shouting. "What in tarnation?" he asked the evening sky.

When he walked into the house, he deposited cookies and candy in a safe place, then went into the living room to see what the racket was all about.

The kids were quiet now, sitting on the floor in a row, looking at a small, but very lovely Christmas tree. It had long needles, the soft kind, and was decorated with colored glass balls. A gold star sat on top. Robert gave out a low whistle. "Well, what do you know about that?"

"Did Santa bring it, Daddy?" Bobby asked.

"I'm pretty sure he must have," Robert answered.

Phyllis stood up and began singing. "Oh, Christmas tree, oh, Christmas tree...how lovely are thy branches...." Mary and Clara joined in. The three girls could really sing. Robert sat in his armchair, amazed at all that was before his eyes. Who could have arranged this? *Cora? The Reverend? The Reverend!* He smiled to himself. That's what the pastor and Jim had been conspiring about.

"Daddy, isn't the tree pretty?" Bobby asked.

"It sure is, son. And doesn't it smell wonderful?" Robert said, taking a deep breath, which the kids imitated. "Let's go make some sandwiches for everybody, now. Girls, are you hungry?"

The girls stopped singing long enough to shout "yes" in unison.

"Well, come on then. Sit at the table and we'll have some supper." Four little ducklings followed their father into the kitchen.

After appetites were satisfied, Clara spoke up. "Daddy, I wish Mommy was home."

"Me too, Squirt. But listen everyone. I do have one surprise for you."

The children stopped squirming and looked at their father.

"We're all staying together this weekend. You're going to be staying here at home tonight, tomorrow, the day after that, and on Sunday, I'll take you back to your other homes."

All four kids jumped out of their chairs and began dancing around the kitchen, laughing and whooping like wild things. Robert laughed as he tried to wrestle back control.

"All right, all of you sit back down for a minute. We've got a couple of things to take care of." The children didn't sit, but stood, quiet and focused.

"There's one very important thing you each must do before you go to bed."

The kids remained mute.

"You must each take off one of your shoes and put it under the Christmas tree."

"Why, Daddy?" Phyllis asked, tilting her head to one side. It was the first time Robert had heard her speak directly to him all day.

"Because Santa comes tonight, and he might have some special treats for you. If you put one of your shoes underneath the tree, he'll know it's yours and leave something special in it for you."

"How will he know which shoe's mine and which one is Mary's?" Clara asked.

Robert hesitated. He hadn't anticipated such a question. "Well, Santa is pretty smart, so I guess he'll be able to figure out whose shoes are whose."

Clara began to skip around the kitchen. "Whose shoes are whose? Whose shoes are whose?" she chirped, singsong.

"All right, now, settle down. Each of you go put one shoe under the tree while I clean up the table," Robert told them, and all four were off in a flash.

Robert whistled a little as he cleaned up the kitchen. The children were laughing together and playing in the living room. It sounded so...normal. He wished Edith was there. How she would have loved this. And he thought about the goodness of friends...as much as he missed his wife, at that moment, his heart could not have been more grateful.

20
January 1937

Edith's roommate, Ruth Baggett was not faring as well as Edith, and today she was coughing hard. She had been coughing all night, in fact. Edith was alarmed at the amount of blood her friend was now spitting out.

"I'm getting the nurses. Ruth, you should lie down or something. I'll be right back."

Ruth was coughing too much to protest. She stayed sitting on the side of her bed while Edith walked as fast as she could to the nurse's station.

"Someone better check on Ruth. She's coughing her head off—lots of blood."

Two nurses jumped out of their chairs, leaving charting and medicines behind, looking concerned. They wasted no time in getting to Ruth's room while Edith stayed back, walking slowly down the hall, looking at the paintings on either side. She was worried about Ruth. At the same time, she caught herself thinking about how well she was finally doing. Plans were being made for her release, and she was chomping at the bit.

"When you know you're getting close to discharge, it's harder than usual to be patient, but you have to give us a little more time," Dr. Elchert told her during her most recent check. "That carrot is dangling in front of you, and you want to just reach out and snatch it, but that's not how it works with TB. You're almost there. You've been patient this long. You can hold on just a little longer."

A clatter raised her head. One of the nurses she had just talked to was running from Ruth's room, calling out to other staff. "Get Dr.

Elchert back here, stat!"

Alarmed, Edith hurried to the door and saw Ruth lying on the bed, the second nurse trying to revive her friend. She almost fainted at the sight. Her knees buckled and she grabbed onto the doorway to steady herself. Dr. Elchert had to pull her out of the way so she and her interns could enter.

"Edith, get away from here. You don't need to see this."

She went to a nearby lounge and dropped into a chair. *You don't need to see this.* But she *had* seen it. Ruth lying on the bed, gasping, her face sallow and her lips blue. Edith was sure she had seen Ruth taking her last breaths. From the room, she could hear the continued commotion, the doctor's questions of the nurses and interns. When did this start? Did she have a fever? What has her sputum looked like the last few days? How did her lungs sound on auscultation? Where's the most recent chest X-ray?

When it seemed like hours had passed, the physicians and nurses came out of the room, all with hang-dog expressions. Dr. Elchert was the last person out, and she was closing the door behind her when she looked to where Edith was sitting. Edith saw her press her lips together and adjust her glasses before walking in her direction. She was silent as the doctor sat in the chair across from her.

"Edith, was this morning the first time you heard Ruth coughing like that?"

"I heard her coughing last night, and she sounded rattle-y. I asked her if she was okay, and she told me not to worry."

"Well, I'm sorry to tell you this, but Ruth has died. Her lungs completely failed. I'm puzzled as to why this happened because she was improving. Not as fast as you, maybe, but...." She rubbed her temples. "I have a feeling she might have developed a pneumonia on top of her TB."

Edith couldn't cry. Her eyes were as dry as her mouth. She felt cold, as if an icy north wind had passed over her. She stared at the physician, who was searching Edith's face.

"Are you all right? Have you been coughing in the last day or so?" she said.

Edith shook her head. She was feeling stronger every day.

"All right, but I'm going to want to see you this afternoon so I can listen to your lungs myself. I'll give the nurses a time for you to be in the exam room. I've got to go write a few notes, so excuse me."

As the physician walked towards the nurse's station, panic set in, and Edith began to tremble. It was uncontrollable. She tried to hold her arms tight against her torso to stop it. She was freezing. She was thirsty. She was scared. She couldn't control her movements.

One of the nurses came to her side. "Edith, we're going to move you to a different room. You'll be in Room 10 now. C'mon. I'll take you there." The nurse helped her to stand, put an arm around her waist and guided her down the hall. She opened the door to the room and showed Edith to a comfortable chair near the window. "Don't worry about your things. We'll get them in here for you." She left as Edith began to sob, great heaving sobs that racked her body.

When she was finally done crying, Edith looked out the window. The sun was shining. It looked like a million diamonds had been dropped on top of the snow that covered the ground.

She had to get out of there.

21
February 1937

It was a quiet homecoming because Robert made *sure* it was quiet. Edith didn't need a hundred family members coming to visit. She didn't need the kids disturbing her rest, and he did his best to keep them entertained. What Edith needed was to continue getting plenty of relaxation and good nutrition.

He was grateful that their extended family brought food over so that he didn't have the burden of *everything* on his shoulders. They happened to be a family of excellent cooks, and the many scrumptious dishes they provided were just what Edith needed. She ate well, saying her food tasted better than ever.

"Look how I'm gaining weight," she said, patting her tummy. "I'm really hungry all the time now, and everything tastes delicious!"

"It's probably because you're getting good home cooking. Besides, you needed to get fattened up a little," Robert kidded her. "You were practically skin and bones when you went to Mt. Vernon."

"Ha! Don't have to worry about that now!" she said.

Edith was almost delirious with joy at being home. That joy often caused her to do more than she really was capable of, and she had to learn to pace herself.

"I'll do the dusting today and the mopping tomorrow. We'll get to laundry the next day." She developed a plan and stuck to the plan. *I am not going back to any hospital* became her mantra.

Almost eight, Bobby was a big help with the girls and with small jobs around the house. He had learned to do a variety of chores at his aunt and uncle's, and he was independent with most of them.

"Mom, do you want some tea? Would you like a cookie? Can I do anything for you?" Bobby was determined that his mother never be separated from them again and tended to hover over Edith. "Would you like me to clean the living room?"

"Son, you've done enough for today. Why don't you go play for a while? Maybe your sisters would like to go out and build a snow fort. Have you ever done that?"

"Sure. I've built them with my cousins…oh, I get it. You want me to get the girls away from you for a little bit." Bobby thought his younger sisters might be pests to his mom.

Edith laughed. Laughing no longer set off a coughing jag, and she was happy that she could let loose, let the belly laughs come out.

"Well, it is time for me to stretch out for a bit, but I probably won't sleep. Let's get the girls dressed up warm."

After the children were outside, Edith reclined on the sofa and said a prayer of thanks that all was going so well with her return to life at home. The kids had not been standoffish with her or with each other as she had expected, and the family's routine fell back into normalcy. She had worried for nothing.

"Lord, we humans need to have more patience, don't we? You're always teaching me new lessons. Maybe now I'll be a better learner. Thank you for getting me home." Ruth Baggett's face passed through her mind. Edith knew she was lucky her own outcome was so different from Ruth's. Part of her felt guilty that she had survived and Ruth had perished, but she decided that as always, God was getting her prepared for something. She was needed here on earth. It hadn't been her time.

***

Edith continued getting stronger and gained weight, so much so that by the end of the month, she decided she better start eating smaller helpings.

"I don't want to get fat. I know I needed to gain a little weight, but I don't want it to get out of control. It's too hard to take back off."

"I think you look wonderful," Robert said, pulling her in close for a hug. "I didn't think you could get more beautiful, but you did." He was as romantic as ever. "No matter that you were sick…I guess something about the treatment you got in those hospitals changed how you look. Or maybe it's just because you're home now. Heck, I think you're actually glowing. That's it—you're glowing."

Robert's words struck her like a closed fist, and Edith, saying nothing aloud, felt her stomach turn over. Glowing. That usually meant one thing.

***

Doc Smith was a bit of a newcomer in Sycamore, but he was familiar with Edith's history from Dr. Montgomery's records.

"Edith, you're pregnant. When was your last period?"

Pregnant. Again.

"They were all messed up while I was sick. I'm not sure...maybe a couple of months ago? I just stopped paying attention to that, in a way."

"Well, you won't have to worry about it for several months. You're going to have a baby, and I'm thinking it will be sometime in October. Edith, I'm going to be very blunt.

"You don't know me like you did Doc Montgomery, but I'm your family doctor now, and I'll always be forthright with you when it comes to your health. You've just been through a serious illness—one that could've killed you. You're just getting back on your feet."

Edith knew what the young man was getting ready to say. His face was earnest and kind, but his tone of voice was solemn.

"It's really too soon for you to be pregnant. Your body is just starting to recover from the TB. To get through this pregnancy and have a healthy baby, you're going to need to do everything I tell you. The most important thing for you will be adequate rest. You already have four children at home, do you not?"

Edith nodded. Four small children and now, one more on the way. They were still strapped financially. The timing was lousy.

"Do you have help? I mean, do you have any family who can help you with things around the house?" the doctor continued.

"Our son, Bobby, is a big help. He's eight, and he's a very responsible boy. He watches out for me."

"Well, he better because you're going to need some watching. I hope you have some older family members who can lend a hand, too. And Robert. How helpful is he?"

"Oh, he's so busy with work and trapping and hunting and shearing sheep...I don't see how he could take on anything more."

"He obviously found time to help get you in this condition."

Edith could feel her face flush with a mixture of resentment and embarrassment. "We hadn't been together in so long…."

"I know. I'm sorry if I sounded harsh. I understand—I do. I'm just telling you that you're going to need help from all able bodies. I'll be watching you carefully through these next few months, but I won't be at your house helping with cleaning and cooking and so forth, and that's the stuff you *really* need help with."

"I'm sure my sisters will help me."

The young doctor took off his stethoscope, sighed, and sat down on a stool across from Edith. He took her hands in his own.

"I really didn't mean to sound so hard on you. We're going to get you through this pregnancy, and God willing, without any complications." Now the young professional folded his arms across his chest. "That will be our goal—healthy baby—no complications."

Complications? Her whole life was complicated.

"Dr. Smith, I'll do everything you tell me to do, and I *won't* do anything you tell me *not* to do. I'll eat properly and get plenty of rest. I'll recruit my sisters to help me out a little. God has chosen to bless me with another baby. So many women never get the chance…I'll be fine, I assure you."

The physician looked his patient square in the eye. There, he saw determination and a will of iron. He extended his hand.

"Deal."

22
Fall-Winter 1937

"Bobby, can you take the girls out to play, please? They're making such a racket upstairs! I've got to lie down for a while." Edith's ankles were swollen, and she needed to prop up her feet. Six months pregnant, her protruding belly pulled her lower back forward, causing it to hurt like a toothache—sharp, unrelenting pain.

He had just come in from chores in the barn, but he answered, "Sure Mom." Bobby was Edith's biggest helper. He never spoke of it, but the fear of his mom being separated from them again ran deep. It was evident to everyone in the family circle because of Bobby's constant checking on his mother. Now, he hovered.

"Can I bring you some water to drink? It's awful hot today."

"Yes it is, son, and humid. Sure, a glass of water would be nice." Edith put her mop away and picked up a bucket full of dirty water to empty outside. The kitchen floor had been a mess, but it gleamed now.

"What are you doing?" Bobby said. "You shouldn't be doing that! Mom, I can do a lot of things you don't know about. You go lay down and I'll take care of this." He was insistent.

"Hey, you're kind of bossy today," she kidded him, ruffling up his hair. "All right, buddy. Thank you for watching out for me."

Bobby smiled, proud to be of assistance. He followed Edith into the living room, where she reclined on the sofa with her feet elevated on pillows. He waited till she was lying down before saying, "I sure hope I have a brother this time. I don't mind playing house with the girls sometimes, but Clara always wants to make mud pies and she tries to get me to *eat* them. I need a brother around here, somebody

I can play ball or cowboys with. You just gotta have a *boy*."

Edith reached for his hand. "I'll do my best, Bobby. I don't have a lot of control over it."

The boy stood by her side, silent for a moment. His face was solemn. "Mom, when you have the baby, I'll still help you. Even if it's a girl."

"I know you will. You're already a big help. Now go have some fun with your sisters."

He rolled his eyes, his shoulders slumped. "Mudpies, here I come...."

***

On October 12, Alton Monette Riedel was born. He was named after Franklin Monette Smith, MD. Edith had come to love her new physician like a brother.

"Well, Edith, you've done it again. Five wonderful children, you have now. A handsome boy right here, if I may say so." The doctor was finishing his exam of the new baby while Edith recovered from the delivery.

"How is he? Strong? Healthy?" Robert asked.

"Oh, yes. Now, how are you doing, Mom?"

"I feel fine, Dr. Smith. I'm happy he's here. I have so much energy right now I could get supper going and clean the whole house," Edith said. She was beaming.

"Good grief. Settle down, my dear. There'll be plenty of time for all that, but not for a couple of weeks. This is a good time to recruit your sisters to help you."

"Oh, don't worry, Doc. I've got that lined up already," Robert said.

"You'd think I was an invalid!" Edith exclaimed, frustrated with the continual restrictions Robert and the doctor put on her. "You don't realize what all I had to do after my mother died. I'm strong."

The physician sat in a chair by Edith's bed and handed the newborn over to her. "Look at this boy, Edith. You've managed to bear and deliver a strong baby. Baby number five. Number *five*. And you are only a few months out from your tuberculosis. Remember your promise to me?"

Edith put the baby to her breast, where he drank hungrily. "I do, Doc. I understand what you're saying. I'll behave." She smiled.

"Come see me at the office in one week. Bring little Alton

148

along with you so I can see if he's gaining weight properly."

"Okay. Thanks for everything."

The physician started for the bedroom door to leave, but he turned back to add, "You did a good job today, Edith. You *are* a strong woman, and I'd like to keep you as my patient for a long, long time."

"Message received," Edith replied. "Don't worry."

***

Another meager Christmas loomed. On December 22nd, Edith finished new dresses for the girls' dolls. She used scraps of material saved from dressmaking she had done earlier in the year. Each doll would have an outfit that matched one of her owner's.

Bobby would receive a BB gun. Edith put up a small protest.

"Robert, are you sure he's ready for a gun like that? I'm afraid he'll accidentally shoot one of the girls or the animals."

"He's been hunting with me so many times that I'm not worried at all," Robert said. "I've taught him everything he needs to know about safety around guns. He's very responsible, and I want him to have it."

She thought about how mature her oldest child had demonstrated himself to be. "All right. We don't have much to put under the tree, but I hope the kids will be happy anyway."

"Well, I do have one surprise up my sleeve..." Robert kept her hanging, waiting for her to take the bait.

"And what is that?"

His mouth stretched into a broad, toothy smile.

"I've saved enough money from trapping to take all of us to a movie—*Snow White and the Seven Dwarfs*." He could barely contain his excitement and pride, crossing his arms over his puffed-out chest.

"Oh, honey! The kids will love it. So will I, come to think of it." Edith was as excited as Robert, now. "When will we go?"

"After the holiday. For Christmas morning, I'll make a special card from Santa that we can all open together. You can read it out loud to the kids."

"Best idea ever," Edith said. "Little Alton's first movie and he won't even remember it, but his big brother and his sisters can tell him all about it."

"There'll be plenty more for him to see later," Robert said. "You know, taking five kids to the movies is getting pretty expensive. I was surprised. We might have to take in our own popcorn."

"That's no problem. I can pop up a grocery bag full. But you're right. Five kids—we better be careful in the future, honey. *Everything* is getting more expensive."

"Five kids. That's enough for anyone. We *will* be careful."

23

1939

Careful wasn't enough to keep Robert Riedel's family from growing again. A baby girl had just been born, much to the dismay of her brothers, Bobby and Alton.

The boys stayed with their great grandmother while Edith delivered the baby. There, they were spoiled with cookies, and Bobby played numerous games of checkers with his grandpa.

Robert went to pick the boys up when Edith had recovered for a few days.

"What did you name her?" the older woman asked Robert.

"We haven't come up with a name yet," he said.

"What? It's been a week since she was born! Something *must* be coming to you two by now! What do you call her when you talk to her? Baby?"

"As a matter of fact...."

"Well, I never! Settle on a name and start calling her that. Gotta establish her individuality. She's a *person*, you know."

Robert chuckled to himself as he drove the boys home. His Grandma Camilla was just as feisty as ever, and she wasn't shy about giving a lecture when she thought one was needed. He decided to consult the boys about potential names. Maybe asking them to pick her name would help them be more accepting of another sister, and since Bobby was almost ten, he might have a good idea to contribute.

"We haven't named your new sister, boys. Mom and I can't decide. What do you two think about a name?" Robert asked.

Bobby looked out the window, sullen. Alton hung from the back of his father's seat in a new device called a car seat. The older boy looked back at his little brother, who appeared unconcerned with the whole matter. Bobby turned his eyes back to the scenery passing by at thirty miles per hour.

"I can't think of any names," the boy began. Several minutes transpired, as they traveled along the highway passing the fields and woods of Wyandot County.

"Why don't you just call her 'Old Tree Limb'?" Bobby said.

"What?" Robert asked.

"Old Tree Limb. Call her Old Tree Limb."

Now Robert laughed. "I don't think your mom will go for that, but I can ask."

Both boys were quiet for the rest of the ride home. One had fallen asleep in his Bunny Bear car seat, and one ruminated over the arrival of another sister.

***

"Lou Gehrig retired from baseball." Robert folded the newspaper, laid it on the end table, nearly knocking over a lamp. He closed his eyes.

"What? What are you talking about?" Edith rocked baby Roma, whose unfortunate 'Tree Limb' nickname stuck, perpetuated by her oldest brother.

"Lou Gehrig. One of the best baseball players ever known. He played for the Yankees."

"You don't even *like* the Yankees. You're a Reds fan."

"I like Lou Gehrig, though. A decent fella. Great ball player. He's got some sickness they can't cure, looks like. Just a young guy."

"Well, that's too bad. Is it some kind of cancer?"

"Not known yet, but he's done. Retired yesterday at Yankee Stadium."

Edith was silent. Robert loved baseball almost as much as hunting and fishing. He needed distraction, and she had an idea.

"Robert, do you s'pose there are any strawberries left down at the Hushour place?"

"Boy, it's July. I don't know about that."

"Why don't you take Bobby and go see. If they have some, pick me a couple of quarts and I'll make strawberry pie."

He stood up and stretched. "That sounds good. I'll go see what's still on the vines."

"If there aren't any strawberries, get blueberries instead."

Robert called his son, but instead of only one child, two boys and three girls showed up, all clustering around his legs. He patted each one on the head.

"Bobby, let's you and me go get some berries for your mom. Clara, you stay here and watch the other kids. Mom's in the house."

"Aw, can't we all go?" Clara asked.

"Not this time. Alton's too little, and Phyllis and Mary can't pick berries yet. You watch them. That'll be a big help while your mom takes care of Roma. When Bobby and I get home, Mom's gonna make you a pie."

A chorus of "yippee" settled the argument. Robert and his namesake picked up berry pails from the woodshed and started for the railroad track that ran along Hushour property line. Robert was quiet as they walked, thinking about Lou Gehrig, only 36 years old. Robert was 33. *Too much life to live and not enough days.* It was hard to believe.

"What are you thinking about, Dad?" Bobby finally asked.

"Son, you've heard of Lou Gehrig?"

"Sure."

"Well, he's really sick. So sick he had to quit baseball."

Bobby stopped in his tracks for a second, then jogged a few steps to catch up with Robert, who was still walking.

"Dad, he's not very old."

"Son, people don't have to be old to get sick and die. Look at my little sister, Anna Lee."

"Oh, yeah. I remember that."

They walked in silence the rest of the way. Bobby, sensing his father's sadness, stayed close by, matching stride for stride. Robert kept a fast pace, the pace of a man walking off an emotional struggle.

They reached the railroad tracks.

"Wow! There are still strawberries here," Robert said. "I'm surprised. Bobby, you go down a-ways with your bucket, and I'll start here with *my* bucket. We'll meet in the middle. Don't pick any green ones or any real little ones...let them grow more."

They worked in silence, the son and his father taking an unhurried approach to berry picking, careful to choose fully ripe strawberries, and just as careful not to bruise them.

After an hour of picking, they were face to face and had filled each bucket to the brim.

"Your mom will be happy to see these. She'll have more than enough for pie."

"Maybe she'll make jam," Bobby said.

"Then we'll have strawberries in the winter, too," Robert

answered. "There's not much better than strawberry jam on toast."

They began the walk back home as quiet as they had been on the way to the berry patch. Finally, Bobby spoke.

"Dad, do you think Lou Gehrig will get well?"

"I guess the doctors don't know how to cure his disease, so probably not."

Bobby was quiet again for a minute.

"Do you know what I think, Dad?"

"What's that?"

Bobby stopped walking and set down his berry pail. Robert stopped also, giving his ten-year-old his full attention.

"I think if Lou Gehrig dies, everyone will remember him like he is right now. A famous baseball player. Maybe the greatest ever. He'll never get old and weak, like great-grandpa did. Everyone will just remember him hitting homeruns and such. I think that's good." He picked up his pail and started walking again.

Robert stared at Bobby's back, moving towards home, then followed his son.

Out of the mouths of children. He pondered how such a young boy could already have such big thoughts.

***

"I'm pregnant."

The announcement caused Robert to stiffen his back, his ramrod-straight posture now tense. He whirled around to face Edith, who was standing behind him in the toolshed.

"What? How far along do you think you are?"

"Not far. A couple of months."

"How can that be?"

"What do you mean, 'how can that be'? You know how it happens."

"You're still breastfeeding Roma. I thought the doctor said that would prevent you from getting pregnant."

"He said it might *help*. It wasn't a guarantee. And it didn't work for us."

"So, you got pregnant around...."

"Right around the time Lou Gehrig retired from baseball, my dear. Remember how depressed you were? Because he was so young? Well, I didn't want you to be depressed anymore, if you recall." She smiled her wide, brilliant smile.

He felt himself flush.

"Edith! You shouldn't talk about such things!"

She took two steps towards him and grabbed his arms, laughing.

"Why not, honey? We love each other. We're married. There's nothing wrong with feeling romantic. We just got a little surprise out of it."

Robert stared at his wife, astounded. Six kids already. A seventh on the way. More mouths to feed, more clothes and shoes to buy, more visits to the doctor, but no more money coming in. And war was brewing in Europe—Germany had just invaded Poland. *Who knows what will come of that?*

Robert turned back to his work, sharpening his scythe. "I've got to get the rest of the garden cut back and turned under." He said no more.

Edith walked back to the house, disappointed and resentful at Robert's reaction. The older kids were playing tag in the side yard, laughing and yelling at each other. Little Alton wasn't quite two, but he was trying to keep up with his brother and sisters. Roma was still napping in the playpen near the kitchen table. Edith sat down in one of the ladder-back chairs that were part of the dining set. This was the place where her best thoughts often came to her.

It's not my fault alone.

It takes two to tango.

She sighed. No wise or profound thoughts today. She poured boiling water into the sink to clean the dishes from lunch. She waited a minute for the water to cool but didn't wait quite long enough. The water was scalding. She started to pull her hands out, then thrust them to the bottom of the sink, allowing the water to burn her skin. It brought tears to her eyes.

"Edith?"

She pulled her hands out of the sink. They were mostly covered by soapsuds, but her skin shone through, lobster red. She quickly hid them in a dishtowel as Robert continued to speak.

"I'm sorry I reacted the way I did. I was just shocked."

She didn't reply, and he crossed the room, taking her in his arms.

"We've got our hands full around here. I wasn't expecting another baby so soon, and I didn't know how to feel about it. I was thinking only about how much everything costs. You know as well as I do that we don't have a lot of money coming in."

"You don't think I haven't thought about all that myself?" Livid, she pushed away from her husband, eyes blazing. "I'm the one who has to carry the baby around inside for nine months and then deal with labor and delivery and taking care of them after they're born. You're out fishing and hunting or listening to baseball on the radio. Who takes care of these kids when they're sick? Who gets them up and dressed every day? Gets them ready for school and does homework with them? Who does the laundry and cooks all the food and...." She took a breath, but she said nothing else, out of steam.

Robert took a step back, fuming at her tirade.

"I *said* I'm sorry. I know it's hard on you." He paused, then quieted his voice and asked, "Edith, do you really feel like I don't help enough? I'm working as many hours as I they give me at the pottery, and I fish and hunt to help put food on the table. I work out in the garden...shear sheep...I'm trying to be a good husband and a good father. I play with the kids...." Now, *he* ran out of words.

Edith finished drying her hands, walked back to the table and sat down. Roma showed no sign of having been disturbed by the louder-than-usual dialogue taking place in the kitchen, and Edith caressed her chubby cheek. Robert joined her at the table, taking one of her hands and examining it front and back. *The hands of a worker.* Outside, they heard the other kids still laughing and yelling, the ongoing game of tag becoming a frenzy. Finally, Robert spoke.

"I'm sorry. I really am. Edith, I love you more than I ever thought I could love a girl. Nothing can change that. Do you understand me? We've been through a lot together, and we'll get through this, too." She didn't smile, but her face softened.

"We don't have much choice, you know."

Robert smiled. "We *do* have a choice...a choice to be happy and to keep making the best of our situation. Sometimes the very thing you didn't expect turns out to be the best thing of all."

Now Edith smiled and relaxed. "That's true. Pretty much every one of these kids has been a surprise, and we're still standing."

Robert laughed. "Just barely, sometimes. Well, I sure hope we can get a boy this time."

"We'd be a little more balanced," Edith said, nodding. "Bobby and Alton would be happy."

"Yeah, and no one ends up with a name like Ol' Tree Limb."

24
1940

Named after his grandfather, Verlin Wooster Riedel made an appearance in early March. Not surprisingly, Bobby and Alton were enthralled with the little guy. Another brother—the boys were saved! The children celebrated most heartily with their dad. On the menu— popcorn and milk, a Robert Riedel favorite, and a treat he was adept at making.

Verlin was a good baby—hardly ever cried, smiled early and often. Of course, he had six brothers and sisters who loved him and spent endless hours entertaining him.

There was nonstop activity in the Riedel household, and Edith was in the middle of every minute of it. She sometimes wondered how she could manage, but she was always thankful for the health of her many children. She began to rely on Bobby, who became even more responsible about helping with all the kids. He made cream of wheat for their breakfasts. He helped get everyone dressed. There weren't many clothes for each child to choose from, so that job was easy to accomplish without much ruckus. Once Bobby, Clara, Mary and Phyllis left for school, Edith was on her own with Alton, Roma, and Verlin. Calm would settle over the house for a few hours. *I couldn't do it without those oldest two.*

Robert was working at the pottery, continuing to shear sheep for local farmers and run his traps for extra income. In the summer, he began a house painting business.

"I've always liked painting houses and it pays pretty well," Robert said.

"I'm not too crazy about the idea of you being up high on a ladder," said Edith. "There are seven kids in this family, and I'd like them to keep their father around for a while."

"There are seven kids in this family I need to *provide* for," Robert answered. "I'll be fine. I'm strong and I've got good balance."

"If you say so."

And so, life for the Riedel clan moved along exactly as it did for many families in Wyandot County. Everyone they knew had the same money pressures—no one had recovered to their pre-Depression financial status. The work was never-ending, but there was great pride in neatly maintained homes and gardens, healthy herds of livestock, and endless fields of wheat, barley, corn, and beans. Robert and Edith had grown up being hard workers. There was no foreseeable change in their destiny.

***

"Let's go fishing, kids." Robert stood up and five kids jumped up, too. The girls ran off to change into shorts while Bobby and Alton stood at their father's side.

"Is Alton going? He can't bait his hook. He's not even three."

"Why don't you teach him, Bobby? That's a good thing for a big brother to do—teach his younger brother how to fish."

"Okay, Dad. But I might have to ask you a couple of questions myself."

"That's all right, son. You know, we'll have to help the girls, too. They're kind of squeamish about worms and such."

"Oh, brother." Bobby rolled his eyes. "Why do we have to take *them*?"

"For two reasons. One, it's good for 'em to learn how to fish, and two, it will get 'em out of your mom's hair for a while."

Bobby seemed to consider this, cocking his head to one side. Then he said, "I s'pose that's a good enough reason right there."

Robert laughed. "C'mon boys. We'll get the fishing poles."

The children followed Robert like ducklings follow their mother all the way to Sycamore Creek. Each child held on to a cane fishing pole except for Alton, whose fishing pole was carried by his beloved big brother.

"Now you kids remember to be a little bit quieter so we don't scare off the fish. Everyone sit down right here till we get your hooks baited." The four younger children dutifully sat on a fallen tree.

"Bobby, you help Phyllis and Alton. I'll get Clara and Mary."

Robert and his firstborn pulled nightcrawlers out of an old Chock Full o' Nuts coffee can which had been filled with moist dirt, leaves, and a few old vegetable scraps.

"Ewww," Clara complained when the first worm was pulled out of the muck.

"Better get used to it, Clara, if you're going to fish with us," Robert said.

"They look so icky. Do they feel icky, too?"

"A little, I guess, but I'm going to put him right on Alton's hook and then I won't have to touch him anymore. Now watch how I do this."

Robert expertly guided the long earthworm onto a fishing hook. The worm wriggled, trying with invertebrate desperation to wrestle free of its torture.

"Oh, Daddy, I can *never* do that!" Clara was hiding her eyes behind her hands now.

"If you can't bait your own hook at your age, you can't fish."

Clara harrumphed her way back to the log she had been sitting on and plopped down, resting her elbows on her knees and her chin on her hands.

In the meantime, Bobby had baited Phyllis and Alton's hooks as well as his own. "We're ready, Dad."

"Good, son. Did you show them how to do it?"

"I tried, but I still think Alton's too little to mess around with a hook."

"I agree. We'll bait his for him till he's older."

Robert and the four young fishermen stood on the bank of the creek, where Robert showed his children how to cast their line out into the water. Bobby was already a fisherman and stood off from his family a short distance, intent on his own line.

"Bobby, help watch your brother and sister's bobbers. If they get a bite, you might have to help them set the hook."

"Okay, Dad." Bobby moved a bit closer to his little brother. "Now just be real quiet and try to keep your pole still," he told the toddler.

"Daddy, do I have a bite?" asked Mary.

Robert looked over at her bobber. "No, honey. That's just the movement of the water making your bobber go up and down. When you have a bite, the bobber will go clear under the water…"

He was interrupted by a splash. He turned to look in the direction of the sound and saw Clara bobbing up and down, thrashing and choking, trying to call for help. She was nearly a hundred feet away, unsuccessful in her attempts to grab onto a half-rotted log that had fallen across the creek.

He dropped his pole and ran along the side of the creek towards his oldest daughter's location. When he reached the log, he dove into the murky creek and swam out to the middle where Clara continued to struggle. In her panic, she made it more difficult for him to grab her and pull her to safety. Robert finally wrapped his arms around both of hers, pinning them to her side.

"Stop!" he shouted as loud as he could, spitting mouthfuls of Sycamore Creek back into Sycamore Creek. She stopped flailing, looking shocked. Then Robert lifted Clara over his head and onto the log, where she lay gasping for breath.

The other four kids had dropped their poles and were running to see what had happened to their sister. Mary and Phyllis held hands while Alton and Bobby stood, mouths open, watching their father rescue Clara.

"Wow, Dad! That was great!" Bobby said.

Robert pulled himself up to join his daughter on the log. He waited to catch his breath, then put his hand on her shoulder. She was still lying prone on the log, her face to one side, an occasional cough producing small amounts of water. "You all right?" he asked.

She nodded, saying nothing. Several minutes passed before she finally raised her head and began to push herself up into a sitting position.

"What were you doing, Clara?" Robert knew he was going to owe Edith an explanation.

The ten-year-old sputtered once more, then began to cry.

"I don't know, Daddy. I just walked out onto the log. I tried to keep my balance…"

"Now Clara, do you know how to swim?"

"No sir."

"Then what do you do around water?"

"Wait for you."

"That's right."

He was quiet for a minute. Clara continued to sniffle.

"I'm sorry, Daddy."

He patted her on the thigh. "It's all right. Were you bored?"

"Yes sir."

He sighed. "Not everyone likes fishing, and I guess it's not for you, Squirt, but what you did was dangerous, and it scared me. Don't ever do anything like that again, okay?"

"Okay."

He put his arm around her shoulder and pulled her close. "All you kids need to learn how to swim. Then we can all come down here and jump in on purpose."

Clara looked up at her father. "Really? We could swim here?"

"Sure. We did all the time when I was your age."

"How did you learn to swim?"

"Your Grandpa Wooster threw me in and told me to start moving my arms and legs. I learned how to swim real fast, I can assure you."

Clara laughed so hard she almost fell back in the creek.

"Whoa, there, Squirt. We've had enough of that for one day," Robert said as he grabbed the back of Clara's shirt. "C'mon. Let's get off this log."

The rest of the kids were watching wide-eyed as Robert and Clara scooted their way back to the shoreline.

"Wow, Clara. Was that ever dumb!" Bobby said.

"Yeah, Cwawa! Dumb!" Alton repeated.

"That's enough boys. We'll say nothing of this to your mother, all right kids?"

Five heads nodded.

Robert looked around at the tangle of fishing lines. "We still need to catch a few fish for supper tonight. What say we get this mess straightened out and try again. Clara, it won't take long for your clothes to dry. Sit in the sun."

"All right, Dad." She found a flat rock to perch on.

They spent the rest of the afternoon catching enough bass and bluegills to make a feast for the whole family. By the time they got home, both Clara and Robert's clothes were dry.

"Look at all those fish!" said Edith when they arrived home.

"Did you kids have fun?"

Robert and the children all looked back and forth at each other.

"Yes, Mom," five voices chimed, dissolving into giggles.

Edith thought it better not to ask.

***

Late in the summer, Robert was mucking out the horse stall when he heard a man's desperate voice calling his name. He dropped his rake and shovel and walked to the barn door, gazing out to see who was doing all the hollering. It was Jack Miller, on a dead run, continuing to yell, "Robert! Robert!"

He left the barn and walked towards Jack, wiping his hands on an old rag. Before he could speak, Jack said, "Come down to the creek. Danny Daugherty has fallen in—he never came back up. He might be drowned. No one has seen him along the creek or anything…"

"Let's go," Robert said. Both men began to run in the direction of Sycamore Creek. Robert's children followed, curious as to why their father would be running.

"You kids stay here. Get back!" Robert hollered at them over his shoulder, then picked up his pace.

"But where you goin'?" Bobby shouted.

"To the creek. Tell your mom."

Bobby and the other kids headed towards the house. Suddenly, Bobby stopped in his tracks. "Clara, you girls take Alton to the house. I'm going to the creek. Tell Mom." He turned and sped off in the direction his father had gone.

"But…." There was no use in asking a question. Bobby was already gone.

The children started towards the house again, when Clara stopped walking.

"Mary, you and Phyllis take Alton to Mom. I'm going to the creek, too."

"But Clara," Mary started, but she was already looking at Clara's back. She turned to Phyllis. "Let's go."

The three remaining kids trudged to the house. Edith was in the kitchen peeling carrots over the sink.

"Hi, Mom."

"Hi, kids." Edith glanced over her shoulder. "Where's Bobby and Clara?"

"With Daddy," Phyllis said.

"Out in the barn?"

"No. They went to the creek."

"Oh!" Edith was surprised. "Are they going fishing?"

"I don't think so, Mama," Mary said. "I don't know why they're going, but they were both running. *Fast*."

Edith froze, cold terror filling her. She dropped her knife in the sink and spun to face the children.

"Running? They were running to the creek?"

"Yeah, Mr. Miller was running, too."

More than one person had drowned in Sycamore Creek. Some parts of the creek were so shallow that a child could wade in it, but there were areas of sharp drops-offs, where one could easily be lost, and there were tangles of old trees and roots. She tried not to show her concern.

"Well, maybe one of the fellas caught a really big fish and they wanted everyone to see it. Why don't you kids go play in the den for a little bit while I finish getting things ready for supper?"

The kids retreated and Edith turned back to her vegetables, praying as her hands worked. "Whatever it is, Lord, let it turn out all right. Please let it turn out all right." The only words she could think of repeated themselves over and over in her mind.

***

At the creek, a group of men had stripped off shoes, socks, and shirts. They dove repeatedly into the water, staying under the surface for a minute, then pushing back up long enough to grab a breath and shout, "He's not over here."

Robert was one of those men. He was a strong swimmer and knew the creek well, fishing and swimming there for thirty years. He made several unproductive dives not far from the other men. Then he remembered the deeper area under the log from which Clara had fallen. He made his way there.

On the shore, Bobby watched from behind a tree. Clara tiptoed up behind him and tapped him on the shoulder. He jumped, electrocuted by the interruption of his covert activity.

"What're you doing here?" he hissed.

"I wanted to see, too," she said.

"Well be quiet and stay down," Bobby said.

The children peeked out from around the huge sycamore tree they stood behind. Sometimes they would look over at each other,

164

puzzled. What was going on? Then Clara noticed Robert swimming towards the log she had fallen from.

"Daddy's going to my log!" she said to her brother.

"Hush!" Bobby said, but he looked in the direction of the log.

Robert reached the half-rotted log, pulled himself up onto it, then looked out over the surface of the creek again, hoping to see bubbles bursting on the surface somewhere. Nothing. He lunged back into the water, diving towards the bottom.

Under the surface, it was more difficult to see. Though sunlight shone through the water, the creek bed was riled up from multiple frantic divers, making it muddier than usual. Robert came up for air briefly, then dove again. *I can't see a darn thing!*

Once more, he resurfaced, stretching upward for air. He sucked in as much as his lungs could hold, then made another dive, deep, deep into the creek. For a second, he got caught on something, momentarily stuck, unable to move up or down. His lungs were ready to burst. He reached behind him and felt a snarl of branches from the log. He yanked as hard as he could, loosening his overalls from the branch—in the effort, he tore his pocket—it had been caught on the branches.

He repositioned his hands in front of him, feeling for other things he could not see. Another smaller branch nearly punctured his hand, and when he pulled back, he brushed against some material not native to the creek. As he reached his hand deeper into the twisted branches, he felt a leg, then another leg, then the back of a child. His lungs were screaming for air, but he worked to remove the body from its trap, pulling as hard as he could do disentangle swim trunks from the branch. The body fell into his arms.

Bobby and Clara watched in horror as their father exploded through the surface, holding the limp body of Danny Daugherty in his arms. Clara let out a scream—she couldn't help herself. Bobby pulled her back behind the sycamore, but not before Robert saw his children. He was too out-of-breath and exhausted to say anything to them. All he could do was swim with one arm towards the shore, pulling young Danny's body behind him.

Clara's scream had alerted the other divers, who came to meet Robert on the bank of the creek. Robert was weak with his rescue efforts, and he began to shake violently as he emerged from the water. The other men rushed forward to assist him.

David Daugherty came forward to receive his dead son into his arms. Dr. Smith was by his side, helping to support him. David held the boy out to the young doctor, who briefly examined Danny's lifeless body, but they all knew the examination wasn't necessary.

"Dave, I'm sorry, but he's gone. We just got to him too late."

David collapsed on the muddy shore, rocking his boy back and forth. The rescuers struggled to hold back their own tears. It could have been any one of their children. All their kids swam in Sycamore Creek.

Robert sat on the ground, trying to control his tremors.

"Take some slow, deep breaths, Robert," Dr. Smith said. "You've got a lot of adrenaline circulating around right now. That's what's making you shake."

Robert looked up at the physician and nodded. He was unable to speak, but he followed Doc Smith's suggestion, pulling air deeply into his lungs and blowing it out slowly through his mouth. The other men were beginning to head for home, helping Dave to carry his drowned son back to higher ground. Robert looked after them, watching how each man took a turn carrying Danny in their arms. He stayed seated for several minutes, continuing his deep breathing. After several rounds of the exercise, the shaking began to subside. He stood up.

"Whoa, don't try to get goin' too fast," Doc Smith warned. "You've just been through a pretty bad experience. Why don't you sit here a bit longer?"

"I have to get out of here. I can't stay around this place. Besides, I've got two scared kids hiding behind that tree over there."

"What?" Doc spun around to look in the direction Robert pointed. "Oh my gosh, what are they doing here?"

"Snuck down here to see what was going on, I s'pose. I don't think they bargained for what they saw."

"I highly doubt it. Well, they've just learned a hard lesson, Robert. I know you and Edith will help them understand."

"I don't know if I understand it myself, Doc," Robert said, squinting and rubbing his temples with his fingers. "I *never* understand how come kids have to die."

Doc was silent, looking towards the tree where the Riedel kids were still hiding.

"Listen, your kids have two of the finest parents I've ever

known. You and Edith have the kind of relationship a family doctor likes to see between parents and children in his practice. It's healthy." Doc extended his hand to shake Robert's. "I gotta go, but listen to me. The kids will talk about all this with you when they're ready, and when that time comes, I know you will handle it well." He trudged up the embankment to his car.

Robert waited long enough to watch Doc pull away in his truck, then walked towards a bottlebrush shrub where he had thrown his shirt. He saw Clara peeking out from behind the sycamore tree. He could see that she was crying. He pulled on his shirt, then held his arms out to her. She left her hiding place and ran to him, crying as if her heart were broken. He hugged her tightly and asked, "Where's your brother?"

Clara pointed back to the tree.

"Let's get him and go home."

As they approached the tree, Robert could see Bobby sitting on the ground, picking up and aimlessly tossing small stones.

"Bobby, you ready to go home?"

"Yes sir." The boy stood up. He looked up at his father, and a sudden burning in his eyes caused him to blink several times.

"It's okay to cry, son."

That was all it took. Tears bubbled up, spilled over, and wet Bobby's cheeks. The three mourners stood in a circle, arms wrapped around each other till the children could collect themselves. Robert put one hand on each child's shoulder.

"You two listen to me, now. This was too much for you to see at your age. I don't want you talking to your brothers and sisters about what you saw here. They're little, and it would scare and upset them too much. When you need to talk about it, you come to me or your mom, all right?"

The children nodded.

"And we're going to talk again about all the swimming rules, all right?"

Again, the children nodded.

Robert began to feel weak and shaky again, thinking about how cold Danny had felt in his arms. He took a few more deep breaths to pull himself together before speaking.

"You two saw a terrible thing...a *terrible* thing. I wish you hadn't been here at all."

"I'm sorry we came, Dad. I know you told us not to," Bobby sniffled. "I'm sorry we disobeyed you."

"Well, let's not worry with all that right now. We've got to get home, kids. Your mom is going to wonder what's keeping us here so long. She'll be worried. Are you all right? Will you be okay to walk home with me now?"

"Yes, Dad," they answered in unison.

They began walking, one child on each side of their father, and though they often felt they were far too old to hold hands with their parents, Bobby and Clara almost simultaneously reached out and grabbed onto the hands of the man who had pulled Danny Daugherty from the bottom of Sycamore Creek.

25

June 1941

"Mom, these curls are too tight! Can't you loosen them up a little bit?"

"Clara, if I don't roll them tight, you won't have any curl at all. Your hair is straight as a stick, child."

Clara sat on the floor in front of the sofa, but she squirmed incessantly. Edith sat behind her, a pile of rag rollers at her side, hands busy with soft, dark hair.

"If only my hair was like Mary's! Her hair is curly without even putting any rag rollers in it." Clara rested her chin on her fists. "It just doesn't seem fair. Don't you think her hair could be a little straighter and mine could be a little curlier?"

Edith sighed. She didn't know which gender was more challenging. *So much drama with the girls…so much rambunctiousness with the boys.* She pulled Clara's hair a little tighter.

"Ouch, Mom!" The protest made Edith feel a little guilty and at the same time, a little satisfied.

"Sorry, dear. I'll try to be gentler but hold still so we can get this over with."

Saturday night bath time was always chaotic, but with six kids and a baby, getting everyone together for church on Sunday morning went much smoother if Saturday night was spent in preparation.

Sunday mornings didn't change much from week to week. In reality, they were scarely more controlled than the chaos from the night before.

"C'mon kids…time to get in the car!" Robert shouted up the stairs. Bobby and Alton were down the stairs so fast Robert had to quickly step out of their way or be knocked over.

"Glad you boys didn't break your necks!" he said to his breathless sons, who were already running out the front door.

Next came Mary and Phyllis. The two remained close after the experience away from their family and were almost always together. Robert noticed a smudge of something tan on Phyllis' mouth.

"Phyllis Corrine, what's on your face?" Robert swiped a little of the thick substance away with his fingers. "What *is* this?"

Phyllis reached up to remove the rest. Her cheeks flushed, and she looked down at her feet. Mary looked sheepish, too.

"All right, girls, 'fess up."

Mary was the first to speak. "Daddy, it's just butterscotch pudding."

"Pudding! Where did you get pudding?"

"We saved it from supper last night and took it upstairs for a treat before bed."

"Are you sure you two didn't swipe it from the icebox?"

Now Phyllis joined in. "No, Daddy, honest. We saved it. We took it up and put it on the windowsill for a treat."

"So after prayers, you had a little treat? Well, there's nothing wrong with that, but why didn't you call me to join you?"

The girls giggled.

"And I have to say you sure didn't wash your face very well, little girl."

"Sorry, Daddy. I saved a little bit for this morning. I'll go clean up right now."

"Well, hurry up. We've got to get going."

Phyllis rushed from the room as Clara was arriving at the foot of the stairs. Her curls were already beginning to fall, and she was rolling the ends of her hair around her fingers, trying to get it to re-curl.

"I don't know why Mom even fusses with my stupid hair," she said. "It never turns out."

Robert rubbed his chin, feigning deep thought. "We could shave your head. Hold on. I'll go get my sheep shears." He turned, as if to head for the barn.

A look of horror passed over Clara's face. "You wouldn't do that! Dad! You couldn't!"

"Well sure I would, if it might help you out." Robert had a hard time keeping a straight face.

"Dad, I can't go around bald!"

"Then stop complaining. Be glad you have hair at all."

"Sorry Dad."

Robert smiled and put his hands on the sides of her face. "Squirt, you're just as pretty with straight hair or curly hair. It doesn't matter. I'll talk to your mom about it. Now cheer up and go on out and get in the car." Clara did as she was told.

Phyllis and Mary returned with Roma in tow.

"All right, you look much better. Take your baby sister out to the car, girls."

Mary grabbed Roma's hand and said, "C'mon, Roma. It's time for Sunday school."

Roma's blue eyes twinkled, and she smiled up at her big sister. She was normally a quiet little thing. Robert thought it was because she couldn't get a word in edgewise with all her brothers and sisters. Today she said in a clear tone, "I like Sunday school."

"I know you do, so let's go," Mary said. "You can sit by me."

The three held hands all the way out to the car.

Finally, Edith appeared with Verlin. "We're ready...I think." Edith laughed.

"It's a job and a half, isn't it?" Robert said as he took Verlin, who was getting squirmy. Just a year old, he was starting to get around on his own very well and made it clear he liked his independence.

"Down! Down!" Verlin said.

"I'll put you down, you little rascal, but you have to hold my hand," Robert said to his youngest, setting him on the ground.

"Me run."

"No, you walk with me." Robert held tightly to the little guy's hand.

Verlin pulled and tugged on his father, anxious to join his brothers and sisters. "Bobby! Bobby!" he called.

"Geeminy Christmas, kid. Bobby'll wait for you. Edith, you all set? This boy's about to pull my arm out of the socket."

"Yes, just had to grab my pocketbook. I'm ready."

It was then that Robert noticed how pale Edith looked.

"Hey, are you all right? You looked kind of cottony."

"I'm fine. It's just wrestling with all these children."

"Well, if you're sure…okay. Let's go."

Edith was quiet on the ride to church, almost as if she didn't notice the racket of seven noisy children. Robert decided he'd make sure she got plenty of rest that afternoon. He'd almost lost her once, and that was enough.

***

That afternoon, Edith rested while Robert kept the older kids busy with croquet and checkers. The girls helped with Verlin, putting together puzzles with large wooden pieces made for small children. Clara and Bobby also helped Robert get dinner on the table, even though Edith protested.

After dinner, Robert read the Bible to the kids. He asked the older kids to read a few passages each so that they got some practice reading out loud. Then they all listened to the radio and the latest news of the war before Robert said, "That's enough of that," and shooed them off to bed. He was thankful that Bobby and Clara were able to help with the younger children.

Edith was back at it. "Robert, you know I'm fine. I feel like some kind of invalid, laying around here."

"Remember what Doc Smith told you? There are going to be days when you just have to take it easy or you'll end up with that TB again. He said you have to 'listen to your body,' remember? Well, you just don't look that good today, so to me, that means take it easy."

Though she tried to make a good show, Edith's wan smile wasn't enough to hide how lousy she really felt. "If I don't look so good, are you saying I'm not appealing to you anymore?" she joked.

"You know darn well what I mean," Robert said, striding over to the couch where she lay. "I can't let you get sick again, Edith." He squatted down beside her. "The kids need you here. *I* need you here. We're all a little lost when you're not around." He kissed her on the lips. Hot. She felt hot. "What do you say I break you off some ice chips from the block? That might be a little treat for you."

"That sounds good. I think I'd like that."

When he returned to the living room with her ice, she was already sound asleep. He decided to keep the ice close by in case she woke up and wanted some. Then he sat in a chair nearby and watched her breathe until he fell asleep himself.

***

On Monday, Tuesday, and Wednesday, Edith was "Fine, fine, fine—I told you I'm fine! Revival starts tonight, and we're all going!"

Robert knew better than to argue, but kept a close eye on her that day, trying to find excuses to touch her skin, make sure she wasn't feverish. He thought she was a little short with the children at times, but that seemed to be a response anyone might have to relentless activity all around. He tried not to worry. Edith carried on her normal functions throughout the morning, though he saw that she was handing more duties off to the kids. That was good for them—they needed to learn how to help around the house. Clara ran the wringer washer with Edith's coaching and hung clothes outside on the line while Mary and Phyllis cleaned the upstairs. Robert was sure he heard a 'dust mop fight' after lunch. It was a play fight, but it was noisy.

"You girls cut it out and get busy!" he yelled up the stairs.

"Yes, Daddy." Two voices replied as one.

Bobby helped put ice in the icebox. It was a job he didn't mind because he got to suck on the small pieces that invariably broke off the block.

Alton, Roma, and Verlin were too little to help. They played on the floor in the living room, and the older girls took turns entertaining them.

Dinner was bologna sandwiches...easy, quick, and cheap. Then it was time for the revival meeting.

It was a beautiful evening in early June. The weather was perfect. Sunny, not humid, with a lovely breeze rustling the leaves on the maple tree in the front yard.

"Let's walk to church," Bobby suggested, and the family agreed. They paired up. Bobby held Roma's hand; Alton walked with Clara. Phyllis and Mary held hands, as usual, and Robert carried Verlin. Edith kept pace, but Robert noticed her shielding her eyes from the setting sun.

"You doin' all right?"

He received a look of disgust in reply. He said nothing more.

The revival meeting started with prayers and singing, then a young visiting pastor gave a rousing sermon. The church grew hotter as the minister got louder, more energetic. Men fanned themselves with straw fedoras while the women agitated the air using lace-trimmed hankies. The pastor paced back and forth behind the altar, sweating and entreating all within hearing to repent. The Riedel children watched, wide-eyed. They had never seen a minister so animated.

Robert whispered to Edith, "Anyone who didn't believe prior to coming in here better think about it a little more." He chuckled, and Edith elbowed him in the ribs.

Finally, the sermon seemed to be winding to a conclusion. The congregation kneeled to pray, and the minister issued a call.

"All who repent and wish to receive Jesus Christ as their personal savior, come forward. I'll pray with you."

The piano player started a familiar hymn, and the congregants began singing as they rose to their feet. "Just as I am, without one plea...."

"Can we stand up now, too? My knees are killin' me." Bobby whispered.

Robert nodded. The children all rose.

"Are we supposed to go up there?" Bobby then asked, watching several people make their way to the altar.

"No, son. You're already a believer. You just stay here."

Robert turned to look at Edith, still kneeling, head down in fervent prayer. Or at least he thought that was what she was doing until he saw her try to pull herself up, using the pew in front of her as a support. He reached over and grabbed her elbow, but when she was halfway upright, she collapsed back to her knees.

Several parishioners close by came to their aid. The children stood with their mouths open, aghast. Robert pulled Edith up to their pew.

"I knew you were sick!"

She was perspiring, pale, lethargic.

"Bob, you better get her home," Martha Crawford said. Her husband, George, was nodding enthusiastic agreement.

"We walked tonight." Robert said.

"We drove. I'll go get the car and bring it 'round front," said George, as he scooted past other people in his pew.

"Bobby, you'll have to get the kids home. You all go ahead and start walking. Do you think you can manage Verlin?"

"Sure, Dad. Clara will help me, too."

"All right then. I'll see you at home. Get going."

Bobby and Clara held hands with the smaller children, and the middle children took care of themselves. Seven Riedel children wasted no time in leaving the church, frightened by the sight of their mother—sick again.

Enough sunlight remained in the sky to shine directly through the beautiful stained-glass windows of the church, casting a pinkish glow over Edith's face, but underneath was the truth of the matter—a pale, ill woman. Robert said a quick prayer before George returned. Trying to draw as little attention as possible, with whole-hearted singing to accompany them, Robert and George guided Edith out of the church and down the front steps to George's waiting car, which he had left running. In minutes, they were home. She spoke only once during the trip.

"I have the worst headache."

A cold chill went up Robert's spine. The very words Anna Lee had said to Robert's mother so many years ago....

The men helped Edith into the house, where they took her directly into the bedroom and assisted her to lie down. Robert took off her shoes.

"Bob, do you want me to get Doc Smith?" George asked.

"No doctors," Edith spoke up. "I'll be fine. I have a headache."

Robert hesitated. Edith always knew what she wanted, and he didn't want to upset her, but he was worried. He motioned to George to leave the room.

The two men stood in the hallway outside the bedroom, talking in hushed tones.

"I think she better have Doc look at her, but she'll throw a fit," Robert said.

"Better her to throw a fit than you end up with a dead wife." George's tone was ominous. What could he see that Robert hadn't noticed?

"All right. Do you mind getting hold of him? He wasn't at church tonight, so he's probably busy."

"I'll find him, don't you worry." With that, George was gone.

The kids arrived home and Robert told his two oldest to get everyone ready for bed, not to come around their mom.

"Dad, is Mom sick again? Will she have to go back to the hospital?" Bobby's concern was plastered all over his face, eyebrows knitted in a frown, his usual crooked smile gone.

"Son, I think she *is* sick, but I don't know with what, and I don't know about a hospital. Doc Smith will come see her and tell us what to do. Don't you worry. We're going to take care of your mom."

Bobby and Clara looked at each other, and though no words passed between them, it was clear to Robert that his oldest children understood that something serious was happening.

"Go on, now, and help your brothers and sisters get ready for bed. Everyone can have a cookie for a snack, but make sure they all brush their teeth. You two can stay up a little longer and read, all right?"

"Okay, Dad."

He watched as the kids went on their way, hoping they would all sleep. For him, it was about to become a long night.

***

Doc Smith arrived early the next morning. Robert answered the door unshaven, dark circles under his eyes, his hair disheveled—it stood almost straight up in front.

"Sorry I couldn't get here earlier, Robert. I was helping deliver a baby, and you know how that goes sometimes. This one was an all-nighter. I thought she was going to be born on Wednesday, but she didn't arrive till Thursday. That baby did *not* want to come out!"

"Doc, I'm just glad you're here now. Edith has a fever, and she's talking out of her head. At least when I can understand her, which isn't much."

"Good Lord! George told me she had a headache and about passed out at church. I didn't know she was this bad off. Not that I could've come anyway, but I might have suggested that she go to Wyandot County Hospital. Let me go see her right now."

The two men went to Edith's bedside. Robert sat in a chair on the left side of the bed, and Doc approached from the right, first taking a moment to look Edith over from the top of her head to the soles of her feet.

"How high has her fever been?"

"I couldn't get her to hold a thermometer in her mouth, so I put it under her armpit. The last time I checked, it was 102."

"Under her armpit?"

"Yeah."

"That means it's really 103."

Doc pulled out his stethoscope and listened to Edith's lungs, heart, and abdomen. "Everything sounds okay at this point." Then he pulled out his pen light and opened Edith's right eye. He moved the light directly over her pupil, pulled it away, then repeated the action. When he was done, he moved to her left eye. Edith tried to squint against the light. She mumbled some garbled words that neither man could understand. Doc put his pen light back in his bag.

"Robert, has she been coughing again? Have you heard her coughing?"

"Golly, no. You think that tuberculosis is back?"

"Well, I think I know what's going on, and it's sometimes related to tuberculosis. Let me do another couple of things. Help me roll her on her side."

Once they had her repositioned, Doc tried to bend Edith's head forward as if to touch her chin to her chest. Immediately, her hips and knees flexed, too. The men turned her on her back. Doc pulled a reflex hammer out of his bag. Using the metal handle, he scratched the bottom of Edith's feet. Both times, her toes fanned out and flexed up towards the top of her foot.

"Okay." Doc sounded upset. "That's enough. Sit down, Robert."

Robert returned to his chair, leaning forward, running his hands through his hair.

So that's why it's standing straight up, Doc mused. Then he sat on the edge of Edith's bed, put his instruments back in his bag, and cleared his throat.

"I'm pretty darned sure Edith has meningitis," Doc began. "Has she been vomiting? Has she been more sleepy than usual?"

Meningitis. Robert couldn't speak for a minute as memories of Anna Lee's death crowded his brain. *Meningitis*. A killer had crept into their house.

Finally, Robert raised his head and looked at the doctor. "She's been a little on the grouchy side. I don't think she's slept any more or less than usual. She hasn't been eating much, but look at how busy she is with all these kids. It's no wonder she doesn't eat—she doesn't have time. And if she's grouchy, well, sometimes I get grouchy, too. She works like a dog..." he trailed off. "What are we going to do?"

"I don't think we should move her. Her brain is very irritated right now. I think we should just keep her here and look after her. Do you have some help you can call on? Your sisters?"

"Oh, yeah. They'll come over and help tend to her. But what about passing the infection?"

"We don't know if it's bacteria or a virus that's causing this…either one could be the culprit. People shouldn't be in here anymore than they absolutely have to be in order to care for her. Try to get her to drink some fluids. She may resist, but keep trying, and you have to be careful that whatever she's drinking doesn't go down her windpipe and choke her."

Robert was overwhelmed, barely able to process what he was being told. Doc could see it in his face.

"I'm going to be checking in on her, and I'll send my nurse down to check on her, too. You know Jenny—she'll be a good help with providing Edith's care."

Robert put both his hands on the side of his head and squeezed, as if he could somehow squeeze out the cobwebs that clouded his thoughts.

"What are her chances?"

"That's hard to say. There's really no treatment other than treatment of symptoms. Try to keep her fever down—give her cool baths with a little alcohol in the water. Try to get some fluids in her, even if it's just ice chips melting on her tongue. Keep the room quiet as possible and keep the lights low. People with meningitis have extra sensitivity to light and noise."

"There's nothing else we can do?" Robert said.

"I'm starting to hear about a new medicine called penicillin, and there's a lot of hope for that drug to treat all kinds of infections, but we don't have it available yet. I'm sorry—I wish there was more I could offer." Doc stood up.

"I'll send Jenny down this morning. The office isn't too busy today. And you call your sisters, all right? I know Bobby and Clara can help keep the other kids occupied and out of your hair."

"Yeah, they're pretty good babysitters. Well, thank you, Doc." Robert stood.

"Listen, you know where I am if something changes—for the better or for the worse. And I'll be back by the end of the day. I'll keep as close an eye on her as I can."

"I know you will. All right, then, thanks again, Doc." The two men shook hands.

"You know I'll be praying, too, Bob." Doc went out the front door, closing it with a quiet 'click.'

"Dad, how's Mom doing?"

A voice from behind him startled Robert back into consciousness of his surroundings. He turned to see Bobby, a concerned look on his face, still in his pajamas.

"Son, come sit down. I need a cup of coffee. Were any of the other kids awake yet?"

"I don't think so."

"Good. Let's talk man-to-man."

Robert grabbed a cup from the counter and filled it almost to the brim with steaming black coffee.

"Could I have a cup, too, Dad?"

Robert looked at his son and realized he was becoming a young man. He was taller, filling out, his dark hair still wavy.

"I don't see why not. You want it black like this?"

"Well, maybe I'll put a little cream in mine." Bobby headed towards the icebox and retrieved the cream. "Maybe a little sugar, too."

Robert laughed, and the sound seemed odd. He realized he was trying not to cry.

The two sat at the kitchen table. Each took a sip of their coffee before Robert finally spoke.

"Bobby, your mom has meningitis."

"Meningitis! Like Anna Lee had?"

"Yes."

Bobby sat his cup on the table. His eyes welled with tears. "Can she get better if she's at the hospital?"

"Doc doesn't think we should move her right now. We're going to care for her here at home. He's going to come by to check on her, and he's sending his nurse down this morning. I'm going to call your aunts and ask them to come over and help around the house and with your mom, too."

Bobby swiped at his eyes with the back of his hand. "I'll help you, Dad. I can help with a lot of stuff now."

"I know, son. You and Clara will both help me with the younger ones. And Clara might even be able to help put on a meal. She and Mary are both becoming pretty good little cooks."

The men of the family were quiet for a minute, sipping their coffee. Then Robert spoke.

"Something else we all need to do is pray, son. Pray hard."
"I will, Dad. You can count on that."

***

For two days and nights, people floated in and out of the Riedel home like specters—hushed in speech, noiseless in movement, going about the business of preparing meals, distracting children, caring for the sick. Everyone wore looks of worry—knitted brows, apprehensive faces, lips often seen moving in silent prayer. But for Edith, unaware of anyone's presence, little changed. Sometimes she was restless, other times deadly still. Sometimes she would take a few ice chips on her tongue, other times she would fight the attempts of those who fed them to her. Sometimes she was burning up and sweating profusely. Other times, her skin was bluish and frighteningly cold to the touch.

Doc Smith kept his promise. He checked in at least twice a day, and Jenny came in between Doc's visits. Jenny tried to give Edith aspirin on her tongue just to break her fever, but Edith usually spit it out. Then Jenny would give Edith a tepid sponge bath, which usually set off a round of shivering like Jenny or Robert had never before witnessed. Both Doc and Jenny were professional and kind to everyone in the family, but they were grim in their countenance. It was not unnoticed by Robert.

Bobby snuck into his mother's room more often than anyone realized. He held her hand. He quietly sang her favorite hymns and prayed for her. And at night, he suffered the restless slumber of a child tortured by memories of the past and fear of the unknowable future.

On Sunday morning, Edith was cool, clammy, unresponsive. Her legs were dappled with purple spots, and the bottoms of her feet were nearly black. Robert stood at her bedside, exhausted, endlessly rubbing her legs. His sister, Cora, had spent the night, and she helped Bobby pile on blankets to keep Edith's legs warm. One by one, Clara, Mary, and the other children crept into the room, quiet and somber. The youngest of the pack couldn't understand how serious the situation was, but even little Verlin recognized that his father, brothers and sisters were scared, and he was, too.

The young pastor who had been providing the revival sermons came to visit, along with Reverend Reinhart. They stood at the bedside and prayed fervently. Suddenly, the younger pastor's head popped up, and he said, "I know what my sermon will be about this morning…faith in the worst of times." The two men left.

Doc Smith came to check on Edith. The children left the room while he examined Edith again, but Robert and Cora stayed, sitting quietly, awaiting Doc's verdict. When he was done with his exam, he turned to Robert, a look of frustration and sadness on his face.

"Robert, it's time to stop praying. Edith isn't improving, and at this point, even if she lives, she'll be an invalid. She'll need total care all the time. Truth is, I don't think she's going to live. If I were you, I'd stop praying."

Robert's mouth dropped open. His shoulders slumped. Doc had never been so grave in his discussions.

"I hate to be so blunt," Doc continued, "but there's just no hope here that I can see. She should've come around by now if she was going to. If she lives, she'll be a vegetable. You wouldn't want her to end up like that, and if I know Edith, *she* would say the same."

Cora began to cry.

Robert sat up, straightening his shoulders. "I can't give up on her. This is my wife, the mother of my children. I love her."

"I know it, but you've got to start facing reality, man. Look at her feet and legs. Her circulation is shutting down. That's what all the purple splotches are about. Her kidneys will go next, and before long, her heart and lungs will stop working, too. It's over, Bob."

Robert shook his head, vehement. "She's got to live. She can't be ready to go, and I'm not ready to *let* her go."

Doc put his hand on Robert's shoulder. "I know this is hard for you but hear me out. You've got to get yourself prepared. She's not gonna make it through this one, Bob. I've never seen a patient in this condition who was able to recover. The odds are against her. I'm sorry to have to say it. Listen, I'll drop in on you later, and if anything comes up in the meantime, you call me right away. I'll be here in a flash." He left.

Robert looked at Cora, who was drying her eyes and patting Edith's hand. She looked up at her brother. "Do you think he's right? Is this really happening to us again?"

"Not if I can help it, it's not." Robert returned to his post, lifting the covers to look at Edith's legs. They seemed more purple than before, and they were freezing cold. He began to rub her legs, trying to stimulate the circulation.

An hour later, he was still rubbing her legs. Her skin was so fragile, it began to peel up in his hands. He was horrified…was he making her worse? Still he rubbed and massaged, trying not to loosen up any more skin.

The children had come into the room and stood around their mother's bed. The girls were crying. Bobby and Alton were stoic, but Robert knew his oldest boy was worried.

"Take the covers off my legs. They're so heavy." Edith's voice, quiet, but clear.

"Mommy!" Alton cried out, and all the children joined his chorus.

Robert stopped his activity. His head snapped up to look at Edith's face. Cora and Robert looked back and forth at each other, then back and forth at Edith. She had spoken! Robert went to the head of her bed.

"Edith? Darling? Can you hear me? Edith?"

"The covers…off my legs."

Cora stood and began removing bed linens. "Edith. Oh, Edith…."

Robert turned to his kids. "I'll be right back. I'm going up to the church. You all tend to her and I'll be back shortly." He left the room, raked a comb through his hair, and left for the church.

When he arrived, the congregation was in the middle of reading the Gospel. He walked up the aisle, catching the attention of the minister, who stopped reading the Bible and looked at Robert. All the congregation did the same thing, many of them with their mouths hanging open.

"I'm sorry to interrupt, but I'm here to ask all of you to pray for my wife, Edith. You all know her and that she's been sick with meningitis. She finally woke up and said a few words. I believe that if everyone in this church prays for her this minute, she'll recover. Please—pray *right now* and keep on praying whenever you think of it." He turned to leave, hearing the minister begin a new prayer. "Dear Heavenly Father, we come to you right this second to ask for your blessing of healing on Edith Riedel…only you have the power…."

The heavy wood doors of the church closed behind him, and Robert nearly ran all the way home. When he arrived, Edith was quiet again, and all the family was with her. Her feet and lower legs were still uncovered, and he was not surprised to see that the purple was fading from her extremities. He fell to his knees, exhausted, relieved, weeping.

The children swarmed around him. They all knelt with their

father, and Cora prayed aloud. Then Phyllis began to sing.

"Praise God from whom all blessings flow…praise him all creatures here below.…"

The others joined in. "Praise him above ye heavenly hosts. Praise Father, Son and Holy Ghost. Amen.…"

Their song ended, they all stood and hugged each other, watching for any sign that Edith might begin to wake up. She remained quiet. Finally, Cora said, "Kids, come with me. None of you have eaten a thing. Let's go make breakfast." She looked at her brother. "That all right with you? Can you sit with her for a bit?"

"Of course."

Robert sat in the chair next to Edith's bed. Something about her face was different. It was less pinched, less stressed. He could feel that her fever had broken, could see that her overall color was improving. Her breathing was easy. He knew she had turned a corner.

This is one time Doc's going to be wrong, and for the first time in several days, he allowed himself to smile.

***

The next day, Edith was able to raise her head off the pillow, sip some water and a bit of apple juice, and the day after *that,* she asked for chicken broth. Every day that followed brought small improvements. Doc was stymied and walked with Robert into the living room after his exam of Edith. He sat down on the sofa and shook his head.

"I've never seen anything like it. Not in all these years of practice, not when I was an intern—never. You all took mighty good care of her is all I've got to say."

"Well, we're grateful for all you did, too," Robert said.

"Ha! I told you to give it up, but you didn't, did you? You kept right on praying."

"Me, the kids and the rest of the family, everyone at church…yeah, we prayed just about every minute. She had a lot of people trying to get to God's ears."

Doc was quiet for a minute. "Bob, I'm a man of science. I try to look at the facts I'm presented with. I read my medical journals and try to keep up with everything new that's happening in my field. But I can tell you there are many things we don't understand and maybe will *never* understand. If miracles exist, I'd say Edith is one of them." He shook his head again and repeated, "I've just never seen anything like this."

Robert was more a man of faith but wasn't one to preach at people. Nevertheless, something in Doc's demeanor made him feel comfortable enough to say, "There's a saint named Augustine I learned about when I was a kid. He once said something to the effect that miracles aren't contrary to nature, but only to what we understand about nature. That always stuck with me. We might never understand why Edith's getting better, but I just accept it as a miracle. Believe me, I'm grateful, and I'm going to do everything I can to keep her healthy."

Doc smiled. "You better. I have a feeling we don't get too many miracles in one lifetime. I'd say she's been the point of *two* miracles already."

"Well, we've got seven other miracles running around the back yard right now, I imagine."

Doc laughed out loud. "Is that what you call all that racket?" He stood to leave.

"Thanks again for everything, Doc."

"Thank you for the words of wisdom. I hope I get to see more miracles in my lifetime."

"I have a feeling you will." Robert tapped his finger to his temple. "Just keep your mind open to it." Then he pointed to Doc's chest. "And your heart."

The two men shook hands, Edith's miracle having created an even stronger friendship than before.

26

October 1941

"When Mom gets home, I'm telling!"

"Go ahead, you brat! I'm gonna tell her what *you* did!"

"Well, it's *my* birthday, so I should be able to eat whatever I want!"

"But not *all* the brown sugar lumps! Mom always gives each kid one! You're just selfish, Clara!"

"There were only three in there! How could she split three between seven of us?" Clara flounced off, having had enough of her brother's accusations. "If you want something to eat, get some bologna out of the icebox," she sniped over her shoulder.

Bobby was disgusted with his sister. How could she? She knew he loved the lumps that mysteriously formed in brown sugar. His mom couldn't use them in cookies, so she always handed them out to the kids. It was one of his favorite treats.

His father was at work, and his mother had gone to see Doc Smith. She had regular check-ups since she was still recovering from meningitis. Old enough to babysit for short periods, Bobby was in charge of the household. Clara was supposed to help—not be a pain. But it was her birthday. Maybe he should be more forgiving and not so selfish himself. *Lumps of sugar aren't worth a dumb fight.* He went out to sit on the porch.

It was a Friday, exactly one week before Halloween. The maple tree was losing its red and gold, and the smell of dried leaves already on the ground was familiar, pungent. The air was crisp and cool, and the sky was a cloudless azure. Bobby drew in a deep breath and felt the calm of the season.

He knew that if they didn't behave, there would be no trick-or-treating. He already had plans to dress up as a cowboy. In imitation of his big brother, Alton had decided to be a cowboy, too. Clara was going as Cinderella. Mary and Phyllis were going to be hobos. Roma and Verlin weren't old enough to go, but the other kids would share bits of popcorn balls or apples or whatever treats they got. Trick-or-treat was always fun in Sycamore.

His father's car turned into the stone driveway. He could see that his mom was riding in the passenger side. *Dad must've picked Mom up at the doctor's office.* He was surprised, thinking his dad should still be at work.

Robert exited the vehicle first and ran around to open the door for Edith. He helped her out of the car and held her arm as they approached the house. Edith looked down at the ground, her face pale.

Bobby jumped up to open the front door for his parents. "Hi, Mom. Hi, Dad. It's a good thing you're home!"

Edith glanced at him and said, "I'm happy to *be* home. Maybe you can tell me why *you're* so excited about it a little later. I've got to lie down for a while."

Robert escorted Edith to their bedroom. He took her coat and purse, and once she had reclined, he left the room, leaving the bedroom door open only a crack.

"Is Mom sick again?" Bobby asked.

"No, son. Just tired. She needs to rest for a while."

"Are you done with work for the day?"

"No, Bobby. I've got to go back. I just left for a little while to bring Mom home from the doctor. I didn't want her to walk home today."

"Why not?"

"Son, can we talk about this later? I've got to get back to work. Now you mind the kids while Mom rests for a while, all right? Make sure they don't bother her. Get Clara to help you with Roma and Verlin." He walked back out to the car without so much as a glance back over his shoulder.

Great, Bobby thought. *I've gotta convince that brat Clara to help me.*

Then he remembered that he didn't really want to fight with Clara, especially on her birthday. He breathed a deep, drawn-out sigh and went upstairs, to where Clara had retreated. She was lying on her bed, reading a book.

"Clara, Mom's home, but she's pretty tired, so she's lying down on her bed."

Clara sat straight up, a frightened look on her face.

"Is she sick again?"

"Dad says no, but she's really tired. She *did* look pretty tired when they came in the house. Dad left work to go pick her up at Doc Smith's, but he had to go back to work, so we have to watch the kids."

Clara put her book aside. "It's my birthday...."

"I know, sis, and I'm sorry I got in a fight with you over something so dumb as brown sugar. I'm sorry your birthday isn't turning out to be much fun. Did Mom make you a cake?"

"Not yet."

"Well, maybe you, Mary, and Phyllis could do that. I could watch the other kids if you guys want to bake."

"We've had to do *everything* since Mom was sick, you know that? Even the little ones have to help out. Dishes, vacuuming, hanging out the laundry...."

Bobby was sympathetic, but firm. "Clara, come on, now. Mom still does a *lot* of stuff. But we hafta help her. Heck, look at all these kids around here! That right there makes her life hard all the time."

Clara fiddled with the pages of her book. "I s'pose you're right." She shook her head a little and pushed her hair back from her face. "Okay. I am eleven years old today. I'm not a baby whiner. I'll get the girls and we'll make a cake. It can be for me *and* for Mom—to make her feel better, you know?"

"Okay, I'll keep the little ones busy outside. We'll play tag or Red Rover or something."

Clara got up and walked over to her big brother. "I love you, Bobby."

"Gees, already! I know it!" Then he laughed, and the two walked back downstairs, the brown sugar fight forgiven and forgotten.

***

That evening, after supper was a memory and birthday candles had been blown out, Edith and Robert retired to their bedroom. The kids sat in the living room playing checkers and reading, but they were distracted by raised voices. What was being said was muffled through the closed door, but the conversation sounded angry at times. The oldest kids looked at each other, cautious not to cause too much ruckus in the living room, straining to hear what was going on behind closed doors. Finally, in hushed tones, they shared their observations.

"Mom sounds mad," Mary said.

"Daddy sounds mad, too," Alton said.

"They *both* sound mad sometimes, and then they're quiet sometimes," Clara said.

"I don't like it when Mom and Dad are mad at each other," Phyllis said.

"It doesn't happen that often," Bobby reassured her.

"Yeah, but when they *are* mad, they get *really* mad," Clara concluded.

Reaching the end of conjecture with this statement, the children turned on the radio, hoping to listen to Gene Autry or Glenn Miller instead of worrisome arguments. The girls danced with each other while Bobby read stories to Alton and Verlin. Eventually, the voices in the other room became quiet and stayed quiet. The door opened, and their parents walked into the living room, hand-in-hand.

Edith's color was better, and she was smiling a little. That eased Bobby's mind. Dad was right—she was simply tired, and no wonder.

"Will all you kids sit down for a minute?" Edith said. "And turn off the radio, if you would, Phyllis." Phyllis did as she was directed as Edith continued. "Dad and I have something to tell you."

Robert led Edith to the sofa, where they sat down. Verlin immediately went to his mother, intending to sit in her lap.

"How's about sitting on *my* lap, buddy?" Robert said, pulling the tot over to himself. Verlin tried to squirm away towards his mother, but Robert wrapped his arms around him, settling him into an embrace.

"Kids, I went to see Doc Smith today. I've been pretty tired, and I know I've been a little grumpy sometimes," Edith began.

"Are you getting sick again, Mom?" Clara asked.

"Well, no, not really, but..." Edith began to cry.

All the kids jumped up and went to their mother's side, trying to crowd in around her as close as they could get.

"Mom, Mom, what's wrong? Don't cry. Please tell us you're all right." Various voices pleaded for Edith's news.

Robert cleared his throat. "Kids, Mom is going to have another baby."

Bobby and Clara both backed up a couple of steps. Mary and Phyllis looked delighted, big smiles on their faces, hugging each other and their mom. Alton looked unconcerned. Roma and Verlin were too young to understand the implications.

"Another baby? That'll be eight of us," Bobby finally said. "Where's it going to sleep?"

"We've got a little time to figure all that out, son," Robert said. "In the meantime, it's going to be more important than ever for you kids to help out around the house. Your mom is going to need each of you to take care of your own rooms and so forth, help out with dusting and sweeping."

"What about cooking?" Clara said. "I'm getting pretty good at that."

"Yes, you most certainly are. That cake you made tonight was delicious," Robert said.

"It was every bit as good as what I can make," Edith now said, a small smile crossing her face again. "Children, you're all very good helpers, and I'm counting on you. In another few months, you're going to have a baby sister or a baby brother. When ladies are going to have a baby, they get tired easy, and that's why I need you all more than ever to help out around the house."

"Well, Mom, you *just* got over being sick. How come you're having another baby already?" Bobby asked. His face was grim. "Isn't seven enough? How many babies do you want?"

"Oh, Bobby," Edith said, her eyes welling again. "I guess the only answer I have is that I'll take as many babies as God sees fit to give me."

The boy glared at his parents. "Seems to me like God ought to realize we have enough."

"Bobby!" Edith exclaimed, but she was talking to his back. Bobby was on his way out to the front porch. She started to get up to go after him, but Robert took her arm.

"Let him go, Edith. Let him work it out a little on his own."

The other children had gone back to their own activities, and Verlin still squirmed to sit with his mother, so Robert handed him over to Edith.

"You're so adorable," Edith said. "I could just eat you all up!"

But she was still crying quietly. Verlin reached up and touched her face.

"Mama cwy?"

"It's all right, honey. Mama's not sad."

Robert knew she wasn't sad, but she was as worried as he.

***

Half an hour passed. The other kids had gone upstairs to retire for the night, but Bobby was still sitting on the porch.

"Robert, go out there and get him. He'll catch his death of cold," Edith said.

"Yeah, it's time for him to come in and get to bed. That kid'll sit out all night if I don't go talk to him."

Robert walked out to the front porch, where his oldest son sat looking up at a bright crescent moon and a sky full of stars.

"Beautiful, isn't it?" Robert started.

"Yeah. My teacher told us that stars make energy. Did you know that, Dad?"

"No sir, I don't believe I've ever heard that. It's interesting, though."

"I was just thinking about something."

"What's that, son?"

"Remember in the Bible when God told Abraham he would make him have as many kids as the stars?" Bobby continued to look at the sky.

Robert chuckled. "Well, Abraham wasn't going to have all those kids himself, but God promised him he'd have as many *descendants* as the stars."

"I don't understand, Dad. What's the difference?"

"That just means that Abraham would *start* a family, but his kids and his kids' kids would also have lots and lots of kids. Enough to populate the whole earth."

"How many kids are *we* gonna have, do ya think? A galaxy full?"

"Maybe enough for a little constellation," Robert joked.

Bobby hung his head. "I'm sorry I didn't act happy when you guys told us."

"It's all right, son. I understand. It was kind of a shock to your mom and me, too."

"How does this keep happening, Dad? How do ladies have babies?"

Robert smiled to himself. "That's a discussion for another day, buddy, but I promise you this…when the new baby comes, I bet you'll love him or her as much as you love your other brothers and sisters."

They were quiet for a minute. Then Robert said, "Bobby, it's past time for you to hit the sack, but I want to tell you one thing before you go in, and I want you to remember it."

"Yeah?" Bobby said as he stood up.

"All you kids are the stars in my sky."

Bobby walked over to where his father sat and hugged him. No other words were needed.

Robert stayed on the porch for a while, thinking about the energy created by stars…so much to know about the universe, yet so much that was unknowable.

"Just like life," he said aloud. "Just like life."

27

December 1942

"Mom, can us kids have a banana?"

Edith didn't divert her attention from ironing. "Bobby, I don't have any bananas right now."

"Well, what about oranges? Do we have any oranges?"

Now Edith stopped and propped the iron up on its end. She put her hands on her hips, let loose a deep sigh, and said, "Robert Riedel, Jr. When was the last time you saw an orange in this house?"

"I don't even remember, Mom. Can't you get some the next time you go grocery shopping?"

"Not likely. First of all, there's hardly any in the grocery store. Second, when they *do* have them, they're way too expensive. Three, we've got plenty of apples."

"Aw, gees, I'm sick of apples. What about peaches?"

Edith considered this. "Tell you what…tonight we can open a couple of quarts of the peaches we canned last summer. How's that? We'll have 'em for dessert after supper."

"Nothing right now?"

"Apples. Or crackers and cheese. Or all three together. That's a good snack."

"Okay," Bobby groused as he went to the pantry to pull out saltines. He opened the refrigerator, looking for and retrieving apples and cheddar.

Edith glanced over to check little Kathy in her playpen. The eight-month-old was napping, peaceful, her face relaxed, mouth slightly open. Child number eight turned out to be a happy, easy baby with deep brown eyes and chubby pink cheeks. They all spoiled her.

"Good thing we got this refrigerator before the war, Mom. When is this darned war going to end anyway?"

Edith's reverie was interrupted by Bobby's question.

"I wish I knew," she said. "Until it does, it's going to be hard to get those other fruits you love so much, son."

"The President could stop it, couldn't he? He's the most powerful man in the world, isn't he?"

Edith continued her ironing as she tried to think how to answer. At thirteen, Bobby was curious enough to ask questions and old enough to understand answers, but the war was more complex than Edith felt she could explain.

"Son, the President isn't the only person making the decisions about all this, and he doesn't have much control over the Japanese and the Germans. It seems like they want to take over the whole world for some reason."

"My teacher said it was because the Germans felt like they got kicked around too much in World War I. And she said the Japanese felt like they didn't get enough credit for helping win World War I. So everybody's still mad about World War I, I guess."

"Your teacher knows a lot more about it than I do," Edith said. "And when people get mad about stuff like that, who knows what they'll do? They might want to fight for a long time, buddy."

"I think we should just blow them off the face of the earth."

Now Edith stopped her work, again propping the iron up on its end and walking over to stand close to her son, who was focused on his snacks.

"Bobby, look at me," Edith began. He complied as she continued. "I don't want to hear you talk like that. War is terrible. So many people have already been killed. Our boys, their boys…it's terrible. We don't want the war to get *worse*…we want it to *end*. We're all proud of our soldiers, but there's a lot of heartbreak. How do you think the Klaiss family felt about their son being killed?"

Bobby hung his head. Edith continued.

"The Germans and the Japanese love their boys just as much as we love ours. Don't get me wrong, son. They started it and we got drug into it, but we want peace as soon as it can be achieved."

Bobby looked up, nodding in the affirmative. "I know, Mom. I know, but in my mind, the enemy has it coming to them. Sorry. Hey, can I go to the movies later with Charlie Dennis? We want to go see 'Gentleman Jim' with Errol Flynn. It's only a dime, which I already have. See?" He pulled a dime out of his pocket as proof.

"Sure, as long as you don't get home too late. What time does it start?"

"Seven. We'll be home by nine. Is that okay?" He picked up the snacks for him and his siblings and walked out of the room before Edith could answer.

She went back to work, pondering her son's comments about killing the enemy. *I hope he never has to be a soldier*, she thought, pushing the iron harder on the shirt she was pressing.

***

That evening, a little after nine, Bobby returned home from the movies. Edith and Robert sat in the living room, Edith darning socks and Robert listening to the war news on the radio. Bobby stomped snow off his boots, unwrapped the scarf from his neck, and took off his coat.

"How was the movie, son?" Edith asked.

"Oh, it was fine. Just fine." He wasn't convincing.

"You don't sound too enthusiastic," Robert said.

Bobby walked further into the room after stowing his coat in the hall closet. He sat down on a foot stool near his parents.

"Do you guys know what's going on in Germany?"

"Well, I was just listening to the news, actually," Robert said. "Why do you ask?"

"Because there's some pretty terrible stuff going on."

Robert got up, crossed the room, and turned off the radio. Edith had put down her darning and looked concerned about what they were about to hear.

"Why don't you tell us what you know, son."

"Over in Germany, the Nazis are rounding up Jews and taking them to camps. They about starve them to death or put them in gas chambers."

Edith put her hand to her mouth. She had hoped her children would never hear of this.

Robert took a deep breath before speaking.

"Son, we've been hearing some reports about this. How did you find this out?"

"The newsreel before the movie."

Of course. Neither parent had thought about the newsreels.

"Bobby, it's a terrible thing. A *terrible* thing."

"I know, Dad. Why in the heck don't we go over there and stop them?"

Robert sat back in his chair. He had thought the same thing many times.

"I'm not sure, son. I think the President and Congress feel that the war is a European war and that we shouldn't get involved."

"Well, if *I* was President, *I'd* put an end to it. They're killing little kids and old people, too, you know…kids as little as my brothers and sisters." He shook his head. "We need to go over there and bomb the heck out of Hitler."

"Tell you what, son…let's concentrate our efforts on praying for all those people. You never know how powerful prayer can be," Edith said.

"Mom, there's a time for prayer and a time for bombs. Prayer won't save those people now." Bobby stood up. "I'm going to bed. I'm going to pray all right. I'm going to pray that Hitler dies." He left the room.

Edith and Robert just looked at each other. Was this really their gentle-hearted son?

"He was going to hear this stuff sooner or later, honey," Robert said. "We can't protect them from everything."

"It's too bad there's something so horrible we have to try to protect them *from*. When do you think all this warring will end?"

"When men decide they're sick of killing each other, I guess. Let's call it a night."

It was a quiet walk to the bedroom, and when they finally stretched out on the bed, Robert could hear Edith's whispered prayers.

***

Christmas wasn't far off. Bobby, Clara, and Mary no longer believed in Santa, but the littler children were making regular mention of toys they'd like to see under the Christmas tree…trains and trucks and new dolls and dollhouses. Looking at her war-time ration book, Edith knew Santa would not be providing much of what they asked for, but she knew how to improve their chances….

Women were working outside the home in far greater numbers than ever. The war effort had pulled so many men overseas that women replaced them in the factories and all kinds of jobs that men had carried out in the past. It was more common in the bigger cities but reading about it made up Edith's mind. She would find a job and go to work. *I'll just inform Robert when he gets home. I'll make a good meal and break it to him after he's done eating and the kids are in bed.*

When Robert arrived home from work, the entire house smelled of meatloaf, homemade bread, and baked beans.

"Is Winston Churchill coming over for dinner?" he joked.

"No, just the prime minister of the Riedel clan," Edith said, smiling. "There's apple pie, too."

"Did you have to sell one of the kids to get the sugar?"

Edith laughed and kissed him on the cheek. "Three of them. Three kids for two pounds of sugar. Turns out they're better than rationing coupons."

She was in a good mood. She felt...*light*...inside. She was going to work. "Supper will be ready in about a half hour."

"Good. I don't mind telling you I'm starved. I'm gonna look at the newspaper till you call me." He left for the living room.

Edith hummed as she worked. She knew Robert would have a lot of questions and she knew how she would answer him—she had mentally prepared all afternoon. As she was setting the table, Mary came into the kitchen.

"Mom, I can help with that."

The kids had become more helpful than ever as Christmas approached. Edith smiled.

"Thanks. That'd be nice." She handed Mary the silverware.

Mary put a knife, fork, and spoon at every place setting except for Kathy's highchair. There, she put a baby spoon and Kathy's baby plate, which was divided into three small sections.

"Why do baby plates have those little spaces like that?"

"I suppose they started making them that way so all the mushy baby food doesn't just get mixed together."

"Well, did we buy that plate for Kathy? I don't remember it before."

"No, your Aunt Cora found it at the dime store."

"Hey, could we go Christmas shopping at the dime store in

Tiffin, Mom? I've been saving my pennies and I'd like to get the little ones a present."

"Goodness! Where have you been getting pennies?"

"Well, sometimes I just find one laying on the street. I found some by the railroad track this summer when Bobby and I went to look for groundhogs. And I've saved them up whenever I get one from my aunts or uncles."

Edith stopped, her mouth hanging open for a minute. "Aren't you clever? Well, I think a shopping trip is in order, then. Maybe we can go next week. I have some things I want to do in Tiffin anyway."

"What do you need to do?"

"Oh, just some different things. We'll talk about it when we go, all right?"

"Sure, Mom. Want me to go get the other kids for supper?"

"Yes, and your dad, too."

Supper was quiet except for the sound of silverware clinking on china plates and an occasional, "pass the butter" or "pass the potatoes." Even little Kathy ate mashed potatoes and applesauce. She couldn't handle her spoon yet, but her adoring big sister Clara made sure she didn't miss a bite. Bobby helped the younger boys cut their food. Mealtime was always a time of shared responsibility. Edith looked at the faces around the table and was grateful for each one. At the same time, she knew she needed something more. She was anxious to share her idea with Robert.

When the dishes were done, Edith gathered the children in the living room for their nightly Bible story. She chose the story of Jochebed, the mother of Moses.

"So when Jochebed heard Pharaoh was having all the Hebrew baby boys killed, her love for Moses made her think of how to save him. She put him in a basket made of reeds. She made it like a little boat so Moses could float out onto the Nile River. Guess who found that basket? Pharaoh's daughter. She loved that little baby boy and adopted Moses to be her own child."

"What did Moses' mom do then?" Phyllis asked. "Did she get her baby back?"

"Well, yes she did because mothers always love their children very much, but she knew that for Moses to live, he would have to be Pharaoh's little grandson."

The children who were old enough to understand looked

disgusted, and the little ones looked confused.

, "Here's the best part of the story, kids," Edith continued. "Moses' mom was chosen by Pharaoh's daughter to help babysit him, I guess you could say, and Moses turned out to be a great leader for the Hebrews. He helped them be freed from Egyptian slavery."

"What's slavery?" Alton asked.

"That's when one person doesn't let another person be free. They make them do all the work and stuff," Bobby said. "Kind of like it is around here sometimes."

The older kids all laughed, rolling on the floor with their hands on their stomachs as if they had just heard the funniest joke *ever*. Even Robert chuckled behind his newspaper.

"It's not really *that* bad, is it?" Edith said. "Kids have to help out when you have a big family like we do. Some kids don't even have their mom and dad at home as much as you do. Their moms and dads work."

Robert peered out from behind the sports page, looking over his glasses at his wife.

"That'd be awful," Mary said before Robert could speak. "I hope you never have to go to work. Who would cook and bake and make clothes for us?"

Edith avoided the question saying, "Okay, time to hit the sack. Skedaddle, all of you, and don't forget to brush your teeth. I'll be up to say prayers with you before you know it, so get moving."

Seven sets of feet pounded up the stairs. Undisturbed, Kathy remained sound asleep in her crib.

A faceless voice came from behind the newspaper. "I assume we're going to be having a talk of some kind after the kids are down."

"Yes, we are." Edith felt confident about her decision.

***

"Edith, we've talked about this before. How in the world are we going to both work and manage all these kids? Yes, Bobby and Clara can help out, but is it fair to put all that on them?"

"I've thought about this a lot. Not only can Bobby and Clara help, but I can ask my sisters to help out a little. They don't have as many kids as we do, and they'd probably be happy to…"

"*Probably*. That's the most important word in the sentence you just said. *Probably*. Edith, darling…think about it. No one is in good shape financially, including us. They certainly can't be expected to provide meals for our kids when we drop them off at their houses. And they can't be expected to leave their own homes and come over here, drag their kids out and so forth…think of what they've already done when you were sick…." Robert shook his head back and forth. "No. I just don't see it. I just can't see how we'd do it."

Edith collected her thoughts. "What about this…I work during the evening and you work during the day. While you're at work, I take care of things around here and at night, you take care of things. Then we don't have to ask *anyone* for help."

Robert was still shaking his head. "I don't want my wife out working at night. And when would I check my traps? When would I go hunting?"

So that's what it comes down to. What Robert wants to do. Edith fought back tears, which always seemed to spring to her eyes when she was mad.

"I think Bobby could watch the kids by himself that long, don't you?"

"Edith, he comes with me. I'm teaching him how to hunt and trap. He's thirteen. This is the age for teaching him."

"Clara is twelve. She surely could manage for short periods."

"A new baby? Three others five years old or less? Edith, Edith…what are you thinking? What's come over you?"

Christmas. That's what's come over me. Christmas and being poor. Being poor and scraping for every nickel. That's what's come over me. Edith remained quiet for a minute, composing herself, then said, "I'm tired of not having anything to put under the tree for these kids year after year."

"What do you mean? They always have stuff under the tree."

"Yes, the same *old* stuff re-made or re-painted or re-sewn. Chocolate drops given to us by the church. Pity candy. I'm tired of it, Robert. *Tired* of it!" She stood up. "Do you know Mary's been saving pennies to buy her brothers and sisters gifts at the dime store? She probably has more money than *we* do." She turned to leave the room.

"Next week, I'm taking Mary to Tiffin to spend her pennies. When I do, I'm looking for a job. Even if it's part time, I'll be contributing something to this family."

Robert followed her into their bedroom. Her back to him, Edith was brushing her hair furiously.

"It's a wonder you don't yank every hair out of your head,

Edith. Calm down." He put his hands on her shoulders, but she brushed him off and turned to face him.

"Don't try to talk me out of this, Robert. I've made up my mind."

"I can see that. I won't try to talk you out of it. I'll let you think on it and over time, I believe you'll see I'm right."

She wanted to shout at him, shake him, slap him but instead, held on to her hairbrush with a death grip. She'd show him.

***

Edith looked through the 'help wanted' ads before she and Mary made good on their planned shopping trip. Edith saw very little she was qualified for. She was beginning to realize that without a high school diploma, it would be challenging to find a job. *If only I wouldn't have had to drop out of school,* she thought with a sigh. *But then, who would've taken care of Dad and the boys?* Life had taken a path similar to other kids her age, but it caused a problem now. Still, she hoped she might be able to find something in retail or a service position of some kind.

On the appointed day, Edith and Mary walked through downtown Tiffin, looking in shop windows, pulling their scarves tighter around their necks to protect them from the cold. Not one store had a "help wanted" poster in the window, but that didn't stop Edith from asking inside. By the time they got to the dime store, she was discouraged. Nevertheless, she didn't let Mary see it.

The young girl's eyes shone with excitement. She had saved about seventy cents and was sure she would be able to find gifts for all her brothers and sisters. As she walked up and down the aisles, she realized how little she could get with her pennies. If Edith hadn't been so before, now she was even more disheartened seeing her daughter's dismay. Mary's eyes welled up.

"Mom, I can't buy anything here. I don't see anything less than ninety-eight cents."

"I know, my darling. But there might be something if we keep looking in every nook and cranny. You just never know what we might come up with." Edith smiled encouragement, fighting back her own tears.

They continued their search, picking up different items only to find the prices higher than they had expected. Pick up a toy, look at the price tag, lay it back down, move on.

A salesclerk approached. "Can I help you find anything in particular?" she asked.

"We're window shopping, I guess," Edith said. "My daughter has saved some money to get her brothers and sisters a gift."

The clerk bent down to be closer to Mary's face. "How many brothers and sisters do you have?" she asked.

"Seven," Mary replied.

The clerk quickly stood back up straight, astonished.

"My. That's quite a family," the clerk said, turning her gaze to Edith.

Edith said, "It *is* quite a family. In fact, do you know if there are any jobs available here at the store? I could use some work to help *feed* that big family."

"Oh, gosh, I don't think so. At the beginning of the Christmas season we were hiring a few people just to get through the holidays, but even *they* have been laid off now. We just don't have as many people shopping this year. And any time we *have* had jobs open, you can't believe the number of people that come in to apply."

Edith bit her lip. "Do you suppose I could at least leave my name and phone number?"

"There's a whole application you have to fill out. Hold on and I'll get one for you. You can fill it out and mail it back to us."

The clerk disappeared. Edith looked around. Even though being time for Christmas shopping, there weren't many customers in the store. *What chance do I have? If only we lived in the city!* But she knew she'd never be happy in a bigger city. She watched Mary pick up another toy and put it back down.

The clerk reappeared. "Here's the application. All I can say is fill it out completely, and good luck. Frankly, you'll need it. Sorry to be so blunt."

The clerk approached Mary again. "Listen, how much money do you have saved up?"

"Seventy cents."

"Come with me. I think I have the perfect present for you."

Mary followed the clerk, with Edith close behind. The clerk stopped, grabbed something, then spun around to show it to Mary.

"How about a game your whole family can play? Tiddlywinks!"

"What? I never heard of that," Mary said.

"It's a great game for kids of all ages. Do you have older or younger brothers and sisters?"

"Both."

"This is the game for you. And it's only sixty-eight cents!"

Mary's face lit up. "And everyone can play it?"

"You bet! Even your mom and dad!"

"Mom, can I buy it?"

Edith smiled. "Sure, honey. It's your money. You buy what you want. I know everyone will think it's a great present. On Christmas, dad and I will teach you all how to play it."

As Mary skipped after the clerk to the check-out register clutching the precious gift, Edith thought about how to face her husband. There were no jobs. She would not find work. She could not contribute the financial well-being of her family.

***

"Look at it this way, Edith. You're the spine of this family. Without you, nothing happens as it should. Isn't that enough of a contribution? You should be proud of yourself. Look at what you've been through..." Robert trailed off, seeing the frustration on Edith's face. Nothing he could say would help, and he knew it.

She wasn't sure she could even find words to describe how she felt. After a minute, she said, "I love you and these kids more than anything in the world, but I need something *more*. I've helped take care of a family since I was seven years old—*seven*. I can do more than clean house and wipe noses and cook a meal. I have the energy for more, the desire for more. I feel like I'm disappearing into the walls of this house."

Now Robert was quiet. She had never expressed anything like this before. He wanted Edith to feel better about what she meant to their family.

"Listen, if you worked, we'd have to hire help for around here, I'm sure. So you're saving us money by being home. And Edith, I've never known someone who can stretch a dime like you. *That's* your financial contribution, don't you see?"

Edith spoke but there was no conviction in her voice.

"Of course. You're right. I just have to learn to look at things the way you do."

"That's my girl. I love you. You're a wonderful wife and mother." Robert pecked her on the cheek and left the room.

Edith sat, thinking. A couple of the kids came in to get a snack, but she was so absorbed in her thoughts that she didn't even notice who. She sighed and shook her head. She was destined to be a housewife and mother. Forever.

28

June 1943

"We got our report cards!" Clara called as she jogged up the sidewalk. "I got all A's!"

"That's great, Squirt," Robert said, taking a sip of coffee. "Let's see the rest of them. Did anyone else get all A's? You kids are way smarter than I was when I was your age, so I wouldn't be surprised."

"Oh, Dad," Clara said as she hugged her father. "You know, you can quit calling me Squirt any old day now. I'm almost thirteen. *And*...you're smarter than you let on. Maybe you're just smart in a different way than school learning."

Robert was surprised by her comment. "I'm glad you think so, Clara. Your mom had to quit school in seventh grade, and I had to quit in the eighth. We had to help our families."

"I know, Dad. You've told me that about a million times," Clara laughed as she went into the kitchen to help with the morning dishes.

Robert opened the other envelopes as he walked into the kitchen. He poured himself one final cup of coffee before work. The kitchen was warm—forewarning of a hot, humid day—and Clara washed the dishes, clinking them together as she put them on the drainboard.

He sat at the kitchen table to review the reports on all the kids. Alton, just a first grader, had good marks. So did Phyllis. Mary's grades were lower than he liked to see, but he and Edith knew Mary struggled to learn. She was timid, hated to ask questions, and would barely speak in class. They even held her back a year so she could be in the same class as Phyllis, hoping Phyllis' presence would improve Mary's confidence. The results were not that encouraging.

Then he opened Bobby's report card.

Bobby's grades were good—all A's and B's. But his teacher had written a long note about behavior.

"Bobby is a good student, but he can be disruptive. You may remember the note I sent home about him cutting Donna Swerline's hair in class right after Christmas. In April, he hid every piece of chalk for the blackboard in his desk. He spends more time joking around than studying. Otherwise, his grades would be even better. Finally, about one week before the end of the school year, he was caught pulling out the choke on one of the school buses, trying to disable it from running. I hope that over the summer you can work with him to correct these behaviors so that in the fall, he will be ready for his freshman year. I consider freshman year critical to development of habits he will need to successfully graduate from Sycamore High."

Robert put the pile of grade cards in the middle of the table. Fuming, he wondered why he hadn't heard a word about any of this till now. A note after Christmas? He hadn't seen any such note. He brushed his hand through his hair. *It's a wonder he didn't get suspended.*

He didn't have time to deal with it. This discussion would have to wait till he was done shearing the sheep over at the McEntyre place.

"Edith," he called, not knowing exactly where his wife was at that minute. "I'm leaving for work. The kids' grade cards came this morning. They're on the table."

"All right," he heard, maybe from the kids' rooms upstairs. "See you at supper!"

He gulped down the last of his coffee, set his cup in the sink a little too hard, and went out to his car. Work would give him all day to think about how best to handle his ornery son.

***

Edith finished making beds, then started the laundry. She poured her own cup of coffee. Kathy was toddling around the kitchen with her favorite teddy bear. *I'm glad she's walking,* Edith thought. *Now, to get her out of diapers.* Roma and Verlin were playing 'chase' in the living room. "You kids quit running in the house! Go outside if you want to run!" she called. The two energetic children ran through the kitchen and out the back door without a word. The older kids were upstairs, supposedly cleaning their rooms.

Time for a break, she thought.

Edith picked up the grade cards Robert left on the table. She was happy to see that everyone was doing so well. Except for Mary—they needed to figure out how to help her. Pairing her up with Phyllis might not have been the best answer but they sure couldn't afford a tutor. Then she opened Bobby's report. She looked at his grades first, satisfied with what she saw. The teacher's message made her sit straight up in her seat.

'You may remember the note I sent home about him cutting Donna Swerline's hair in class right after Christmas.' Not only did Edith not remember it, she was certain she had never seen it. She called upstairs to her oldest.

"Robert Riedel, Jr., come down here right now!" She returned to the table and sat, arms folded, stern set to her jaw.

Catching the tone of her voice, Bobby wasted no time in heeding his mother's call. He knew 'mad' when he heard it.

"What is it, Mom?"

"Sit down. Take a look at this note from your teacher."

Bobby's face went white. "What do you mean?"

"What do I *mean*? I mean take a look at this note from your teacher." Edith sounded as disgusted as she felt.

Bobby looked first at his grades, saying them out loud. "Arithmetic, B. Civics, A. English, A. Geography, B. Science, B." When he finally got to the teacher's note, he read in silence. When he was done, he put the report card on the table and looked at his mother.

"Suppose you tell me what happened to this note your teacher sent home at Christmas time? And maybe you can tell me a little more about the bus."

Bobby fidgeted in his seat. He knew better than to lie. His mother could sniff out a lie before three words were out of his mouth.

"I'm sorry, Mom." Best to start with the apology. "I didn't want to bother you with anything. I mean, you just had Kathy and everything..." He trailed off, trying to think of any other reasonable excuse.

"At Christmas time, Kathy was already eight months old. I hadn't 'just had' her. Try again."

Now Bobby made a full confession, the words pouring out of him. "Mom, it wasn't any big thing. I just cut the ends off Donna's pigtails. She wasn't even really that mad. And yeah, I hid the chalk, but it was just a little joke for April Fool's day."

"What about the bus?"

He looked down at his feet. This was *most* embarrassing.

"Well, see, Mom, I like this girl. Her name is Jean—Jean Walton—and she's real cute and nice, and I thought if I made the bus so it couldn't run, I could sit by her for a while longer while they figured it out."

Now it was all Edith could do to not laugh out loud. She hadn't expected this answer at all. She was glad her son was looking at his feet and not at her eyes, which would have given her away. She composed herself.

"You can bet that when your dad gets home, we're going to be talking about this again, and you can expect some discipline. I don't know what that will be right now but get ready to explain all this to your dad later. Now go on…go finish cleaning your room."

Bobby slunk away. Edith knew his dread of further discussion would be the worst punishment they could inflict. She chuckled to herself. *If all eight kids get into this same kind of mischief, God help us.*

***

"What's for supper?" Robert walked in the back door and sniffed the air—something wonderful awaited.

"Oh, just meat loaf," came Edith's reply.

"One of my favorites. I'm starved."

"It'll be ready before long. You're kind of late today."

"I stopped over at Bud Pittman's to talk to him for a few minutes after I got done at McEntyre's."

Edith stopped mashing the potatoes. "What about?"

"Our number one son." Robert washed his hands, grabbing Edith's apron to dry them on while she gave him a kiss on the cheek.

"This should be interesting," she said. "What sage advice did Bud give you?"

"I didn't ask his advice…I asked him to give our boy a job."

"A job! Doing what?"

"Just helping around the farm. I figure baling season ought to be a good way to work off some of Bobby's extra energy. Wish I had as much energy as that kid." Robert sat at the kitchen table.

"Are you considering that a punishment?"

After a moment, Robert replied. "More than punishment, I think of it as discipline. Bud will pay him a little, so he'll not just be working for free, but he'll definitely work *hard.*"

"I've been thinking about this all day, too. Wait till you hear why he pulled the choke on the bus. I almost laughed right out loud. Anyway, I think he should do some work at the school this summer...help clean classrooms or something like that."

"That's a good idea...that would be more like punishment, so he gets the message that actions have consequences. I like the idea of him working for Bud, too, though."

"Me too. Let's talk about it more after supper." Edith put a pat of fresh butter on the pile of mashed potatoes and yelled, "C'mon kids. Supper's on."

A herd of elephants headed toward the kitchen, *or at least that's what it sounds like*, Edith thought. Last to arrive, she picked up Kathy and put her in the highchair. The other seven elbowed their way to the table.

Robert chucked Kathy under the chin. "How's my little pumpkin?" The tot smiled and said, "Daddy!" Then Robert said, "All right, the rest of you...settle down. There's plenty for everyone. Who's saying the prayer tonight?"

"I will, Dad," Bobby said as he folded his hands and bowed his head.

"Make it good," Robert said. Bobby's head shot up and he looked at his father, stern and unsmiling.

"Heavenly Father," Bobby began, "thank you for the delicious food my mom has made for us to eat. Thank you for my family and all the love we have for each other. Thank you for forgiving us when we make dumb mistakes. Please take care of our soldiers in the war and bring them home safe. Amen."

"Nice job," Edith said as the free-for-all of supper began. There was little noise beyond the clinking of spoons against serving bowls and occasional giggles from the children. Bobby helped Roma and Verlin get their food, then waited till everyone else had a plate before he finally filled his own.

After everyone had finished and the little ones had been excused, Edith asked, "Whose turn is it to help with dishes?"

"My turn," Phyllis said.

"Phyllis, why don't you let Bobby take your chore tonight? Why don't you go play the piano for us? I'd like to hear some hymns. Clara and Mary, you go with her and the three of you can sing," Robert suggested.

The girls jumped at the chance to get out of kitchen clean-up. "Okay, Dad!" They practically ran out of the room.

Now it was down to Robert, Edith, and Bobby. Edith began scraping away scraps from dirty dishes and packaging up viable leftovers. Bobby started picking up dirty dishes to transfer to the sink. Robert remained at the table, drinking his coffee. He watched his son work as he thought about how and when to start his questioning. From the living room, he could hear Phyllis, Mary, and Clara. *Those girls have good voices. Phyllis is getting better at the piano all the time*, he thought. The music was a bit of a distraction, so he refocused.

Their backs to Robert, Edith was already washing dishes, and Bobby was drying them.

"Bobby, what would you like to tell me about your grade card?" Robert began.

Bobby stopped drying for just a second—the only sign that Robert's voice had startled him. He put a dry dinner plate on the counter and turned to face his father.

"Dad, I'm sorry. I know I pulled some jokes this year and that I probably shouldn't have, but…"

"*Probably*? Did you say *probably*? You know better than that."

"Yes sir."

"Go on. I'm waiting for an explanation."

Bobby sat down across from his father. He wasn't sure his legs would hold him while he relayed his story.

"Well, the first thing that happened was me cutting Donna's pigtails. I sat behind her in class."

"Do you still sit behind her?" Robert interrupted.

"No, not anymore. Mrs. Peterman moved me after I cut her hair."

"All right. Go on."

"Well, see, her pigtails are real long, and they were hanging on my desk. She was kind of moving her head back and forth, and they brushed through the ink on my paper and smeared it all up so you couldn't read my writing."

"I can see how that might be a problem since your writing is kind of sloppy anyway," Edith interjected over her shoulder.

Bobby looked over at his mother but decided he might be wise to refrain from any comment.

"Yes, Mom." He looked back at Robert and continued.

"I got out my scissors and just trimmed up the inky part of Donna's hair. Since I cut one pigtail, I had to cut the *other* one, too, so they would match. At first Donna got mad. Then when I told her what happened, she wasn't really mad anymore, but Mrs. Peterman was."

"What about the note your teacher sent home?"

"I threw it out the bus window."

Robert, his elbows resting on the table, put his index fingers up to the bridge of his nose, closed his eyes and shook his head back and forth. After a minute, he lifted his head, looking back up at Bobby.

"What about the chalk?"

"Aw, Dad, that was just an April Fool's Day joke. As soon as Mrs. Peterman realized it was gone, everybody had a laugh and I gave it back to her right away."

"Okay. That all seems fairly easy to understand. Now tell me about the school bus. Why were you messing around with the choke?"

Bobby's face turned crimson. He glanced at Edith, whose back was still toward the men. Bobby noticed her shoulders shaking. Was she laughing or crying? He hoped she wasn't crying. He hated to see his mom cry. He turned back to Robert.

"Dad, I know I shouldn't have done that."

"Darn right you shouldn't have! If something would have gone wrong, I'd have had to pay for the bus repairs. What on God's green earth ever possessed you?"

"Jean Walton. I mean, Jean didn't tell me to do it or anything, but see, I kind of like her and I try to sit by her on the bus whenever I can. She's pretty, and she's nice. Oh, and she's really funny, too."

For one second, Robert had a hazy memory of feeling that way about his beautiful Edith.

Bobby continued. "I wanted to have more time to sit by Jean. I didn't think I was doing any harm…just delaying the ride home for a while. Guess I shoulda just called her on the phone."

"You don't think you've got plenty of time for girls, son? You're only fourteen."

"Well, I might get drafted."

"Drafted?! What in the world gives you that idea?"

"You know, Dad…the war. Lots of guys from Sycamore High are going to the war. Pretty soon it'll be my turn." He hung his head.

Edith whirled around, a frightened look on her face. Robert emptied his coffee cup and sat it down quietly.

"Look at me, son."

Bobby raised his head.

"By the time you're old enough to join the service, I hope and pray this war will be over. In the meantime, what you did was a type of vandalism. You're lucky the school isn't pressing charges."

Bobby looked shocked, eyes wide, mouth hanging open.

"You wasted the bus driver's time, the maintenance man's time, and you caused other children on the bus to get home late. Their moms were probably worried about them."

"I didn't think of all that," Bobby muttered.

"That's obvious. Look son, you've got good grades. They're not as good as they could be, but I'm not mad about them. But all this joking around stuff has got to end. You've got to get serious about school."

"I will be next year, Dad. I promise you that." Bobby started to get up from the table.

"Sit back down, young man. Your mom and I have something to tell you."

"She's not gonna have another baby is she?"

It was Robert's turn to look shocked. "Good heavens, no! You're not, are you, Edith?"

Edith's face was somber as she dried her hands on a dish towel. Robert prepared for the news. Then she smiled wide. "No! I most certainly am not."

Robert's relief was evident. "Okay. Come sit with us."

"Sure," she answered as she joined the men.

Robert returned his attention to their boy. "Son," he began, "you're getting ready to start high school where they don't put up with such shenanigans. They'll kick you right out of school. Do you understand? I want you to graduate high school."

"I want to graduate, too, Dad."

Edith spoke up. "You don't know what your dad and I would give to have our high school diplomas. We didn't have that opportunity, Bobby."

"I know, Mom. I know how important it is."

"Then why in the world aren't you behaving like it's important? Bobby, you're smart. Way smarter than either one of us, but you don't always show much common sense. That's part of growing up, too. It's not just your age. It's the common sense you show."

Bobby looked down again. "I'm sorry, Mom...Dad."

"Your mother and I have been talking about this. We have some ideas about how you can gain some wisdom from all this."

Bobby looked back and forth between his parents, not sure what to make of this pronouncement. He knew he was too old for a paddling. Grounded. Maybe he was going to be grounded.

"First of all, tomorrow morning we're going up to the school to talk to the principal. We're going to see if she can't find some jobs for you to do around the building, whether it's cleaning classrooms or burning all the trash or cleaning the buses. I'm sure they've got something for you."

"I agree with your father about this," Edith jumped in. "You caused problems at school, and this is a way you can repay them."

"Yes ma'am," Bobby said.

"There's one more thing," Robert said. "You're going to work for Bud Pittman this summer."

"What will I do for him?"

"Any old thing he asks you to do, that's what. You'll work for him till about a week before school starts back up."

Bobby didn't know what to say. Mr. Pittman had a big farm— huge expanses of wheat fields and soybeans and corn. But he had a tractor. Maybe he'd get to drive the tractor.

"Anything else, Dad?"

"I want you to apologize to your teacher and to the bus driver and maintenance man at school."

"Oh, I already did that," Bobby replied. "I apologized to Donna, too."

"All right, then. I guess that's it. After you dry the dishes, you're excused." Robert stood up. "And son, remember this. We don't have much, maybe, but we have our good name. You always want to protect your good name. Oh...and try not to worry about the war, now, okay?"

"Yes sir." Bobby stood, also, and headed for the dish rack. "I'll have these done in no time, Mom."

"Don't forget Bible reading. When you're done, come on in the living room. I'm going to get the kids gathered up."

"All right."

Edith and Robert went out to the front porch and sat on a glider they had there for evenings like this. They watched the sun setting, pushing the glider forward and back with their feet.

After a few minutes of silence, Robert spoke. "I should have known it had something to do with a girl," he chuckled.

"He's turning into a young man, you know, and he gets all that orneriness right from you," Edith said, her eyes laughing. "He's just like you, up and down."

"Ha! I think he's just like *you*." Robert pecked her cheek.

Edith stood to go get the kids together for Bible time. "Who chased who, exactly, in this relationship? I'm pretty sure *I* didn't make the first move."

Robert stood up and grabbed her by the waist. "Do you regret it? Do you ever regret marrying me and having all these kids? Our life together hasn't been easy."

"Regret it? Never in a million years."

They kissed—a deep, warm kiss that comes of abiding love.

"Better watch it or we'll be adding a ninth," Edith said.

"After eight, what's one more?" Robert kidded as Edith groaned and pulled away, opening the screen door to the house.

"You sleep on the couch tonight, all right?" she kidded.

Robert winked, and she turned to go in the house, calling, "Kids! You kids come on in the living room…."

The moon was just starting to be evident in the darkening sky. Robert enjoyed its pale beauty for a few seconds and whispered a prayer of gratitude before going in to join his family.

29

March 1944

March is a fickle month, Robert thought, looking around at the landscape. *Doesn't know whether it wants to snow or send up flowers.*

His gas ration having run out for the month, he walked home from work tired and worried. Another child had entered the world during this vacillating month—Richard, fondly dubbed "Dickie."

Number nine—he's doing fine, played over and over in his brain, giving him a rhythm to walk to. Richard was strong and healthy, thankfully, but Robert wasn't making one penny more than before the newest was born, and he wasn't always getting his full forty hours at the pottery. The pottery was one factory that had not been re-tooled to meet the needs of the military. Nevertheless, he stayed gone all day and didn't let Edith see his paychecks so as not to worry her.

Rationing of many goods continued, making it more difficult to feed and clothe his brood. He was hunting and trapping all he could, trying to make extra income with the animal hides and putting meat on the table. He felt discouraged. It was his job to provide for his family. *But how much more can one man do?*

Then he thought of Edith. She worked day and night to provide for the family, too, in her own way. *It might be woman's work, but she's busy from sun-up till sundown.* He was thankful that the girls could help her more now. Clara tutored the younger kids. Mary was an excellent cook. With her joyful outlook, Phyllis kept the little ones occupied with games and music. *If not for those three...*he thought.

Yet he also knew that Edith was more than capable of handling a large family. She had demonstrated it over and over.

Thinking about his wife and kids helped him adjust his own attitude as he walked. He knew he was blessed.

Things could always be worse. Put that one on repeat.

As he strolled up the sidewalk to his home, he heard laughter and squealing coming from inside. He walked through the door to find A.C. Cewalt sitting at the kitchen table, performing card tricks for the children. Edith looked up from the sleight of hand to greet him.

"Hi, honey! Mr. Cewalt came over and washed windows today. He's staying for supper tonight." Edith beamed—her smile always lifted his heart, even when he was exhausted.

Robert didn't show his fatigue for entertaining. "That sounds good. A.C., we're happy to see you," he said as he crossed the room to shake Mr. Cewalt's hand. "I have to go get cleaned up, but I'll be right back, and we can catch up on how you've been."

Edith followed Robert into their bedroom. "I can see how tired you are," she began. "I didn't know what else to do. He needed a meal, but you know A.C.—he won't accept anything he hasn't worked for."

Robert sat on the edge of the bed for a second before answering. "He's a good man, but it seems like he shoulda found work by now. *Regular* work. There must be some unfilled jobs out there."

"Honey, I don't think he *can* work. You should've seen him cleaning the windows. He moved as slow as molasses in January, and I don't believe he was malingering. I think he's physically unable to work. He must have bad rheumatism or something."

"Well, I'm not upset about him being here, don't get me wrong. If he did the windows for you and we have enough to feed him, all the better, right? We've gotta help each other in this world. These are rough times." He brushed his hand through his hair, pushing it back from his forehead.

Edith smiled at the familiar gesture and looked intently at his down-turned face. Something else was wrong, but she knew he'd talk about it in his own time. "I'm gonna go finish up a couple of things for supper. You want a cup of hot coffee while you visit with A.C.?"

"Nah. I think I'll just drink some plain old water."

"I'll get a glass ready for you." She left the room.

Robert stared ahead at Edith's closet door. There weren't many clothes in that closet. Certainly not the kind of clothes he would've liked for her to own. There weren't many clothes in his *own* closet, but he didn't care like a woman might. He made himself a vow—if he *ever* made extra money again, some of it would go into Edith's wardrobe.

He rose. Time to go out and engage in conversation with A.C. and put on a happy face and play with the kids; time to go a little hungry so that the children might be filled up.

***

Dinner was finished in a heartbeat, it seemed. With eight growing children (*not including little Dickie*) and two adults at the table, food never lasted long. Tonight, there had been *three* adults. Robert poured himself a cup of coffee and turned to Mr. Cewalt.

"Cuppa coffee?" he asked.

"That sounds good right now. Sure."

Robert poured a second cup and handed it to their visitor. Edith had rounded up the kids for Bible reading, and the two men retreated to the front porch to enjoy the spring-like evening.

"Robert, you sure have a fine family," Mr. Cewalt began as he sat down on a wooden ladder-back chair. "Your Edith is a heck of a cook."

"Yes she is, and she's teaching the girls how to cook, too. Whoever marries those girls someday will benefit from Edith's instruction." Robert laughed and patted his stomach. "I have to keep busy just to keep from growing a gut."

"You *do* keep busy all the time. Edith was telling me about all the hunting and trapping you do. Do you get much for the pelts?"

"I get the going rate, whatever it is at the time. Of course, minks are usually pretty good, but most everything else rises and falls based on how many people are looking for that kind of pelt."

"Is it hard to trap?"

"Not really. Just time consuming. I have to get up early to go check the traps every morning before I go to work and a lot of times in the evening on the way home."

Mr. Cewalt considered this idea for a moment. "When do you get to have time with your kids?"

"What do you mean?" Robert raised his coffee cup to his lips, but Mr. Cewalt's next question stopped him before he took a sip.

"Do you get to have much time with the family?"

Robert held his coffee cup between his two hands. The mug

felt warm, and the evening was quickly cooling down. He shivered, took a sip of the warm beverage, and considered his answer.

"Of course I get to have time with the kids on the weekends, but during the week, not too much. By the time I get home from work, it's supper time. Then the kids get rounded up for Bible stories. Before long, they're off to bed though the older kids stay up later now. I usually get a little more time with *them*."

Mr. Cewalt tipped his chair backwards so that it sat on its two rear legs. He rocked the chair back and forth with his feet. Finally, he sat straight up again.

"Could you teach me how to trap? I mean, maybe I could go to work for you, check your traps and so forth. I wouldn't need high pay. Just a little portion for doing the leg work."

Robert hadn't considered that this kind of 'ask' might be coming. He was caught off guard and struggled to come up with a truthful answer that didn't reveal how worried he was about money.

"A.C., I can see how that would be a big help to me, but honestly, with this family I need every dime I make from trapping. Yeah, it's keeping me away from them to a degree, but like I said, I go early in the morning—the kids are getting off to school then, anyway—or I go in the evening before I get home. The kids don't know the difference. To them, I'm still just at work. I'd love to help you out, but..." He trailed off, not knowing what else to add.

"It's all right, Robert. I just thought I'd check."

"Haven't you been able to find any work, A.C.?"

"Oh, I still do odd jobs. I get by all right. I did think maybe we could figure out something that would be helpful to both of us, but it's okay if you don't think it would work. It really is." Mr. Cewalt leaned back again. "Yep, yep. You've got a big family to support. I reckon every penny comes in handy these days."

Robert shivered again and said, "It's getting chilly out here. Let's go into the den." The two men stood up, but before they opened the door, Mr. Cewalt put his hand on Robert's shoulder.

"I admire men like you. Men who will do anything to keep body and soul together and make sure their families have all they need. If I had been a little more like that as a younger man, I'd be in a better situation now. I appreciate that you and your family even let an old toad like me show up and have a meal."

"Well, A.C., you always earn your meal. A lot of people just walk around with their hands out." Robert opened the door.

"Come on. Let's have another cup of coffee."

"No, no, I need to head home for the night. I enjoyed talking to you." He set his cup in the kitchen sink. "No need to interrupt Edith and the kids. Tell her I said thanks and good night, will ya?"

"Sure thing. Sure thing." Robert set his own cup in the sink and reached out to shake Mr. Cewalt's hand. "Come back any time, and if things start turning for the better, maybe we can still work out something on the trapping."

Mr. Cewalt smiled. He knew that was unlikely, but he said, "Thanks. I believe I'd enjoy working for you." He walked to the door, placed his hand on the doorknob and turned back to Robert.

"Don't let the years fly by you, Robert. Keep your kids close to you for as long as you can. Spend every minute you can with them. And hold on to that wife of yours. She's a gem. See ya 'round." With that, he was out the door and gone. Robert could hear his whistling floating back on the wind.

Someday I have to find out more about his life, Robert thought. He heard each of the kids taking a turn at prayer, their attempts full of the innocence and simplicity of childhood. He felt his heart swell for a minute, then he remembered.

Soon I might have more time with the kids than they would want. I sure hope things pick up at work. He straightened his shoulders and went to join his family, determined to hold his baby son, tuck the rest of the little ones into bed, and spend some time with the older kids before they all retired for the night.

He walked into the living room. It was the usual scene. Edith on the sofa, holding Richard, who was squirming, but quiet. Eight kids seated on the floor in a semi-circle with their heads bowed, murmuring their prayers.

Edith looked up and smiled. She beckoned him over with her free hand. He sat on the sofa beside her and reached for Richard. Edith looked surprised, then handed the baby over.

"And all God's children said…" Robert said aloud.

"Amen!" returned by eight voices.

"All right, you hooligans. Go get your PJs on," Edith said.

The thundering herd retreated to their rooms. Robert and Edith could hear them upstairs talking and laughing.

Robert looked at his infant. *A handsome baby if ever there was one.*

"Penny for your thoughts," Edith said.

"Hmmm. Well, where did we get all these kids?"

Edith laughed, throwing her head back and letting the sound bubble up from somewhere deep inside. It was like music to Robert.

"You big dope," she said. "From the stork, of course."

He smiled at her. "Well, they're all okay, but let's stop with this one. I'm not sure we could do much better than the kids we already have."

"Fine by me!" she laughed. Then Edith realized how serious he was.

"Are you okay?" she asked.

"I'm just tired and worried about money. As usual, right? Tonight A.C. asked if he could run my traps for me and I had to turn him down. Honey, I have to tell you something. I wasn't going to, but you should know. I'm not getting a full forty hours at work right now, and we're going to have to tighten our belts a little more again."

She leaned back against the couch and said, "You really *are* a big dope. Did you think I didn't know something was going on? I've seen the worry on your face. I've seen your lunch still in your lunch box, too. That told the tale, you know."

"Oh gees. I never thought of that."

She laughed again. "Robert Riedel, if there's one thing we've gotten good at, it's rubbing two nickels together to come up with a few extra pennies. We'll make it. But think about this. I still could try to find work. The older kids can help with all these little ones, and if you're home more, we wouldn't need someone to babysit."

Robert knew that Edith had been thinking about this for some time. *Why did I ever think I could hide anything like this from her? She's too smart for that.*

"Do you think there's anything out there? Remember, you tried once."

"Yes I did, and I can try again. Let me at least try."

"All right. It does make more sense now than it did before considering that I'll be here on the home front a little more."

"We're out of gas rations, too, aren't we, my darling husband?"

"Yes, but we get our new coupons before long."

"When we do, let's go looking for work."

"I never knew a girl so determined to work a regular job."

"For your information, I'm not a girl. I'm a woman, but I'm ready to do more than 'woman's work.'"

It was Robert's turn to laugh. He laughed partly out of relief that she had taken the news so well, but partly because he could never fool his wife, anyway, and she was the most stubborn, persistent, resolute woman he had ever known.

"You'll always be *my* girl."

"Well, that's okay, I guess. C'mon. Let's hit the sack."

Richard had fallen asleep, despite the conversation and laughter.

"He's a blessing," Edith said.

Number nine—he's doing fine, Robert thought as the couple made their way to the bedroom with the newest Riedel in his arms.

30

September 1945

On an unusually warm day that included an azure sky embracing puffy white clouds, Robert and Edith made off for Sycamore Creek with nine kids, multiple fishing poles, and a picnic lunch of bologna sandwiches. Sunday school and church had been almost unbearable because of the humidity, and the kids had squirmed their way through the sermon. Now they were barefoot, in dungarees, and free. The younger children skipped ahead and sang. The older kids lagged behind, talking about which boy each girl liked. Bobby, Jr. was instructing them as to why they should pick other fellows. Robert would have held Edith's hand if he had one free from fishing gear.

"You kids don't go too far ahead," Robert called after the kids. He chuckled at the sight of Richard, now a year and a half old, trying to keep up with his brothers and sisters.

"It's a wonderful day, Edith. Wonderful."

"It's a *hot* day, but yes, it's wonderful, too. Do you think the fish will be biting? It's so hot, won't they be down deep where the water is cooler?"

"Probably, but that's all right. This will give the kids something to do and keep them from driving us crazy this afternoon. Maybe we'll get lucky and hit something so we can have a fish dinner."

"I think I'd just as soon have watermelon tonight. Doesn't that sound refreshing?"

"Sure does. Does anyone still have watermelon around?"

"Oh, golly, I don't know. Probably not. I might have a muskmelon out in the garden, still. I can check when we get home."

"Fish, fried taters, muskmelon. Sounds good to me."

"Pop, can we put our feet in the water?" Roma called over her shoulder. "I'm hot!"

"Let's talk about that when we get there," Robert answered, picking up his step. He was sweating, and he understood how the kids felt. He wouldn't mind putting his feet in the water, either.

A lazy afternoon passed, and all nine kids got their feet wet. The older kids waded with the littler ones, making sure no one got the bottoms of their rolled trousers too soaked. When horseplay and splashing started, Robert reminded them that they were 'scaring the fish.'

"Do you ruffians want fish for supper? Then you have to settle down a little." He smiled over at Edith, who was watching her bobber. Deep in concentration, she didn't see him glance her way.

"What are you thinking about?" he asked.

"Why I've never been able to find a job," she said. Blunt as ever, she kept her eyes forward. Her tone was even. "I think it's because I didn't finish high school. I should've finished high school."

"We *both* should have, but that wasn't the way it worked back then. We were expected to help our families. Then we had our *own* family. Now we help *them*, right? I work at the pottery. You work at home. It's just a continuation of how life goes." Robert reeled in a nice bluegill, unhooked it, and put it on a stringer. "I s'pose someday you'll find a regular job if you really want one."

Edith looked up at him. He was standing right beside her, now, and the sun was so bright that it was hard to see his face. She shielded her eyes with her left hand and held on to her fishing pole with her right.

"Robert, what do you think will change? I'll tell you what— nothing. No one will hire a woman who didn't even graduate high school. I know that now. I've figured it out. I'm just a housewife and mother. That's it." She turned back to her fishing. "That's it," she repeated.

Robert knelt down beside her. "That's a *lot*," he said. "Edith, you are so impatient to have a job. You already have the most important job in all the world. Isn't that enough for you?"

"No." She turned to face him again. He could see the frustration on her face, her eyes burning into him.

"But why, honey? Are you unhappy?"

Her face softened. She turned back to the creek. "I don't think I'd qualify it as unhappy," she started, "but it's not *happy* either." She paused.

"I feel unfulfilled," she finally said.

Robert stood up. His legs were cramping from kneeling. He was taken aback by his wife's answer. *Unfulfilled.* What did that mean? What was it about a job that would make her feel any better? Was anyone *ever* fulfilled by a job? He was more fulfilled by hunting or fishing or teaching the kids some new skill. Work was just work. He walked back over to his fishing pole. Unsure of how to respond, he said nothing.

Edith regretted her frankness. She knew Robert wouldn't understand. *He gets out of the house. He doesn't see think about the fact that I talk to children all day long. It's not that I don't love them, but I need some adults to talk to once in a while. I do laundry, cook, and clean up messes every day. The sameness of it is getting to me.*

She set down her pole, brushed some loose hair back from her forehead and re-fastened the strays with a bobby pin.

"I didn't mean to sound ungrateful, Robert."

"I know, honey. But trust me...work's not all it's cracked up to be."

Edith looked out over the creek once again and gave a deep sigh. The water was only a little muddy today, and the sun made it sparkle. Clara was guiding the little ones over the log she had infamously fallen from years ago. "Clara, I don't think that's a great idea," she called.

"All right, mom." Clara began figuring out how to shoo the children back in the direction they had come from, and realizing it was impossible to do without falling in the water, she led them to the opposite shore.

"For Pete's sake," Edith muttered. Then she called Bobby. "Bobby, go help your sister get those kids back over here."

"Okay, Mom." He took off for the log.

This is what I deal with day in and day out. Cleaning up little messes everywhere.

***

A decent catch led to a delicious fish dinner. Clara, Mary, and Roma worked on the dishes while Phyllis played the piano. All the girls sang. Even Kathy, only three, was learning the words to favorite hymns and singing along with her older sisters.

"I think we ought to see if we can get those girls on the radio," Robert said to no one in particular.

"They're good," Edith agreed, but she was distracted. Her conversation with Robert earlier in the day had left her feeling discouraged. She knew she should be happy, and she tried to fend off the feeling of *emptiness* inside her.

Phyllis had stopped playing and the singing had subsided.

"I think I'll turn on the radio," Edith said. "Maybe we can listen to some Glenn Miller. Girls, are you done?"

"Yes, Mom."

She crossed the room to the Philco and turned it on. Glenn Miller's Air Force band was always a pick-me-up. To her surprise, the President's voice had replaced music this evening.

Robert put down the paper. "What's that?"

"The President," she replied, and she sat back down.

President Truman spoke.

"*My fellow Americans, Supreme Allied Commander, General McArthur and Allied representatives on the battleship Missouri in Tokyo Bay, the thoughts and hopes of all America, indeed the civilized world, are centered tonight on the battleship Missouri. There, on that small piece of American soil, anchored in Tokyo Harbor, the Japanese have just officially laid down their arms.*"

Robert jumped up, throwing his newspaper aside. Edith froze, her hand to her mouth. Had they heard it right? They had heard it might be coming, but....

"Kids, kids...come in here!" Robert shouted. Children came running from all over the house, hearing the urgency in his voice.

"Be quiet now...listen."

"*They have signed terms of unconditional surrender. Four years ago, the thoughts and fears of the whole civilized world were centered on another piece of American soil. Pearl Harbor. The mighty threat to civilization which began there is now laid at rest.*"

There was no need to listen to anymore.

The older kids knew what this meant. The littler ones stood by, silent and wide-eyed. Suddenly, the room erupted with cheers led by Bobby, the little boys jumping up and down, girls dancing around in a circle, Edith with tears in her eyes, Robert grabbing her by the waist, hoisting her up out of her chair and pulling her in close for a kiss.

"It's finally over. I think we need some popcorn!" Robert declared.

"Yeah, yeah," shouted nine kids.

"I'll make it, honey" Robert said. "You sit down and get your Bible story for tonight ready for the kids."

Edith eased herself back down into her chair. She picked up the Bible and began leafing through it to just the right story…something about forgiveness. The world would need to know how to forgive if future wars were to be avoided. Ephesians. She knew there was something there.

Then she stopped. Her heart was overflowing with gratitude that the war was finally over, but something else occurred to her in that moment.

The boys would be coming home. They would need jobs. The jobs women had been handling. Her dream of work outside the home was over.

A few tears trickled down her cheek again, but she brushed them away. How could she even think such a thing? *I'm being selfish*, she thought. She heard laughter, corn popping, and happy voices in the kitchen.

You're lucky. Be happy. Stop reaching for something you can never have and be grateful for what you do have.

She found what she was looking for—Ephesians 4:32. A story about forgiveness and how important it was in God's eyes. Perfect for this evening with the kids.

Tomorrow, I better find something in here about gratitude she decided, and as her family rejoined her, she smiled her biggest smile. *They must never know….*

31
April 1946

"Did you see Mom when she came in the house?" As she spoke, Clara waved a feather duster in the air as if it were a magic wand.

"No. Why?" Mary said, keeping her focus on her dust mop.

"She threw her purse on the table and ran to her bedroom. She was crying."

Phyllis and Mary stopped their motion and sat on the bed. Clara sat opposite, facing them.

"Well, you know what *that* means," Phyllis said, and all three nodded.

"Pregnant," they said in unison.

The girls were quiet for a minute. Downstairs, they could hear their siblings playing. It was too chilly for them to be outside much today, and the noise of the four younger children could be deafening. As usual, Bobby was off in a corner somewhere, reading, doing nothing to direct their play to a quieter endeavor.

"C'mon you guys. We better go settle those kids down or Mom will be out there yelling pretty soon. Are you both done?" Clara asked.

"I still have to finish the boys' room," Mary said. "You and Phyllis go ahead. I'll be down in a few minutes."

Clara and Phyllis started for the stairway but were stopped in their tracks.

"If you kids don't settle down right now, I'm going to send every one of you to your rooms without supper!" Edith was already on the warpath. The noise in the den came to an abrupt halt.

"Holy moly. Let's get down there quick!" Phyllis muttered, and the girls raced down the steps to head off further shouting. They knew their mother was upset about something other than noise, but the little ones didn't know that.

Clara was first to cross the den and embrace her mother. Phyllis took Dickie and Kathy by the hands while directing Verlin and Alton to come along with her. "Let's go get a graham cracker, you guys."

As the biggest share of her offspring left the room, Edith's eyes filled with tears and she dropped to the closest chair. Clara knelt by her side.

"Mom, what's the matter? Are you pregnant again? You can tell me."

Edith looked at her daughter. Clara was becoming very grown up all of a sudden. Fifteen years old, and already the boys were coming around like moths to a flame.

"Clara, I need to tell your father first, but yes, I'm going to have another baby. I don't want you to say anything to the other children yet."

"Mom, I won't, but I have to tell you…Phyllis, Mary, and I all guessed it."

Edith dropped her head to her chest and dabbed her eyes. "I'm not very good at hiding things, am I?"

Clara wanted to laugh but squelched the impulse. Her heart tender, she said, "Mom, we've seen you crying when you come home from Doc Smith's with the last three kids. It was pretty easy to figure out."

Edith lifted her head. "You know it's not that I don't love each of you. It's just a lot sometimes."

"I get it, Mom. Really I do."

"Well, remember it when all these boys are hovering around, okay? You know what I mean, right?"

Clara blushed. "Yes, Mom. You don't have to worry about any of that. I'm going to go help Phyllis."

"Where's Mary?"

"Finishing cleaning upstairs. Is there anything else you want us to do?"

"Maybe you three could think about starting dinner. There's

two chickens out there to put in the oven. We'll open a couple of quarts of green beans and make some mashed potatoes."

"Got it." Clara left the room.

Edith stared into space, trying to process the idea of another pregnancy. How in the world could they manage another child?

She tried to think. Bobby was seventeen. He'd be graduating next spring. *Push one out of the nest, pull another in.*

In what way could she tell Robert? And how would he respond? *Work has picked up since the end of the war, thank God,* she thought, *but will it be enough? Ten kids.*

She shook her head to clear the negative thoughts, but she was despondent. She practiced smiling, but it was hard to make the muscles do what she wanted them to do. She could feel her brow wrinkling involuntarily. Her mouth was suddenly dry, and she felt nauseous. She closed her eyes and leaned back in the chair. A few seconds of deep breathing would make it all pass.

"Hey Mom. Are you sick?"

Bobby. His first concern was always whether she was sick.

"No, son. Not sick. Just tired."

"Okay." He left the room, oblivious. *My girls pick up on things faster than my boys.* In this case, that was probably just as well.

Her nausea was beginning to subside. She rose from a sitting position, careful not to stand too fast. *The last thing I need is to get dizzy and fall.*

She headed for the kitchen where four mouths were busy chewing graham crackers. She tried her hardest to smile, sitting with them at the table. They looked at her with round eyes, unsure if they should say anything.

"Kids, I'm sorry. I just had a little headache and you were being pretty loud. I didn't mean to get so mad."

"It's okay, Mom," Alton said. The other three shook their heads in agreement.

Edith reached over and ruffled his hair. "You know I don't like to be like that to you kids. I'm sorry."

"Mama feel bettow?" Dickie chirped.

"Yes, buddy, I sure do. I feel better." Edith stroked his cheek. His vocabulary was improving all the time. She was sure it was because Bobby read story books to him and the other kids. They were *all* developing a good vocabulary.

Mary bounced into the kitchen with a smile on her face but stopped in her tracks, her smile fading to uncertainty.

"Everything okay?" she asked.

"Well, certainly. Why don't you help your sisters with dinner? Maybe you can come up with some dessert for us," Edith said.

"How about baked apples?" Mary offered.

"Delicious. Let's have that."

Mary crossed the room to join her sisters, warily eyeing her mother's interactions with the younger children.

"She doesn't look mad anymore," she whispered to Clara and Phyllis.

"I'm not," Edith said without looking at Mary. "My hearing is very good, you know."

Clara, Phyllis and Mary looked at each other without another word, then set about their tasks. Phyllis started singing a hymn.

"This little light of mine, I'm gonna let it shine…"

It wasn't long before all the children in the room were singing, Edith right along with them. Bobby came in with a copy of "Moby Dick" in his hand.

"Gees, what's going on in here? A revival meeting?"

Roma got up from her seat and skipped towards her big brother. "Bobby, will you play cowboys and Indians with us? Mom, can we go outside now?"

"If you put on jackets, you can play outside till supper."

The singing stopped and a loud 'hooray' went up.

"All right. C'mon, Old Tree Limb. What are you gonna be? A cowboy or an Indian?"

"Indian!"

They were off.

"Well, at least Bobby is finally helping with something around here," Clara said.

"And God bless him for it," Edith said mostly to herself as she left the kitchen for the quiet of the living room. "Hope he's up for more of that."

***

Edith didn't tell Robert that evening, or even the next evening, that she was pregnant again. She couldn't decide how to approach the subject. Just spit it out? Soften him up with some ice cream or homemade pie? *Oh, that's stupid. It's not gonna be exciting news either way.*

Edith hated feeling so low about a pregnancy. Pregnancy was supposed to be cause for celebration. Could the baby sense that she was so down? She knew deep down that wouldn't be good.

She started a load of laundry. The third for that day. Then she went into the kitchen to lay out the plan for supper that evening. Roast with carrots and potatoes. Easy enough. The girls could help with that when they got home from school.

Kathy's birthday was in a few days. Edith had been working on a new dress for her...a sun dress for this summer. It was made from the flowered cotton cloth of a pillowcase Edith picked up at a thrift shop in Tiffin. She had some cotton eyelet lace trim that she could put around the neck to dress it up a little. It would have to do...it was all she had.

All of a sudden, her eyes filled with tears. She sat with her head bent down on her arms on kitchen table and began to sob. She was glad the kids were at school. The youngest two were playing outside, so wouldn't hear her. She allowed herself to continue weeping for several minutes, and then, just as suddenly as it had started, it ended.

Edith raised her head. She brushed the tears from her eyes and the hair from her forehead. *I've gotta pull myself together. These kids need me.* She felt a little numb, but numb was better than sad. She went to the back porch, looked out the back door, and saw Kathy and Dickie playing in the dirt. *More laundry.* This time, she chuckled, but bile rose in her throat, strangling her small laugh. Bitter. She felt bitter. This was no good. *Some way or other, I have to rid myself of this awful feeling.*

She pulled out a pad of paper, grabbed a pencil from the junk drawer and sat back down at the table. Sun was shining in from the open door into the kitchen. She prayed for a minute, then began to write.

> *God made me quick to see*
> *Each task awaiting me,*
> > *And quick to do.*
> *Oh, grant me strength, I pray,*
> *With lowly love each day*
> > *And purpose true.*
> *To go as Jesus went,*
> *Spending and being spent,*
> > *Myself for God.*

She felt better. She actually felt better! She was proud. It was a good poem! Putting her focus on God made her feel better. Writing helped her feel better. She discovered something inside her that she now knew could help her through any hard time. She *could* do something besides being a wife and mom. Edith Riedel could write.

***

When Robert got home, the house was filled with wonderful aromas, as usual. *Roast beef. Apple pie.* Sure enough, two apple pies were cooling on the kitchen counter.

He took off his work boots, and called out, "Hi everybody, I'm home."

He could hear the thundering herd as they began their descent down the steps, calling out, "Hi, Daddy!" The little kids were always first to welcome him. The older kids were still in their rooms, now too 'grown up' to run to greet their father. That was okay. *Teenage years,* he mused, remembering when he felt the same way about his own parents.

"Hi, honey." Edith had entered from the back porch with a load of clothes she had just pulled off the clothesline. "How was work?"

"Just a usual day. Nothing special going on. I'm glad we're back to full steam, though. There's plenty of work for us now. In fact, a few of the men are working a little overtime."

"Are you going to do overtime?"

"Not if I can help it. I've got enough to keep me busy around here," he answered, looking down at the four children still clamoring for his attention.

Edith laughed. "No foolin'! Join the club!"

Robert tousled each child's hair, then crossed the room to kiss Edith. "You look beautiful today. You look...happy. *Extra* happy."

"Well, I am. After supper I want to show you something. Right now, I've got to go fold these clothes, and then I'll get supper on the table."

She walked to the foot of the stairs and called out for the girls. "Clara...Mary...Phyllis...can you all come down here and help me for a few minutes?"

"Sure, Mom! Be right there..."

The next set of footsteps rumbled into the kitchen.

"Hi, Dad."

"Your mom is in the living room. You girls go out there and help her fold clothes, okay?"

The girls went to find their mom. Robert got himself a glass of water and went in to join them.

"It was sure a beautiful day for hanging out the wash."

"Yeah, Kathy and Dickie were playing outside most of the day today. It gave me a chance to get Kathy's birthday present done, too," Edith said.

"Is that what you wanted to show me?"

"That and something else."

"Now I'm curious."

"I hope you'll like it."

"Is it something for me?"

Edith stopped her folding and tipped her head to one side, thinking.

"No. I think it's something for *me*."

Robert smiled. "All the better, honey."

"I hope you'll like it, too, though," she said, beaming. "I can hardly wait to show you!"

Her excitement was contagious, filling Robert's heart. Now he could hardly wait, himself.

***

Dinner was finished. The usual household sounds echoed throughout their home...the girls singing...dishes clanking as they were washed and dried...Phyllis on the piano...the little kids running around in the back yard, their shouting and laughter carried in on the April breeze.

"What did you want to show me now?" Robert asked.

"Come with me." Edith took his hand and led him into their bedroom, where she indicated he should sit down on the bed. She went to her dresser drawer and pulled out a notebook.

"Read this and tell me what you think."

Robert looked at a page with Edith's handwriting. A few cross-outs and restarts made him smile. She had written a poem. He read it in silence, then looked up. Edith was smiling.

"Edith, this is wonderful. You did this yourself?"

"I sure did." She looked...young. Radiant.

"It's so good! It's a *beautiful* poem. Better than some of the poems they made us read in school."

"I was hoping you'd like it," she said as she sat down next to him.

"How did you get the idea? I mean, where did this come from? Have you been thinking about it a long time?"

"No. It just came to me this morning."

"But why this morning?"

Edith took his hand. "I'll tell you why. I was feeling really blue. Depressed. And God just touched my heart and pulled me out of it through writing."

Robert's face displayed immediate concern. "Honey, what are you depressed about?"

"I *was* depressed. I'm not now. But here's the thing. I'm pregnant again."

Robert pulled his hand away, shocked. He stood up and began pacing. Then he sat down again, staring straight ahead. Edith remained silent, awaiting his response.

"Ten kids. *Ten.*"

"A nice round number, I guess."

"A dozen people in this house."

"Yup."

He looked at his wife. "How do you feel? Are you feeling okay?"

"I've had a little nausea off and on, but nothing I can't deal with. I've mostly just felt blue. Tired and blue. But this…" she waved the paper she had written her poem on. "This helped me feel a lot better today, and now I know that whenever I'm feeling bad, I should just write. Read the Bible, pray, and write."

Robert rubbed his forehead. "I don't know how we're gonna do it."

"Neither do I, but we'll manage. We always do."

"Pretty soon we're gonna run out of names."

Edith laughed. "We'll have to invent some, I s'pose. Or start naming them after presidents."

"What if it's a girl?"

"Then we'll name them after the Queens of England."

"Mom! Dad! Where are you guys?" Multiple kids were calling them, an urgency in their voices. Edith and Robert both stood and quickly walked into the living room. An extraordinarily unpleasant odor hit them full in the face.

"Good grief, what is that?" Robert said.

"You know what it is…poop," Edith said.

"But where in the world…"

Bobby was first to make his way to them.

"Uh, you're not going to believe this, but one of the calves pooped on the back porch."

"What?!?"

"One of the calves pooped on the back porch."

"How in the heck did a calf get on the back porch?"

Verlin and Kathy appeared from behind their big brother, holding hands, heads lowered.

"We let him in, Daddy," Kathy said, sniffling. "Me and Verlin. He was cold."

"Honey, he has a fur coat on. I'm pretty sure he wasn't cold," Edith said.

"Gosh, he made an awful mess," Verlin said.

"Yeah, we can *smell* it," Robert said. "Who's going to help me clean it up?"

All the kids had joined the family in the living room, and all had the same horrified expression at their father's request.

"Dad! We can't clean that up!" Clara said. "It's a mess! Wait till you see it." Phyllis, Mary, and Alton all nodded agreement, with looks of disgust on their faces.

"May as well have a look." Robert turned to Edith. "Wanna go with me?"

"No, not particularly, but I *will*."

They walked through the living room, into the kitchen, and out to the back porch slowly, almost tiptoeing, as if they anticipated some monster popping out to devour them. Robert surveyed the incident first.

"Edith, don't even come out here. It's not as bad as all that, but it's definitely a mess. I'll take care of it."

Edith ignored his words and followed him to the scene of the crime. It was bad enough. She gagged a little, then began to laugh. And laugh. She couldn't control herself.

Robert looked in wonder at his wife. *She's lost her marbles.* But her laughter infected him, and he began to laugh, too. The couple embraced each other and laughed till tears rolled down their cheeks.

Finally, Robert caught his breath enough to say, "If number ten gets into as much as the first nine do, we're in trouble. Where's the mop?"

"Mop!" Edith said. "First you're going to need a shovel!"

32

May 1947

"Edith, you've lost all sense of yourself. You have completely lost your identity."

Doc Smith's words made her look up but elicited no other response.

"I know you love your family. No one else I know has raised such nice, well-adjusted kids as you and Robert. But Edith, number ten was…well, I don't know how you've survived ten pregnancies with the health issues you've had over the years."

Her face downcast, she said, "I didn't mean to have ten."

"I'm not criticizing. Traditionally, people around here have had large families. You're not that unusual except for the fact that you've haven't had the best health history. Like I said, it's a wonder you've been able to bear it all. What's more, I know you well enough to know that you want more for yourself."

Edith stared at her physician. "I guess I've told you about writing…"

"Yes, you have, and I strongly encourage you to continue that. But here's what my prescription *really* is…."

She waited.

"Get a job, Edith. Go out and find a job that will get you out of the house a little bit. Get away from your family. Do something more for *you*."

Tears welled up in Edith's eyes. "Don't you think I've *tried* to find a job? I have. No one wants a woman who never graduated high school."

"Edith Riedel, how old are you now? Thirty-six, isn't it? And you've produced ten kids. It's time to find out what you *can* do and stop worrying about what you *can't* do. Trust me. Someone's looking for an employee exactly like you to do a job that no one else could do without the kind of experience you have in your life. You know how to organize. You know how to set priorities. You know how to do a million things at once without batting an eye. Who wouldn't want an employee like that?"

She looked down at her hands, developing the knobby knuckles associated with arthritis. She had used these hands a lot in thirty-six years. What else could they accomplish?

Doc Smith continued. "Listen, I'm gonna boot you on out of here because the office is full today, but you mind my words. Find a job. A *job*. Get out of that house and do something for yourself. And keep writing. Your writing is good."

She got off the exam table. "Thanks, Doc." But she walked out with her head down, pondering the possibilities and what seemed like *im*possibilities.

***

"Mommy, the phone is for you," Kathy called out. She always liked to answer the phone and frequently got to it before anyone in the family.

Edith quickly dried her hands. She had been cleaning chicken for dinner. Her large family now needed at least two chickens to fill up growing children.

"Hello," she said once Kathy handed her the phone.

"Edith, it's Lois."

"Hi, Lois. How's Ross and the boys?"

"Oh, everyone's fine. I don't need to keep you, but I wondered if you'd like to ride to Tiffin with me tomorrow."

"I think I could do that. What're you going to Tiffin for?"

"I'm going to apply for a job at GE."

Edith almost dropped the receiver. A job. Lois was going to get a job.

"GE? General Electric is hiring?"

"Yes. In fact, why don't you apply, too? It'd be fun driving back and forth to work with each other."

"Oh, Lois, I don't know…" Edith wasn't sure whether Lois knew she hadn't graduated high school. Edith was hesitant to commit.

Her past experiences had left her embarrassed and cynical.

"Why not? C'mon, Edith. You apply, too. They're hiring for the evening shift."

Evening shift. That would mean Robert was alone with all ten kids all evening. But it would save them from having to hire a babysitter.

"I'll have to talk to Robert about that idea, but I'll ride along with you. Maybe we can stop at the dime store while we're over there."

"Sure. I need a couple of things, too, so let's do that. I'll pick you up around ten tomorrow morning. See ya then!"

"All right. 'Bye." Edith hung up.

A job. It was almost too much to hope for. She felt anxious, restless. She could hardly wait for Robert to come home so she could talk with him about it.

In her restless energy, she cleaned the entire house, did a load of laundry, and hoed the garden. She played with Kathy and Dickie till it was time for their naps. She fed, changed, and rocked Jimmy, the youngest Riedel. She still felt keyed up.

She got supper going—baked chicken and mashed potatoes. The kids came home from school, and she reviewed papers and helped with homework. Once the kids had finished and scattered themselves to other activities, she sat down and made a list of the household chores that would need to be done if she was gone eight hours every day. Could they do it?

She was continuing her list and considering what child could help with each duty when Robert got home from work. He crossed the room, kissed her on the top of the head, and looked over her shoulder at the list she was making.

"About time you assigned these guys to specific chores."

She looked up. "What do you mean?"

"I mean you let them off too easy sometimes."

"Robert Riedel! I can't believe you just said that to me. Why haven't *you* made some decisions about chores? I'm not the only parent!" Her eyes flashed.

"Gees, I'm sorry. I wasn't trying to pick a fight. Let me see your list."

He sat down and she pushed the list across the table toward him.

He read the list. "This all seems reasonable. Even the littlest ones have something. That's good…they all need to learn about responsibility, and they need to learn it early. What possessed you to take this up today?"

"I'm applying for a job tomorrow."

"What? Where?"

"GE in Tiffin. I'm going with Lois."

Robert shifted in his chair, looked intently at Edith, and said, "Were you going to talk to *me* about this idea?"

"That's what we're doing now."

"Well, it looks like you've already made up your mind."

"We've talked about it before. I didn't think you'd object."

He leaned back. "I don't think I *do* object, but it means a lot of changes around here."

"Yes, it does. Especially because it would be an evening shift job."

"Evening shift! That means it'd be me and the kids alone every evening."

Edith stayed quiet. She wanted him to think about what he had just said. Finally, she responded.

"Robert, you *do* realize it's been just me alone with the kids all day long every day for all these years. Even on the weekends you were off hunting or fishing or trapping. I'm not complaining about that. You were putting food on the table and so forth. But I think that since half the kids are older, they could help you with the little ones, as they have helped me so much the last few years. They're getting more self-sufficient every day. Just little Jimmy—he'd take the biggest part of your time."

Robert knew he had to play this carefully.

"Honey, you'll never know how much I admire you. I know you've wanted to get a job. I know Doc told you that you *should* get a job. I'm not going to stand in the way of you trying to get a job now. But what if you don't get hired? Are you going to sink down in the dumps again?"

Edith didn't have a good answer. It was the very thing she was most worried about.

"I guess I'll just have to see."

Robert remained quiet now. She had been through so much in her life. She wasn't frail, but somehow, he saw her as *fragile*.

"I hope you get a job. I really do." He looked at her list again.

"We can manage this. We *absolutely* can manage this."

She smiled at him. "I've never had a doubt. Look at what you were able to manage those times I was really sick. You're a good husband and a good father."

He stood up, walked around the table, leaned over and embraced her from behind, wrapping his arms around her neck.

"And you're a good mom. Love you."

"Love you, too."

***

Edith combed her hair, applied lipstick, and straightened the seam in her nylons. She wanted to look perfect. She put on her best Sunday dress and pumps. She was ready.

At precisely 10 a.m., she heard Lois' car horn.

"Mary, I'm leaving. See you after while!" Edith called. Mary, her only child that did not like school, had volunteered to stay home with the youngest kids.

"All right, Mom. Have a good time," came Mary's reply from the den where she was playing with her little brother and sister.

Edith went out the door. It was a gray, gloomy day. She was already nervous, and she hoped the weather didn't portend the outcome of her trip.

"C'mom, get in. Let's go!" Lois said as she approached the car. Lois's excitement was contagious. Edith could feel her heart beat a little faster.

The trip to Tiffin was made faster by the women's chatter. Before they knew it, they were parked in front of the GE plant. Lois opened her car door, but Edith was now frozen, looking at the large factory in front of her, wondering if she was ready for another let-down.

"Edith, c'mon. What're you doing?"

"I don't know, Lois...I don't know if I can go in there."

Her face exhibiting surprise and puzzlement, Lois put a gloved hand on her hip. *Why didn't I think to wear gloves,* Edith thought. *So professional-looking.*

"Edith, don't tell me you're scared. I've never known you to be scared of *anything.*"

"I'm not exactly scared. I'm...well, I don't know *what* I am."

Lois began to tap the toes of her left foot. "Well, *I'm* going in there and *I'm* getting a job. Come if you want. Don't come if you don't want." She turned and headed away from the car with a determined strut, disappearing into the large plant.

Edith wanted to cry. She'd been disappointed so many times before. Lois didn't know how many times she had hoped for a job.

As Edith sat in the car, feeling low about her chances, her mind wandered to Robert and his encouragement. She closed her eyes and saw his face.

"We can manage this. We absolutely can manage this."
"I know you've wanted a job. I want you to get a job."
"Are you going to be down in the dumps again?"
"I want you to get a job. I really do."

She lifted her head and opened her eyes. She opened the car door and got out, straightening her dress as she stood up.

"Doggone it! I'm going to go get a job!" she said aloud.

***

Inside the General Electric offices, Edith followed a line of people toward an office marked 'Personnel.' She saw Lois further along in that line. She wished she had come in when Lois did. When Lois, glancing around, noticed Edith farther back in the line, she motioned for her to come and join her, but Edith shook her head 'no'. It wouldn't be fair to cut in front of others who also hoped for a job.

The office door opened, and an older woman, whose glasses sat low on her nose, announced, "We'll take the first five of you in now. The rest of you wait here and we'll continue taking five at a time until everyone has had a chance to fill out an application."

The first five applicants entered, the door closed, and those left in the hallway began to murmur various opinions about the process.

"This'll take all day."

"Why can't they just let us get an application and take it home?"

"Doesn't seem like a very good way to go about this."

Edith remained silent. She was just grateful for an opportunity. She began to count people off in groups of five. It wasn't so bad. She'd be first in the fifth group to fill out an application. Lois would be in the third group. She hoped Lois wouldn't be mad about having to wait for her.

After about fifteen minutes, the door opened again, and the

next group of five entered the personnel office. *At this rate, it'll take about an hour or so. That's not bad.*

"Cripes, it's going to take an hour to even get in. I'm coming back later," groused a burly, bearded man ahead of her in line. He broke ranks, heading for the exit. Another man and one woman followed him, shaking their heads. *Now I'm the last person in the fourth group!* She began to feel an excitement rising inside her. *Don't get too excited, Edith. You don't have a job yet.* She took a couple of deep breaths, letting each one out slowly. *Don't get nervous.*

Lois' group disappeared behind the door of the personnel office. Edith's group would be next. She thought about the kind of questions that might be asked on an application. The question that worried her most would be about education. She knew it could be a drawback. She began to pray silently.

"Lord, you always know what is best, so I'm not trying to question your judgment, but if it's in your will, please help me in this process, and if possible, let my lack of a diploma not be such an issue for GE. I've tried to be smart in other ways, so if you can see to it, please let me have a chance to show what I can do and not be pushed away because of what they think I can't do. I don't mean to be selfish when you have so many big problems to attend to, but look down on your servant today, and help me put my best foot forward. Thank you for thinking of me and loving me and getting me through so much in the past. Thank you for listening to my prayers. Amen."

The personnel office door opened, and the lady with the low glasses motioned for the next five people to enter. It suddenly occurred to Edith that she had never seen any of the first three groups of people exit the office. Where did they go from there?

Inside the office, they were instructed to sit at five school desks that had been set up. The lady began to speak as the applicants were seated.

"I'm Mrs. Hoover. I'm the manager of Personnel. Right now, I'm going to give you each an application to fill out. Then, my assistant will escort you to several different department managers who will review your application and interview you."

Edith was shocked. *They're having interviews today!* She instinctively reached up and fluffed her hair. It was important to look her best. Mrs. Hoover handed out the applications. At first, Edith could barely focus her eyes on the paper. She took two deep breaths, gave her head the tiniest shake, and began to fill out the application.

There was nothing on the application Edith hadn't expected. *Name. Address. Phone number. Highest level of education.*

There it was. She had to write 'seventh grade.' She winced. *Go on. Next question.*

Last five years work experience, beginning with most recent.

She almost dropped her pen. The question took her breath away. *What do I write now?*

She could feel the sting of hot tears beginning to well up. Then she got mad. She thought about what Doc Smith had said to her and began to write in the margins of the paper.

For the last nineteen years, I have been a wife. Eighteen of those years have been spent raising my family. I have carried out all the duties of a wife and mother of ten children while going through the Great Depression and the second World War. I know how to organize work. I know what jobs need to be done and in what order. I know how to work as part of a large team of people. Without teamwork, nothing of worth gets accomplished. I know how to take the ideas of others, put them together with my own, and come up with the best plans for getting things done. I know what it means to have to be economical. I have a good sense of humor and can see the light on the darkest of days. I have fought back from two serious illnesses because I am strong and I never lost faith in God, who helps me in all things. Just so you know, the only reason I didn't graduate high school is because I had to drop out to care for my father and brothers. But in the meantime, I have read every book I can get my hands on, and I think I could not only learn whatever job you need me for, but I believe I could excel at it if you'll give me the chance. Thank you.

She reviewed what she had written. Did it sound too pushy? She was confident she could learn any job. She just needed someone to get past that 'highest level of education' and 'work experience' issue.

She noticed Mrs. Hoover looking at her.

"Are you finished with the application?" Mrs. Hoover seemed slightly annoyed. The other four members of her group had already disappeared. Edith hadn't even noticed.

"I am now," Edith said.

Mrs. Hoover took the application and surveyed what Edith had written.

"Well, this is interesting. Come with me."

Edith stood and followed Mrs. Hoover to a door at the rear of the office, where another younger woman was waiting.

"Dottie, take Mrs. Riedel to see Mr. Majors."

"Yes ma'am. Mrs. Riedel, will you come with me?"

Edith followed down a long hall. She didn't see any of the other applicants anywhere. It seemed strange and was a little unnerving. Dottie opened the door to another office and entered. Her hand on the doorknob, she turned to Edith and said, "We're here, so come on in and have a seat. This is Mr. Majors."

Edith walked in as Mr. Majors stood to greet her. Edith offered her hand. It seemed a professional thing to do.

"Welcome, Mrs. Riedel. Sit down and let's talk for a few minutes. Thanks Dottie." Dottie disappeared, the door closing behind her with a loud click.

"May I call you Edith?"

"Oh, yes. I'd prefer it. I usually think of Mrs. Riedel as my mother-in-law."

Mr. Majors laughed. "Not quite old enough to go by that moniker yet, eh? I understand."

"Oh, I don't *mind* being called Mrs. Riedel. Don't get me wrong. I just think it seems awfully formal." She was babbling. She had to stop that.

Leaning back in his chair, Mr. Majors took time to look at her application. She could see him raise his eyebrows when he got to her written statement. Then he leaned forward, putting her application aside and resting his forearms on his desk.

"Edith, I'm going to be frank. We generally employ people who have at least a high school education."

She had to maintain her composure. "I understand," she said, keeping her tone even.

Mr. Majors stood up. Edith thought the interview was over, and her heart sank. But Mr. Majors had been at this game a while and knew a good worker when he saw one.

"Listen, I'd like to talk to you about a job I think you could do. It's a job that doesn't really require a diploma, if you want to know the truth, but it's an important position nonetheless. Do you mind walking with me out to the line? Let me show you what I'm talking about, and then you can tell me if you think you could do it."

Just as quickly as she had started to despair, her spirit was lifted, and it shone on her face through a huge smile.

"I'd love to know more about it."

Edith followed Mr. Majors away from offices and break rooms

to a huge area where motors were in production. They stood in the doorway for a few minutes while her potential boss talked to her about what was happening there.

"Edith, do you know much about motors and how they work?"

"Not really. I know a little something about threshing machines from my childhood."

"Well, it's not important for you to know every intricacy of how a motor works but let me tell you just a little so that you know the kind of work you would be doing.

"Inside a motor is a compartment known as a stator. The stator is the area where energy is generated. The energy that is created inside that stator charges batteries. That's the basics. Right now, we're looking at the biggest motor GE makes. This is where you'd be working, but just because it doesn't require a degree doesn't mean it's an easy job. It requires some physical strength and attention to detail."

Edith blinked and swallowed.

"What you'd be doing is winding wire into those stators. The wire has to be wound just so. You have to be sure there's no defects in the wire as you're winding it. You have to make sure the finished product is perfect before it moves down the line to the next part of making the motor."

"What comes after the wire winding?" she asked, curious to learn about the entire process.

"The stator is put into a flywheel. The flywheel has magnets in it, and the stator spins so fast that it creates an alternating current."

"Alternating? So the voltage goes off and on? That helps the motor run *how*? What comes next?" Edith asked.

Mr. Majors was impressed by her question and by how quickly she picked up that this wasn't the end of the process.

"Good question. The alternating current goes into a regulator rectifier. The name of that part tells you exactly what it does. It rectifies and regulates the voltage so that it comes out as direct current."

"Okay. I get it." She had folded her arms and reached up, tapping an index finger against her cheek. Mr. Majors chuckled.

"I think you *do*. What do you say? Do you think this is something you could do? Do you think you would like it? You're just doing one job all shift. Winding wire."

"It seems like a pretty important job, though. Yes. I believe I could do it and I think I'd like it just fine."

"Then let's go get you processed."

What did he say? Did he just offer me the job?

"All right." She followed him as he walked toward his office. Once there, he indicated for her to sit down. He picked up his phone, dialing a number, clearing his throat before he began to speak.

"Hi, Fran. It's Berdell. I'd like to hire Mrs. Riedel for the winder position. Yes. I'll send her back down to you, okay?" He hung up.

"Can you find your way back to Personnel?" he asked.

"I'm pretty certain I can."

"It's just straight down the hall from where you came in, and when you get to the end of the hall, turn left. It's right there—the first door on the left-hand side of *that* hall."

"I remember." She stood up. He extended his hand, and she shook it.

"Welcome to the team."

"Mr. Majors, can I ask you something?"

"Sure."

"What made you decide to hire me? I've tried to find jobs before, but no one wanted to hire me without a high school education."

He paused before answering.

"Edith," he finally said, "there are benefits to an education, that's for sure. I'd probably never qualify for the job I have if I hadn't gone to college. I'm one of the lucky ones who got to go. But I truly believe that we acquire skills in life that you don't necessarily get in high school or even in college. We pick up attributes that can't be taught in books or lectures. And when I see someone who has those attributes and skills, I like to get them on my team. That's why I'm hiring you. What you wrote on your application said a lot about the kind of person you are, and you're the kind of person I want to work with. You're the kind of person we want at GE."

She stood, quiet for a minute as she considered his words. She extended her hand one more time.

"I appreciate your confidence. I won't let you down. I'll never make you sorry that you hired me."

He produced a hearty laugh. "I have no doubt! I'll see you in just a week or two, all right?"

"You bet!" She exited the office. Restraining an impulse to leap into the air, she instead bowed her head, a broad smile on her face, and said, "Thank you, Father."

In the personnel office, she was given documents about her starting wage and benefits, the dress code, and general information about where to go on her first day of work—June 28. She could hardly believe someone was actually handing her *employment* information. She left the office, as joyful as when her children had been born.

Lois was standing near the front door of the building. "So?" she asked Edith.

Edith beamed. "I'm in!"

The two women embraced, equally excited about what lay before them.

"Let's get out of here," Lois said. "I can hardly wait to tell Ross." She continued to chat, going on and on, but Edith was barely listening as she stepped out into bright sunshine.

Guess the rain is gone, she thought. She closed her eyes and raised her face to the sky, smiling at the warmth of the sun.

Edith Riedel had a job. A whole new world was waiting for her.

A Final Note...

My grandmother worked for GE until her forced retirement in 1976. She was 65 years old, and at the time, GE did not allow people to work past the age of 65. She was none too happy about retirement because she loved her job, and being a gregarious person, she loved her co-workers. Nevertheless, she and Grandpa had many years to spend together without other obligations. The kids all grew up, each successful in own their endeavors. Grandma and Grandpa finally had some time to vacation or become involved in undertakings they enjoyed. They began woodworking projects together. I still use a wooden paper towel holder and a cooling rack they made.

Grandma never stopped writing. The poem you read in the chapter about 1946 is her own. To the best of my knowledge, her writing was always faith-based, a reflection of how she lived her life. Please enjoy the following works, all penned by Edith Riedel.

<u>Untitled</u>
Oh, glory to Jesus, my blessed Redeemer
Who suffered and died, redemption to bring.
I'll water my soul in the well of salvation,
And shout hallelujah to Jesus, my King.

The Sovereignty of God

Through waves, through clouds and storms,
God gently clears the way,
We wait His time, so shall the night
Soon end in blissful day.
We comprehend Him not,
Yet earth and Heaven tell
God sits as sovereign on the throne
And ruleth all things well.
Trust Him when dark doubts assail thee,
Trust Him when thy strength is small.
Trust Him when to simply trust Him
Is the hardest thing of all.
Trust Him! He is ever faithful!
Trust Him for His will is best.
Trust Him for the heart of Jesus
Is the only place of rest.
Trust Him, then through cloud and sunshine
All thy cares upon Him cast,
Till the storms of life are over,
And the trusting days are past.

Finally, this is a prayer Grandma wrote which shows the sense of humor and humility she demonstrated all her life.

<u>Prayer for the Golden Years</u>

Lord, you know I'm growing older. Keep me from becoming talkative and possessed with the idea that I must express myself on every idea or subject.

Release me from the craving to straighten out everyone's affairs.

Keep me from the recital of endless detail. Give me strength to get to the point.

Seal my lips when I am inclined to tell of my aches and pains. They are increasing with the passing of years, and the love to speak of them grows sweeter as time goes by.

Teach me the glorious lesson that occasionally I may be wrong.

Make me thoughtful but not nosy...helpful but not bossy. With my vast store of wisdom and experiences, it does seem a shame not to use it all. But you know, Lord, I want a few friends in the end.

Amen

ABOUT THE AUTHOR

Theresa Konwinski is a retired registered nurse, a wife and mom to two adult children. Besides writing short stories and poems, her previous books include:

An Extraordinary Year
Ragged Road
Seven Secrets